PURSUED

Susan had always loved New York City—but now suddenly the city seemed a savage, alien place, a human jungle that hid whoever was stalking her through the night.

Trying to keep panic from her movements, her voice, Susan hailed a taxi, gave her home address. With relief she saw the old familiar brownstone building that housed her apartment, and she could feel herself at last relax as she slid the bolt of her front door behind her.

It was only then that Susan realized that something was strangely, terribly wrong. Quickly she picked up her phone, her only lifeline to the outside world, yet even as she did so she knew it would be dead, the line cut.

Someone had entered before her—and now there was nowhere to run, nowhere to hide. . . .

"This new mystery novel offers Eberhart fans their favorite kind of people and adventure!"
—*Houston Post*

OTHER MIGNON G. EBERHART MYSTERIES YOU'LL WANT TO READ:

WITNESS AT LARGE

R.S.V.P. MURDER

THE CUP, THE BLADE OR THE GUN

DANGER IN THE DARK

ANOTHER WOMAN'S HOUSE

HUNT WITH THE HOUNDS

WOMAN ON THE ROOF

JURY OF ONE

DEAD MEN'S PLANS

THE UNKNOWN QUANTITY

MAN MISSING

HOUSE OF STORM

DEADLY IS THE DIAMOND

RUN SCARED

POSTMARK MURDER

ESCAPE THE NIGHT

WOLFE IN MAN'S CLOTHING

UNIDENTIFIED WOMAN

THE PATTERN

FAIR WARNING

THE HANGMAN'S WHIP

THE GLASS SLIPPER

THE CASES OF SUSAN DARE

All available in Popular Library Editions

MIGNON G. EBERHART

DANGER MONEY

POPULAR LIBRARY • NEW YORK

POPULAR LIBRARY EDITION
February, 1976

Library of Congress Catalog Card Number: 74-9091

Published by arrangement with Random House, Inc.

PRINTED IN THE UNITED STATES OF AMERICA

One

Tall wrought-iron gates loomed up in the lights of the car as it came to a smooth halt. Its lights went on and off in a swift dot, dot, dot code. This code, Susan knew, was changed once a week. As the flashing ended there was a slight pause; then the wide gates opened under electric power. At the same time a uniformed guard, with a huge holster on his hip, stood squinting through the dusk. He saw Greg and grunted. "Oh, it's you. The great man told me you were coming today."

"Well, here we are," Greg said.

The guard, one of the Clanser relatives whom the great man rather sourly called pensioners, leaned nearer to squint past Greg at Susan, who sat in front beside Greg. "The young lady?"

"Miss Beach. One of Mr. Manders' office staff. She's to take charge of the house for a few days."

The guard gave another grunt and moved to look in the back seat. Milly Clanser indignantly piped up, "You know me! I'm to stay in the house too and oversee things properly."

And I'll have trouble with you, Susan thought. If you expect to have breakfast in bed, you're mistaken. As usual, however, she knew when to speak and when not to speak.

The guard gave a third heaving grunt. Daylight was fading fast. There were no lights in what could be seen of the house beyond curving thickets of pines and shrubbery which lined the long driveway ahead of them.

"I guess it's all right," the guard said.

"Oh, come on, Col. You know me and Miss Clanser perfectly well," Greg said good-naturedly.

"Well, anyway the great man is here."

Nobody who worked for G.M. was ever surprised at anything he did, but in the faint dash light it seemed to Susan that Greg's face tightened a little in surprise. None of them had expected G.M. to precede them. "Oh," Greg said.

Col Clanser gave forth a grunt, this time in a rather

pleased way. "Sure. Came up in his helicopter a while ago. Heard him. Helicopter hasn't left yet. So he's still here. Didn't want to ride with you, huh?"

"Maybe he just didn't like our company." Greg grinned.

Col grinned too. Milly said from the back, "Let's go on to the house. It's going to be dark in a few minutes."

Col leaned into the open window of the car on Greg's side. "How are you, Milly? How are things with you?" he asked.

Ludmilla Clanser apparently did not intend to take any lesser Clanser to her ample bosom. "What happened to that filling station dear Rose bought for you?" Her voice was icy. "You couldn't make a go of it, could you? So you have a job here."

Col said, "Well now, she is *my* cousin Rose, you know. Same as she's your sister."

"Let's go on to the house," Milly said again.

"All right?" Greg asked Col, sticking to the formality of being passed on by the guard. Col nodded. Greg started up. As they swept along a paved drive, Susan had a swift impression that Col Clanser had made a very disrespectful gesture toward Ludmilla Clanser.

It was a long driveway, and as the trees pressed closely around it, the October twilight seemed to thicken with blue shadows, beyond the path of lights from the car.

Suddenly they turned and there was a full view of the secret house. It was certainly secret, and what Susan could see of it was certainly ugly. She had a glimpse of shiny red brick and iron grillwork everywhere. The trees and shrubbery pressed so closely here that there was the barest pocket handkerchief of lawn, looking rather brown and parched in the lights from the car. Greg brought the car up to an entrance, all glass and grilled iron. "Here we are." He shut off the engine.

Immediately the stillness of woods fell upon them. Then Milly began to struggle with her mountain of coats and scarves. Greg opened the door and started to extract the bags and boxes of groceries they had brought up from the city. Susan crawled out of the car and went to help him. "Look out!" she said. "I think the eggs are in that box." She and Greg had done the shopping together before leaving the city.

"Isn't anybody going to help me?" Milly asked.

Greg replied, "Susan and I will just get these things out of your way." He and Susan went on into the house. The huge glassy door was not locked, so Col must have been right when he said that the great man was there. Greg knew where the electric light switches were and, his arms full of bags and boxes, he contrived to turn on a light in the surprisingly formal vestibule; this apparently opened upon a larger entrance hall. "I'll put these in the kitchen," Greg said.

There was also a small door leading off the amazingly marbled, glassed vestibule. He pushed it open, and Susan followed him down a short passage and then into a kitchen; there was still enough light to perceive the shining white of range and refrigerator, and the remarkably long counter tops. A box was slipping in Greg's arms. He made a kind of dash toward the nearest counter, but a bag of tomatoes slid to the floor. He uttered a word and bent to scoop them up. Susan went on past him to the counter near a window. As she unloaded her own boxes and bags, she glanced out the window and saw a man running hard toward the woods and the wall which she knew enclosed the house. "Greg!"

"What?"

"There's a man! Look—"

Greg slipped on a tomato, swore and caught himself as the running man turned to give the house a swift glance. Susan could see him, but barely; his hat was pulled low over his face. Then he disappeared just when Greg got his balance and came to look.

"No, he's gone. But he was there. I saw him. He was running."

"Was it G.M.?"

"No. No, I'm sure it wasn't."

"Probably the helicopter pilot. Snell Clanser."

"Why was he running?" There had been something furtive, something out of place in that running figure and in that swift look cast back to the house.

"Expect he wants to get back to the heliport as soon as he can."

The great man's helicopter was kept in the Madilson heliport in New York. But he'd had woods cleared beyond the house and its high encircling wall in order to construct a flat landing place, not visible because of the high brick wall and the trees close to the house.

They waited, listening; moments lengthened. Finally there was the starting thump and roar of a helicopter. "Sure, it must have been Snell Clanser." Snell was, Susan knew, another of the tribe, a former airman. Office gossip was that when Snell became a periodic drunk Mr. Manders took pity on him and gave him a job.

They watched and listened; it seemed a long time before the whirring roar of the helicopter diminished slowly in the distance.

Milly spoke angrily from the front door. "Isn't anybody going to help me with my suitcase?"

It wouldn't hurt her to do a little exercise herself, Susan thought tartly. She was enormously fat but she couldn't have been—Susan didn't know what age and didn't care to guess. She turned from the window and stooped to gather up tomatoes. Greg muttered something and went out, past Milly.

"Just which room is to be mine?" Milly demanded.

The great man's long-time confidential secretary, Dora Clanser, had given Susan minute instructions about the secret house and her duties. But if the great man himself were in the house it seemed proper to announce her arrival to him. She looked up to reply to Milly, but Milly had gone outside again. Susan went back into the vestibule and then into the huge entrance hall. A stairway with wrought-iron balusters and red velvet covering its railing led upward. Since the great man had not come from the rooms opening off the entrance hall and they showed no lights, Susan assumed that he was upstairs in the big bedroom which, she had been told, he used very little. It was darkening upstairs, too; she found an electric light switch, flicked it on, and as a sparkling chandelier above scattered lights like many candles, went up the stairs. Apparently her employer, Gilbert Manders, had not heard their arrival. She had been told which room she was to occupy: a small room at the top of the stairs to the right which had a safe set into the chimney. She felt for a light switch there too and found it.

She also found Rose Manders.

Rose had not heard their arrival.

She lay sprawled on the floor. There was a spreading splotch of red across her tight pale-green dress. Her eyes were open. Her mouth, her whole face, sagged. A fur wrap lay beside her.

Susan didn't realize she had screamed until she heard Greg's hard footsteps pounding up the stairs and realized that she must have called him.

He came into the room, saw Rose, and knelt swiftly down beside her. He put his head close to Rose; he felt for a pulse; he held his wrist watch at her lips. That, Susan thought vaguely, was to see if Rose could possibly still be breathing. Finally he squatted there, just looking at Rose. "I don't know what to do," he said as if to himself.

Milly panted into the room, took a look at Rose and Greg and screamed, too, like a locomotive. Nobody human could scream like that, Susan thought dully, but Milly did and then collapsed. She had the foresight, however, to collapse on the bed, which was a good thing, for neither Susan nor Greg could have carried her. Greg rose slowly. "I'll try to find G.M. There are some hot lines downstairs. Direct wires . . ."

He was off, running down the stairs; evidently he ran down some further stairs for Susan could hear his footsteps. There was only one thing to do; they had to call the police.

Milly stirred suddenly, shoved herself upright, and waddled over to stand beside Susan, who felt frozen. Milly looked down at Rose for a long time. Then she stooped, picked up something that glittered, and said, "Of course she did it with this."

This was a revolver, held in Milly's fat, cushioned hand.

Some faraway warning stirred in Susan. "You mustn't touch that. We mustn't touch anything. The police—"

Milly's gooseberry-green eyes popped. "The police!" She opened her mouth probably to scream again, but she thought better of that and thrust the revolver into Susan's hand. "I never thought of that. Here, take this—put it somewhere."

"But I—" Susan couldn't bear the touch of the revolver. She also realized too clearly at once that it had Milly's fingerprints on it and her own. "I'm afraid of guns," Milly said.

So was Susan. She looked around the room, which seemed unsteady as if it were a cabin on a ship, moving yet not moving. She started to put the gun on the mantel of the fireplace. Milly gasped, "The safe! It's open! The safe!"

She pressed her bulk around Rose and peered into the safe. "Why—why, there's nothing in it! Nothing! A thief!"

Susan was going to be sick. She couldn't stay there in that room with Rose. Somebody ought to pull that tight green skirt down over Rose's bulging legs. She sat down on the bed. Milly stood, staring into the safe. Greg came running up the stairs again and into the room. "I can't find him or Dora. My God, Susan, that conference is next week. We've got to do something."

"There's the gun," Susan nodded at it. He crossed swiftly to the fireplace, looked at the gun without touching it, and turned to her. "Did you touch it?"

"I—yes. Milly found it and picked it up—and gave it to me."

"You fool," Greg said to Milly.

"But she killed herself. Obviously. She killed herself. Poor Rose. She couldn't stand Gilbert's goings-on any longer. Sending this girl, Susan Beach, up here to stay." Milly whirled her great bulk toward Susan. "I suppose you expected to take Dora's place. The next mistress. Rose couldn't stand that! It's clear—"

Greg took her by her massive shoulders. "Shut up!"

She opened her pallid mouth where the bright lipstick stood out like streaky blood, and closed it again. Greg said in a voice Susan had never heard from him, "G.M. sent you here precisely to prevent gossip about him and Susan. Surely you've got sense enough to know that."

Milly rallied slightly and meanly. "You can't tell me that Dora spent so much time here with Gilbert for business reasons. It's perfectly clear. But he's had enough of Dora and now—"

"That is none of your business!" He turned back to Susan. "We've got to call the police. I used the direct wires from the switchboard down in the basement. I got the White House first," he said with what would have been a kind of wry grin except for the look in his eyes. "Whoever answered didn't know where G.M. is. Then I got the office—closed. I found a note for Dora's apartment—she didn't answer. I don't know all the numbers on the direct wires. I stopped trying. I was afraid of getting London or Paris or God knows what next. There's an ordinary phone in G.M.'s bedroom here. I'll call the police."

He seemed to wait for Susan's agreement. She nodded. "That is what Mr. Manders would tell us to do."

"Mr. Manders!" Milly said derisively. "You don't call him that when you're alone with him."

Greg was running along the hall and didn't hear her; lucky for you Susan thought, eyeing Milly. "I call him Mr. Mander because that's his name. He is my employer. He was a friend of my father's."

"Dear, dear," Milly said. "So he sent you up here to this—this love nest. Hardly aired out after Dora—"

"Dora is his confidential secretary and assistant and has been for years!"

Milly nodded. "Oh, yes, for years."

"It's not—not—we mustn't stand here and talk like this!"

"Rose can't hear us," Milly said, coolly now. "Besides, she's known all about Dora."

Dora Clanser was the great man's first assistant. She was the head of his New York office. She knew all about the great man's affairs—or at least was said to know. She had given Susan her instructions. She was Susan's superior in years and far her superior in the office hierarchy of authority.

Susan heard Greg's voice from a bedroom down the hall. ". . . that's right. I don't know what happened. I—we have just arrived . . . No, Mr. Manders is not here. We didn't know that Mrs. Manders had come. One of his secretaries came with me and Mrs. Manders' sister . . . Tell Col Clanser at the gate to let you in. No, I'll tell him. I'll use the house phone . . . All right."

Susan couldn't stay in the room with Rose, but she couldn't leave her with her fat legs sprawled out like that. She was aware of Milly's watchful eyes as she went to Rose. She couldn't look at that sagging face, but she gently pulled down the green skirt.

Milly shrugged, started toward the door, went back to snatch Rose's fur jacket and came trudging and panting out of the room after Susan. Greg met them in the hall. "I talked to the police. They'll send for the medical examiner. Nothing else to do. But I wish I hadn't had to—that conference next week—"

"What conference?" Milly asked swiftly. "He told me to come here for a few days, but he said nothing of any conference."

Greg gave her a harassed glance. "Money men. Industrialists. This meeting was supposed to be secret. That's what this house is for."

"Oh, *I* know what this house is for." Milly lifted scant eyebrows. "It's for his mistresses—"

"It's his home away from home. It's a place where he can entertain his guests formally yet—oh, intimately. Where they can talk without danger of being overheard. Or being seen. What do you think Col Clanser is guarding the house for?"

"Oh Col—"

"Great men come and go and sometimes there must be no whisper of their talks. G.M. built the house for that purpose and you know it!"

"He sent this girl here."

"Of course. He has to have a hostess, somebody to see to dinner—"

"You mean *cook?*" Milly's eyes turned a darker, scornful green.

"Oh, no," Greg replied absently. "He sends caterers for that. They bring food, serve it, leave. They're well chosen and are paid to keep their mouths shut. I'll phone down to Col and tell him what's happened and to let in the police."

He knew his way about the house. He went to another telephone on the wall. Someone—Col—must have answered as soon as Greg lifted the receiver. "Col, there's been—been trouble here . . . Never mind. Just let in the police when they come . . . Yes, I said police. There'll be a doctor too . . . Hell, let him show you his credentials if you want him to, but it's not necessary . . . No, I can't tell you now. I've got to get in touch with Mr. Manders." He put down the receiver and took Susan's arm gently. "You two women go into G.M.'s bedroom and close the door. You'll have to talk to the police sometime, but there'll be things that they have to do first. No sense in your watching—I mean—"

"Thank you," said Susan.

He led her to a big bedroom at the far end of the house. Milly followed swiftly, panting.

"Now, just stay here. I'll come back as soon as I can." He turned on a light and left, closing the door firmly behind him.

"Well," Milly said, "I must say that young man seems to think he's got some authority around here."

"Yes, I think he has. He's Mr. Manders' assistant."

Milly glanced hurriedly around the room. A lamp stood on a table near the bed and was obviously designed for reading. The room was almost Spartan in its simplicity. Milly's glance lingered hungrily on a desk and a chest of drawers. Susan almost said, "He keeps no papers here." Again she didn't say it. She was still in a kind of paralysis of thought and motion. She sat down, for her knees felt curiously unsteady; Milly chose the only comfortable chair in the room; it creaked under her weight. She stroked the fur jacket and stared at Susan. "Rose left a handsome will. She had plenty of money. That's how Gilbert got his start."

Susan knew something of the story, not much. Milly went on thoughtfully, "Rose hadn't died more than a few minutes when we found her. I could tell."

Only then Susan remembered the running man she had seen and, later, the whirl and roar she had heard as the helicopter rose and gradually departed. The man must have been Snell Clanser, the pilot.

Two

But Snell Clanser could not have known of Rose's death; he'd have summoned help; he wouldn't let Rose shoot herself; he was one of the Clansers who depended upon Rose for a job.

That meant that he depended upon the great man.

The great man really was a great man. He was called that by some of his office staff; others, such as Greg, called him by his initials, G.M. But whatever anybody called him, he *was* a great man. Susan knew that much of him, for her father had been one of G.M.'s friends; when her father died, the great man had taken the time to write a note to Susan offering friendly assistance if she needed it. Very soon she realized that she did at least need some kind of job; she took what money she had, went to a good school and learned all she could learn there of stenography, filing, accounts, general office work. She then took her courage in hand and asked G.M. for a job.

He had remembered her; he had given her an interview at once; he had given her a job. He had told her that Dora—that is, Mrs. Clanser—would show her the ropes. He had added some encouraging words, given her a little pat on the shoulder and said that she mustn't be nervous; she'd soon get the hang of things. She had begun then to develop a kind of hero worship for him.

She guessed some of his activities even though he was reticent; the whole office force was supposed to keep mouths shut. Yet his name was known and respected in very high and discreet circles; his advice was sought by other great men. He had a kind of genius about money. He did not advertise his place in the world. He kept meetings with other great men a secret whenever he could. He appeared in no magazines and no newspapers if he could help it. Yet his status was known. He was a good friend. He was also believed to be a bad enemy.

But Milly was right; he had got his start with Rose's

money. He had begun as a messenger in a brokerage house; he had soon become a customers' man and he had met Rose. She was Rose Clanser Whitelaw then. Her elderly husband had recently died, leaving a sizable fortune to Rose. G.M. had married Rose; whether or not her money had influenced him was open to question, but in any event he had certainly used it to start him on his upward path as a financier. Everything he touched turned to money. This was not luck; it was due to his study, his uncanny observation and money sense; he had a shapely finger in many successful pies. There was oil money, there was bank money, there was mining money; there were all sorts of bonds and stocks bought carefully and wisely. His quiet fame among other financiers grew. Yet he was an anomaly. He never gave to any political interest; he never bought or sold what could be called influence. In the wide world of money some tentacles of companies which he owned or controlled spread out over the world; certainly most of these companies were autonomous; his control lay behind the scenes. But his main interest was business at home, not in foreign concerns. Greg had explained something of that. "Plain old garden patriotism," he had said. "And also he's a loner. Likes it that way."

But G.M. had ability and an instinct. He knew the market; when everybody sold he seemed to know the exact point at which to buy.

Greg, too, had told Susan an odd and revealing story; the afternoon of the tragedy of President Kennedy the brokerage firms went wild for a time; everybody sold. There was an effort to close the stock market; it had to remain open until the board of governors could agree to its closing. In the meantime, with stocks plunging like mercury, the great man had bought and bought. It was, Greg had said, not because he needed the money; it was, again, simply because he was a patriot—he couldn't see the stock market go to pieces.

The fact that his newly acquired holdings almost immediately recovered their value was, Greg had said, incidental. It was also indicative of his financial genius, if anybody wanted to look at it coldly.

Susan did not look at it coldly. Neither did Greg.

She also knew from Greg, who rarely talked of G.M. and his affairs, that since the great man had made his start with Rose's money he had paid back to her every cent which he had used. Also—partly because Rose wished it but mainly, Greg thought, because he felt he owed it to Rose—he had taken on practically an army of Rose's relatives. The two guards, Col Clanser and another, Wilfred Clanser, were connections of Rose's—cousins, Susan remembered, or possibly second cousins. Milly was given a house in upstate New York and enough money to live on comfortably, although she took advantage of Rose's generosity (and possibly Gilbert Manders' forbearance) to make frequent and long visits to the lavish Fifth Avenue apartment which Gilbert Manders had bought for Rose and where he rarely lived.

Susan had seen the apartment once when Dora sent her there with an envelope of papers for G.M., who was at home then but whose visits, Susan couldn't help suspecting, were not frequent. Once she saw Rose and the apartment, she couldn't find it in her heart to blame him. Milly had been there too and had given Susan a searching, green-eyed stare. Rose had come out to meet her too, at Gilbert's request. Two small dogs, barking because Susan was a stranger, had come into the ornate library where she met Gilbert Manders with Rose.

Rose was enormously fat. Her face was like a pink-and-white balloon; her hair was violently blond and tousled. She looked incredibly sloppy in a bedraggled pale-pink negligee.

The dogs sniffed at Susan's heels and grumbled a little. A Siamese cat strolled in and gave Susan an intent blue-eyed look. Rose picked him up, which he didn't like; he struggled for a moment in the clasp of her plump white arms and then dug in a claw, so Rose screamed and put him down. He then walked away, with no suggestion of effort leaped to the back of the chair from which Gilbert had just risen, and stayed there, still eyeing Susan with that intent blue gaze from the black mask of his face.

She gave G.M. the papers and left, taking the bus homeward and thinking of the apartment. It could have been beautiful; it was obviously enormous. Just as obviously it had been decorated originally by some good decorator. But Susan couldn't help feeling that Rose's fat, white hands had got at the drawing room, of which Susan had had a rather shocking glimpse; there were ruffled pink taffeta draperies; there were many small laced cushions, none too clean; there was a scattering of supposedly French armchairs that were so bogus in their gilt and satin that no good decorator would have permitted their presence for an instant. She also saw in that flashing glimpse that there were sundry spots and stains on an Aubusson rug and—perhaps unfairly—judged that the dogs hadn't had the outdoor walks they required. There had to be some sort of arrangement for the cat. It struck her that there was definitely a kind of cattish smell in the apartment, with a heavily perfumed overlay. No, she didn't blame G.M. for permitting his business to take him from home so often.

She hadn't known then that in fact he kept a small hotel apartment. Even Rose hadn't known that. Susan knew it only because one day when Dora had gone to Washington with G.M. some accounts had been turned over to Susan and she had found a check for its rent. There was also a check for the maintenance of the Fifth Avenue apartment—and a huge check, it seemed to Susan. But although G.M. paid for it, he couldn't have borne to live there with sloppy pink-and-white Rose, the dogs, the cat and the ruffled taffeta draperies. And the smell.

She had wondered then how on earth Rose managed to keep household help. She learned later that she didn't; one of Susan's chores, given her by Dora, was that of seeing employment agencies far too frequently and offering what seemed to Susan far too large salaries.

Another of G.M.'s customs was a very small office staff, small in comparison with his money and the huge amount of business he actually controlled. There were typists, accountants and secretaries, such as Susan. There was a legal department in offices one floor removed from G.M.'s own offices. Susan saw little of the legal department but believed it was sparsely staffed, too. He did not maintain a public relations staff; he employed no lobbyists. He was indeed, as Greg had said, a loner—but a remarkable loner whose counsel was sought by other great men. They in turn might hold counsel with men in government; Susan knew nothing of that.

Comparatively small though his office staff was, there was little office gossip. G.M. was not a man to permit it, and everyone in the office knew it. Nevertheless, some gossip seemed to seep out by itself: G.M. wouldn't hurt Rose, to whom he owed so much, but the whisper was that Dora Clanser was his mistress and had been for a long time.

She was another Clanser, but that was her married name; her husband had been Ligon Clanser, divorced years ago. Dora was an excellent office worker; efficient, alert, sharp-minded and undoubtedly good-looking, even beautiful, with her naturally blond hair, her languorous but also on occasion very resolute brown eyes, her velvet skin, her trim yet inviting figure, her clothes which certainly were expensive but were always appropriate and elegant. Oh, yes, Dora had lasted a long time.

It had taken a long time, too, for Susan to put the scraps of innuendo together. G.M. remained an object of hero worship to her. After seeing Rose she wouldn't have blamed him for keeping a harem. But it would have to be an extremely discreet kind of harem.

She couldn't think of Rose now—that fat, disheveled, pathetic figure, sprawled so dreadfully in the room with the safe. Yet she could not dismiss the picture from her mind; it would remain there forever, she thought with a chill, feeling as if the house had grown suddenly cold. Rose might have had reason to kill herself. Suppose she had known how tragically she had lost G.M. Suppose she had driven herself to a dreadful and final act. Somehow, little as Susan knew of Rose, it didn't seem likely that she would commit suicide. Yet of course there were only a few answers to that shocking event. Suicide. Or accident, or burglary. The safe *had* been open.

A man had been running away from the house, casting back a furtive glance before he disappeared and presumably went away by helicopter.

He had to be Snell Clanser. Someone had brought Rose to the house. Suppose that someone had shot her.

Oh, no, Susan thought with sharp revulsion. It couldn't have been murder! Perhaps the police would call it an accident. Perhaps—oh, yes, surely it was an accident.

It was definitely dark outside the windows when she heard voices and the footsteps of men tramping up the stairs and into the room where Rose lay, a pathetic heap of blowzy hair and blowzy dress and bulging legs. She was thankful that she had pulled down Rose's skirt.

The safe in the room *was* open. But Dora had told her that G.M. never kept valuables at the secret house; the safe was meant only for a depository of notes after some conference at the house. The notes were then taken to the New York office or to G.M.'s solitary hotel apartment in New York.

At last there were more and heavier steps on the stairs. So the first medical examination had taken place and they were taking Rose away, carrying that grossly heavy body down the stairs. Susan was thankful that she could not see the driveway and the car lights which by now must have gathered: police cars, an ambulance, the medical examiner's car. It was now fully dark with the quick twilight of October.

Milly also knew what was happening, for she went to the door, pressed her face against it and listened. When she turned to Susan, she quickly placed one hand over the cushions of fat at her breast, as if to quiet her heart.

"My Rose! My dear Rose! Gone forever," said Milly.

There were several books on the table at the bedside, along with a small clock. Susan's fingers itched to throw a book at Milly—that or the clock. But that might injure the clock, she thought meanly, and then reproved herself; she really must learn self-control if she and Milly were to stay in that house together.

But then of course they might not stay there; G.M. might change his mind, change the date set for the conference, do anything in consideration of Rose's shocking death.

Milly listened again. "They're leaving. I heard the door of the vestibule close. There! There's a car starting up!" She opened the bedroom door and stared into the hall. "No, I can't hear a thing. It's been a long time, I don't understand. I think I'll just take a look." She disappeared in the direction of the room where they had found Rose.

It *had* been a long time, Susan thought with a dazed recognition of the fact that she had sat there, huddled on the long bed with its plain white counterpane, thinking in circles of all she knew and didn't know of Rose and G.M.

Then she heard Greg coming up the stairs—Greg or some man with quick and hard footsteps. It was Greg.

He apparently met Milly, who cried, "What have they done? What have they done with my poor dear Rose?"

"Taken her away," Greg said shortly. "Where's Susan?"

"In there. Sitting like a stone. Not even a tear."

"Susan didn't know—" Greg stopped himself shortly and came to the door as Susan rose.

"I got Dora on the phone," he said. "I told her what had happened. She'll try to get in touch with G.M. The police want to talk to you. Are you up to it? They'll not ask much. I told them everything."

"All right." Susan smoothed back her hair, smoothed down her brown skirt and shook her jacket into place.

"They'll not bother you," Greg said. "I told them why we were here, everything. Take it easy."

Milly came after them down the stairs, padding along like an overweight elephant.

The entrance hall led into what was obviously a formal living room. Lights were on, so Susan could see through the beautiful room into an equally beautiful dining room so large that it could easily seat at least thirty guests. Ranks of polished chairs glimmered against the walls. The rugs were lovely patterns of soft colors and depth. She thought the picture over the white mantel was a Cézanne. Milly, still behind them, grunted rather like the distant cousin Col she had clearly not liked. "Huh! Love nest," said Milly.

It was anything but a love nest. The living room had an austere but very beautiful grace and dignity, which Susan felt just then rather than saw, for Greg led her down two steps into what was a large library. She felt its beauty, too, and thought suddenly that here the great man could entertain guests in a suitable way; he couldn't possibly have done so in the musty, sloppy apartment on Fifth Avenue, with Rose as his hostess and the smell of cat for atmosphere.

She pulled herself and her scattered fancies together; a plain-clothes man stood waiting for her. Two men in uniform waited too.

The plain-clothes man was introduced; his name was Lattrice and she gathered that so far he was in charge of investigating Rose's death. The two men in uniform, police, had guns in their holsters and didn't say a word. In one corner, behind a polished writing table, Col Clanser stood, looking scared.

Lattrice—a detective sergeant in rank, she soon discovered—asked her politely to sit down. "Mr. Cameron"—he nodded a neat head at Greg—"has told us how you happened to arrive just when you did. We just want *your* account of what happened—that is, if you are perfectly willing to have a record made of it. If you prefer to consult a lawyer before you make any sort of statement, you are within your rights."

"Why, I—" It bewildered Susan. "I don't need a lawyer."

Lattrice ran a well-kept hand over his neat dark hair and cleared his throat. "Well, you see, Miss—Beach, is it?—you see, we have every reason to believe that Mrs. Manders' death was due to either accident or suicide, but it is our duty to explore every avenue of investigation. You do understand that."

Susan sat down. She happened to sit in a large and very comfortable upholstered chair which was meant for men; her toes barely touched the pale yellow and green Oriental rug, and her sense of being off balance was in its way disconcerting. "Yes, of course I understand. But you see we just—found her, like that."

"You had barely arrived?"

"Yes. We—that is, Greg—Mr. Cameron and I took some groceries to the kitchen. Then Milly—I mean, Miss Clanser and I went upstairs and found her—Mrs. Manders."

"Did you have any impression of how long she had been dead?"

"No. No—"

Milly burst in. "Only a few moments. She was still warm."

Lattrice nodded gravely. "Col Clanser—" He glanced at Col, who seemed to shrink back behind the desk; Col had rather mean little eyes and needed a shave. "Col Clanser says Mrs. Manders did not come in at the front gate. He says she must have come by helicopter. He heard a helicopter arrive. He heard it leave after you three had entered the house."

"Yes, that's right."

"So there wasn't any time for anybody to escape. Except the pilot of the helicopter, of course."

"But he— Oh—" She turned to Greg. "That man! The running man!"

Nothing about Lattrice seemed to change, yet Susan felt a kind of stiffening about him. He said to Greg, "A running man? You didn't mention that."

"I didn't think of it," Greg said.

"But you saw him?"

"As a matter of fact I didn't. We had just got into the kitchen and were unloading the groceries we had brought. Susan—Miss Beach—went to the window and said she saw a man running. I started to look and I—well, I dropped some tomatoes and slipped on one and by the time I had got to the window he had disappeared. We waited until we both heard the helicopter leave."

"Did you get a good look at this man, Miss Beach?"

"In a way—that is—" She bogged down. "Not really but—" But he wasn't G.M., she thought unexpectedly.

"Was it the pilot Mr. Manders employed? Snell Clanser?"

"I don't know. I've never seen the pilot."

"But you can identify this running man if you see him again?"

Susan hesitated again. She shut her eyes trying to summon a mental picture of the running man and Lattrice said, "Tall or short?"

"Why, medium. He had a hat pulled down over his face. He looked back at the house."

"But you could identify him?" Lattrice said again.

Greg made a sudden motion as if to warn her but she was too confused, too shaken by the ugly event of Rose's death, to grasp his meaning. She said slowly, "I might be able to. Yes, in the right light—yes, I think I might be able to."

Lattrice nodded. Greg shoved his hands in his pockets and looked at the rug. Col Clanser cried, "I didn't see him! You can't see the back gate, the gate that leads into a path through the woods and to the helicopter landing—you can't see that from the front gate where I was stationed."

"Ah," said Lattrice. "Well, now, Mr. Cameron says that this is the first time you have ever visited this house, Miss Beach."

"That's right."

"He told me that you work in Mr. Manders' office and that you and Mrs. Manders' sister—"

"That's me." Milly was still standing, arms folded across her vast body in a belligerent way.

Lattrice nodded politely and went on. "That you were both to stay here and see to the house and arrangements for some business meeting which Mr. Manders had planned for next week."

"Yes," Susan replied.

"When did you last see Mr. Manders?"

"Yesterday afternoon."

"What did he say?"

"Nothing much. Just that Miss Clanser was to come with me. He said that Mrs. Clanser—"

"You mean Mrs. Dora Clanser?" The detective appeared to have taken some pains to inform himself, probably by way of Greg.

"She told you what your duties were?"

"Yes. Only to see that the house was in order for the guests who were coming. Mr. Manders wanted me to act as hostess for dinner. Then I was to leave the dining room. I mean go upstairs and join Miss Clanser but first make sure that the caterer and his assistant had gone."

"*Hostess!*" said Milly scornfully.

A voice rose from the vestibule, two voices, one of them shouting angrily. The detective went to the door of the library. "Bring him in here."

Another uniformed policeman, holding a man by the arm, came down the steps into the library. Col Clanser started forward. "Gosh, Wilfred, you don't know what's been going on—"

The newcomer stared at Col, at the policemen, at Greg, at Susan and rumpled his already disheveled gray hair. He moistened red, wet-looking lips. He got around to Milly and grinned. "So you're here. Never can leave Rose alone, can you?"

Milly did not speak. Greg said rather hurriedly, "Wilfred, there's been an accident. Mrs. Manders was shot."

"Rose! Why I didn't—I can't believe! Why, who shot her?"

"It was an accident," Greg said firmly. "She must have taken out that gun that's kept in the safe."

The newcomer, Wilfred Clanser, shook his head. The vestige of a grin lingered on his loose red mouth. "Too bad. Didn't kill her, did it?"

Milly whirled around as if she intended to slap him; Wilfred had the same impression, for he dodged out of her way. Milly said with dreadful majesty, "She killed herself! Just as we came up the driveway and she saw that girl. That Susan Beach. Rose knew that she was Gilbert's new fancy. His new mistress. So my poor, poor Rose couldn't take it any longer. She killed herself."

Three

For a blinding second of sheer red rage Susan wished she had something more lethal than a book to throw at Milly. Milly! G.M. had asked her to call the gross woman Milly because he had said it made it simpler. He had sighed a little and said that there were so many Clansers. He had then sent her briskly away to take Dora's dictation.

So all the way out from town she had repeated it to herself: Milly, Milly. Susan could feel the alerted gaze of every man in the room except Greg, who, she suddenly perceived, was engaged in keeping his own self-control. He turned to the detective. "There's not a word of truth in that accusation."

Wilfred Clanser grinned openly. "How do you know? The great man is pretty sly. And he certainly liked ladies. Cousin Dora Clanser—he's had her a long time. Where is she?"

Greg got himself in hand. "Mrs. Dora Clanser is now on her way here."

Wilfred wiped one hand over his mouth. "Where's the great man?"

"I don't know."

"Was he here today?" Wilfred asked with a touch of the same greedy curiosity that had suggested itself about Milly. A family trait perhaps, Susan thought coldly, and not pleasant.

"He was not here today," Greg said definitely.

"Are you sure of that, Mr. Cameron?" the detective asked. "You and Miss Beach and, I gather, Miss Milly Clanser arrived at the same time. He could have been here earlier in the day."

"He could have been, but I don't think he was. Col, at the gate, would have known it."

Lattrice addressed Susan. "Are you sure the running man wasn't Mr. Manders?"

So her inner denial that the running man was G.M. had been based on a subtle but very accurate instinct. "I'm sure," she said steadily. "I'd have recognized Mr. Manders."

"She saw somebody running?" Wilfred asked again with a kind of gluttonous curiosity.

"Never mind about that," Lattrice said crisply. "Now as for you—I take it your name is Wilfred."

"Wilfred Clanser, sure. I'm on the front gate at night, Col in the daytime. That is, we take turns for day or night duty. There's a little sort of shed there, hidden in the pines, for cold weather."

"You mean that the house is always guarded?"

Wilfred and Col both nodded, and one of the policemen spoke respectfully. "I live in the village, you know, Sergeant. Everybody knows this house is here. They know Col and Wilfred are guards. They both have permits for guns. It's—" He swallowed rather uncomfortably and went on, "It's been a kind of joke, you know, around town."

"Joke?" Lattrice said.

"Well, you see some people do say that it's a place for the great man to keep his—his girl friends. Either that or he keeps valuables here, money maybe, or jewels or something he's careful about. A joke," he repeated rather feebly.

Greg said quietly, "May I speak to you privately, Sergeant?"

"Why, certainly."

The two men walked up the steps; the sound of their footsteps was softened by the thickness of the rugs. There was not the faintest murmur of their voices; they must have gone on into the kitchen—where she had stood at the window and had so briefly seen the running man, who could not possibly have been G.M.

There was a heavy silence in the library as if everybody there was straining ears to hear what the private conversation might be about.

Susan absently looked around the room. Its walls were lined with bookshelves; there were deep chairs, a deep sofa, a long writing table, a hassock or two of Morocco leather. The brass fender at the fireplace, black marble streaked with pale yellow, gleamed softly and brightly; the fireplace tools were also brass and glowed in the light of the big lamp on the writing table. The lamp's pale-green base looked as if it had once been a very fine Chinese vase. There was a picture over the mantel here, too, a Utrillo this time—an original, she thought. G.M. was not a collector in the accepted meaning of the word, he had only an intuitive flair for beauty.

Rose must have been beautiful once.

The reaction from shock and horror was beginning to crawl along her nerves like a chill. The house though was now warm, almost too warm. Col and Wilfred drifted softly, almost furtively, together, as if they would like to talk but didn't dare so near the ears of the policemen. Milly was, Susan knew now, a woman to be feared. She had had no excuse or right to accuse Susan and she had done so with a kind of vicious pleasure. Decidedly Susan was beginning to think that she did not like the Clanser family in any of its sprawling connections.

Dora, of course, had not been born a Clanser. If the whispers were based on fact and she had been G.M.'s mistress for years, then he had good taste, Susan reflected, and for the first time she felt a little pang of distaste for Dora. Yet if Dora had been G.M.'s mistress it was none of Susan's business. It occurred to her, but very briefly, that her sudden distaste was like jealousy. But she couldn't be jealous of Dora. She had not acquired the experience or the time at the office to compete with Dora.

Col's head jerked up; so did Wilfred's. All at once the policemen looked as alert as terriers, listening for prey.

Milly had lifted her fat face too and said, "It's the helicopter."

Then Susan heard it coming nearer and nearer, so suddenly loud, it seemed almost to hover over the house. The strong beating of the engine roared and roared; abruptly it stopped. Perhaps everyone in the room took a breath. Milly said, "It must be Gilbert." She started for the drawing room but a policeman stood before her.

"Get out of my way, young man," Milly shouted.

"Please, ma'am. The sergeant expects me to keep everyone here."

Milly eyed him, pale eyes bulging. "Do as I say!" She looked as if she might try to shove him aside, but he stood his ground like a rock. She didn't snort, she only breathed heavily and angrily. The young policeman said, "If you please, ma'am."

So Milly waited, listening again. All of them listened. It seemed a long time, and indeed it was sufficient time for anyone arriving in the helicopter to walk along the path from the landing, through the back gate and into the house before there was any sound at all from beyond the drawing room, and when it came, it was unexpected, for it was the indignant yell which only a Siamese cat can produce. At almost the same instant a small, shaggy brown dog came bounding across the living room and stopped at the steps, his bright eyes glittering from behind an unbrushed pompadour. His gaze took in the entire room and fastened upon a leg of the enormous writing table. Another equally shaggy and unbrushed dog appeared behind him and also looked swiftly around the room.

"My God," Milly said, "it's the whole menagerie."

Unexpectedly Susan felt a slight wave of empathy for Milly. But the first dog made a beeline for the table leg and gravely lifted his leg. The second dog seemed inspired by this action and settled herself in the middle of the handsome rug. A little circle of moisture spread on the rug before the policeman who had said he lived in Medbury Hills sprang forward. "You can't do that here!" he cried. But there was no stopping the two small fountains. Col gasped, turned red and cried, "I've got to clean it up. There's paper towels in the washroom."

"Go and get them," said the policeman near the door. Col waddled hurriedly up the steps and thudded across the living room. The invisible cat let out another enraged cry from somewhere. Milly seemed to feel that this was too much and sat down heavily in a chair. The dog at the table leg shook himself. The small one in the middle of the rug continued to pour with apparent satisfaction, looking with interest at everyone in the room. The policeman who said he lived in the village snatched up the male dog, who offered no resistance. He was obliged to wait for the female but at last stuffed her under his arm. He didn't wait for permission but shot across the living room; in a few seconds the heavy vestibule door opened and closed.

"They'll run away. Maybe," said Milly callously.

"Oh, no!" Susan said. "Oh, no!"

"Never mind, Miss," said one of the policemen. "He'll see to them."

The cat, still outside the library, made another uncomplimentary remark and seemed to claw at something that was brittle.

"It's his basket," Milly said to nobody. "G.M. is here. He must have brought them."

The cat's yell and scratches came nearer across the living room. Dora appeared at the steps, carrying a violently agitated basket. She glanced around the room, pinned Susan with her lovely dark eyes and said, "You can take care of him." She put the basket down; the cat must have got a claw into a strategic place, for suddenly the latch for the basket fell open and the cat emerged. At once he became sedate, dignified and reproachful, even though his brown-and-beige fur was rumpled, his black, slightly crooked tail lashed and his blue eyes shot crimson lights.

"Do you mean—" Susan began and Dora cut in, "I mean G.M. means you to stay here for the present. We couldn't leave the—those creatures," she said distastefully, "alone in the apartment. So he said to bring them here. He said you would take care of them."

She took off her gloves with an air of having completed a mission and detaching herself from any consequences. Susan eyed the cat, the puddle in the middle of the rug and asked coldly, "Did you bring a sandbox?"

"A sand—" Dora's eyes widened. Col reappeared, muttered some kind of apology to Dora, and ran past her to start mopping the rug. Wilfred chuckled and tried to hide it. Dora grasped the idea. "Just let him outdoors. You'll not need a sandbox. Good heavens, there's all the woods to run around in."

Susan took a hard grasp on her own common sense. She also remembered the smell of cat in G.M.'s apartment. "I want a sandbox and I want it immediately," she snapped.

Dora lifted silky eyebrows but Wilfred, still chuckling, lunged forward. "I'll fix a box for him, Miss," he said. "That is, if the policemen will let me."

The remaining policemen looked harassed, but one of them nodded at Wilfred. "Go ahead. Better take the cat with you."

Having scrubbed vigorously at the puddle on the rug, Col waddled swiftly toward the desecrated table leg, waving what looked like yards of paper toweling. Wilfred advanced toward the cat, who perceived his intention, glared at him, and instantly chose a place that apparently promised safety, for he sprang with no warning at Susan's skirt, clawed his way upward to her shoulder, dug in his claws and growled hoarsely at Wilfred.

She was thankful that the shoulders of her brown suit jacket were slightly padded. She said, "May I take him outside?"

Again a policeman answered, although in a rather frustrated voice: "I don't know what else to do. Yes, go on. But don't leave the place."

The cat seemed to sense victory as Susan walked up the

two steps, passing Dora and getting a sniff of Dora's expensive perfume; he balanced himself neatly on Susan's shoulder. She heard Milly behind her. "Where is Gilbert?"

She heard Dora's reply. "In the kitchen. He's talking to Greg and a man, I think a detective. You'd better tell me everything. What exactly happened?"

Milly's voice began. Nobody stopped her. Susan went into the big hall and into the vestibule. The door in the vestibule that led toward the kitchen was firmly closed; she could hear no voices. She opened the grilled iron door. Lights streamed from the vestibule windows and fell upon the uniformed figure of the dog-watching policeman. He turned abruptly as he heard her footsteps on the driveway and automatically, it seemed to Susan, his hand went to his revolver holster. It gave her a kind of tremor up her spine. She said, "They said I could let the cat out. Do you think he'll be all right? I mean, he'll not get lost?"

"No. Just let him down. You can't lose a cat. Wish I could say the same for these dogs. They act as if they'd never been outdoors before. I can't even see them."

Susan stooped and the cat condescended to let himself down on the driveway. He then licked back a hair that had apparently been disturbed, sniffed, looked around and modestly disappeared behind some shrubbery.

She could see neither of the dogs. Lights from two cars streamed thinly into the dark. "Try whistling," she advised the policeman.

He tried but gave up, for only a kind of *whishing* sound came from his earnestly puckered lips. He said, embarrassed, "Never could whistle. Something about my teeth."

Susan took a deep breath and whistled nervously; it came out with such unexpected and piercing success that the policeman jerked around again.

"*Where* did you learn to whistle like that?"

"I always had dogs when I was a child. Cats, too. Do you think the dogs heard me?"

"I don't see how they could help hearing," the policeman said with a certain amount of feeling. He rubbed one ear as if to assure himself that he did not have a burst eardrum, and then said, more kindly, "Don't you worry about them. They'll come back as soon as they've had a good run and get hungry. Animals have a lot of sense."

More than I have, Susan thought; how did I ever get into such a situation? But of course she hadn't known, she couldn't have guessed that an office job, working for G.M., could conceivably result in almost becoming a witness to tragedy. But not really a witness. She had only seen Rose dead. She had only seen a running man. The October night was growing chill; her tweed jacket was warm but not warm enough. She wished the dogs would come back. She wished she could go back to New York, to her own small but safe apartment. She wished she were anywhere but here—and at the same time she wanted to see G.M., wanted to see him take charge of everything, wanted to see him with his magnetic force and vigor and intelligence act in an emergency. He would know what to do.

Meantime Dora had said she, Susan, was to stay at the house and take care of what Milly had called the menagerie. The chill of the night was creeping into her bones. The policeman knew it and said kindly again, "I'll see to them, Miss, if you're cold. Feels like we might have an early frost."

"No, I'd rather stay out here."

The policeman understood her. "Can't say I blame you. I've been a policeman for eight, going on nine, years. Never like accidents. As for shooting—well, I can't say I've seen many shootings. Never want to either."

Susan mutely agreed. The cat came into the light from one of the cars; he had a complacent air, settled himself at Susan's feet and began a vigorous grooming of his coat.

The vestibule door opened. Susan and the policeman whirled around. Two men emerged, clear against the lights in the vestibule. One of them was G.M.

He walked steadily toward them. He was a tall man who always held himself vigorously erect, liked exercise and got it no matter what the office pressures were. The detective looked thin and slight beside G.M. As they approached they entered the lane of light from one of the parked cars and G.M. saw Susan. He came quickly to her and put his arm around her shoulders. "Poor child," he said. His voice was low but carried an enormous sense of confidence. She could almost feel her spine stiffening. "I'm sorry I sent you here. Snell must have brought her in the helicopter. I haven't been able to find Snell. Couldn't find my helicopter, as a matter of fact. Hired one and a pilot to bring us up here. Oh, there's Toby."

Toby was obviously the name of the cat, for he looked up appreciatively and uttered a deep-voiced mutter. "Take care of him, Susan dear. I have to ask you to stay on here for—for a bit. You and Milly. Will you do that?"

She couldn't possibly have refused. Nobody could refuse G.M. when he spoke in that tone. In the light from the car he was so close that she could see his face with its deep-set and perceptive eyes, his hard-looking cheek, his strong nose and chin, even the sprinkling of gray in his black hair. He had a certain magnetism; she had known that, but she hadn't before then felt her pulse quicken as though her heart was taking its own course of action. She said—she couldn't have said anything else—"Yes, of course I'll stay."

"Good girl. Greg was explaining to the detective sergeant my reasons for this house when I arrived. I'm going into the village now with Sergeant Lattrice. There are some things I must see to. Now you'll be all right. I've sent Greg to tell the helicopter pilot to take his machine back. I had told him to wait in case of need. Now then—oh, here they are."

The dogs had ignored Susan's whistle; they heard G.M.'s voice and came, their unclipped curls flying, to jump at him. "It was a good idea to give them a run," said G.M.

The policeman cleared his throat nervously. "I'm afraid it was too late, sir. I mean—"

G.M. lifted his head. "I know what you mean. Susan—"

Susan liked dogs but she stood no nonsense from them. "I'll see to them," she said firmly. Something about the firmness pleased G.M. His arm around her shoulders tightened. "I'll be back as soon as I can. All right, Lattrice."

He moved away with the detective toward one of the cars. Its door opened, the light flashed for a moment on G.M.'s tall figure, and then the door closed. The policeman said, "Might be as well to take the dogs in, now, Miss. What're their names?"

"I don't know. Come on, you," Susan said to the dogs, not expecting obedience.

The dogs, however, gave her intelligent glances from under their frowzy pompadours and followed with docility. Toby came too with a rather stately air of obliging for courtesy's sake. "They'll be hungry," the policeman said, opening the heavy vestibule door for the procession.

Susan thought rapidly over the groceries she and Greg had assembled and remembered with gratitude the chopped beef Greg had insisted on. "You never can tell," he had said. "It's always convenient to have hamburger. Besides, we can freeze the meat."

She led the way to the kitchen; the door was open and somebody had stepped on another of the spilled tomatoes.

The policeman turned slightly green. "Looks like blood." He snatched up paper towels, as Col had done, wet them at the gleaming chromium sink and mopped up the remains.

In giving Susan her orders Dora had told her to stock up on groceries and supplies, anything she and Milly might need for a few days. She had been indefinite as to the time; she had said merely that G.M. didn't as a rule have groceries delivered from Medbury Hills; it was too long a drive for prompt delivery. So Susan would have to use her judgment about what might be needed. Somebody, Greg probably, had put the enormous package of hamburger meat in the refrigerator. Susan got it out.

"They're too fat, all three of them," she said. "But they really are hungry."

"A way to get them used to a new place. So they feel at home." The policeman dropped the red-stained and damp paper towels into a trash basket.

"You must have a dog." She found three saucers and a spoon and ladled out what she thought were sufficient amounts.

"Three of them! As good setters as you'll ever see. Not much like these tangled brown mops. But then"—he sounded apologetic—"I guess they are city dogs. My setters wouldn't like the city."

Greg opened the door and came in. He smiled briefly when he saw the dogs wolfing down hamburger; Toby was eating daintily, but eating. "I told you hamburger would come in handy." Greg's voice was strained and tired. He rather looked like G.M. really, tall and erect, with good strong features, although his face was wider and there was no gray in his thick black hair.

He looked at the policeman. "Will you let Mrs. Clanser come in here for a moment?"

"Why, I—well, I'll ask." The policeman reached for the door and turned back. "Don't forget they'll need water," he told Susan and went away.

"Got him out of the way." Greg sat down wearily on the low kitchen stepladder. The lights were so bright that they seemed to take the color out of his face. "Susan, they couldn't find Snell Clanser. Dora got hold of G.M. just as he came back to his hotel suite. They tried to find Snell but couldn't. G.M.'s helicopter hadn't been returned either. G.M. had to hire a man to bring him up here."

"G.M. told me." She found a large dish and filled it with water.

"The point is, somebody had to bring Rose here. She must have died just as we were arriving."

Susan put the water dish on the floor under a table. "Wouldn't that man at the gate, Col, have heard the shot?"

"No. G.M. has the whole house soundproofed. You can't hear a thing from outside. He even soundproofed this kitchen."

"Why on earth did he do that?"

He shrugged.

"To shut out kitchen sounds so his guests wouldn't hear the clatter. At least that's what he told that police detective, Lattrice. His real reason, I suppose, was to prevent anybody at all—the caterer, his assistant, anybody—from hearing his conversations with his guests. Of course, sometimes Dora must have heard and then taken notes. I don't know about that. Susan, do you think there was time while we were here in the kitchen fussing with the food and looking for the man you saw running—and then listening for the helicopter which we heard only a short time—do you think there was time for Milly to go upstairs and shoot Rose?"

Susan leaned against a table. "Milly!"

"We wouldn't have been likely to hear the shot. Milly stood to inherit something over three million from Rose. G.M. told me."

Four

Strangely, the natural little episode of the dogs and the cat had seemed to restore Susan to a natural and everyday world. Even the kind and everyday chat with the policeman about the dogs had provided something like a shield against the unnatural fact of Rose's tragic death.

She leaned against the table, thinking hard. "Yes," she said at last, "I think there might have been time. I didn't know the kitchen was insulated."

"Everything but the windows. You can't hear a thing from the house itself. You can hear—as we did hear the helicopter—through the windows. But G.M. said positively that nothing in the house could be heard. Especially a thirty-two."

"A thirty-two? Was that the gun?"

Greg nodded. "The detective has it. And Milly—if she shot Rose—could have very cleverly got her fingerprints on it—and your fingerprints on it in a way which would seem natural."

"She'd have wiped off her fingerprints."

"But she'd have to hurry. I don't see Milly as a murderer. But she had a motive for getting rid of Rose. And that could have been very quick work about the fingerprints." He paused, thought and said, "A thirty-two doesn't make as much noise as, say, a thirty-eight. Certainly not a forty-five. Milly knew the gun was in the safe. G.M. told the police Milly had been here a time or two with Rose. Well—" He rubbed his eyes wearily. "I also knew about the gun. So did Dora."

"Dora wasn't here."

"Oh, no. And you did see a man running. Might have been Snell. If he'd had a crash with the copter it certainly would have been reported at once. Snell is really a good and experienced pilot. Somebody had to bring Rose here. That detective sergeant, Lattrice, questioned G.M. about that. Lattrice seemed to feel that whoever brought her here must have been someone Rose knew. G.M. agreed. Lattrice asked if there ha been any threats to Rose; G.M. said no, she'd have told him Then Lattrice asked G.M. if he himself had been threatened G.M. said no to that, too. But someone must have told Ros something, anything to induce her to come here. She hate the helicopter. If we could find out who brought her here an who induced her to come—"

The door opened. There had been no sound of Dora's hig heels on the tiled floor outside. Susan remembered that sh had strained her ears to hear the voices of G.M., the polic detective and Greg while they were talking there in th kitchen. Everybody in the library had sat listening. Ther hadn't been the slightest murmur of voices. But surely a sho would have penetrated that insulation.

Dora came into the kitchen in a lithe, graceful way whic was her natural walk. She saw the dogs eating, lifted an eyebrow at Toby who had sat down to wash, and said to Susan "Why didn't you grab them before all that in the library?"

"Why didn't you? You brought them from the helicopter You could have let them run—"

"No, I couldn't." It was curious how Dora's velvety-brow eyes could become, not steely or hard, but oddly opaque a though an intentional curtain came down over them to hid her thoughts. It was an unconscious trick, Susan thought, bu an unusual and rather frightening one. Susan herself had ha few occasions to observe it, but she had seen its effect upo others in the office. It brought forth apologies and instan obedience. Dora said, "G.M. had all he could do to han onto them, one under each arm. I carried the cat basket. hope you'll not be so careless again, Susan. I'm not going t let this house become another apartment like Rose's. I'd ge rid of them if I were G.M."

"But you're not," Greg said softly.

"You sent for me, Greg," Dora said.

"Yes. I don't know the switchboard downstairs. I saw you name and number and G.M.'s but nothing else. So after getting the White House—"

"The White House! What for?"

"Oh, I didn't mean to. I was going to say, if you can rin Snell on that switchboard, it'd be a good idea to try."

Dora considered it. "All right. You reached me, you know Greg, just as I walked into my apartment. I'd been havin cocktails with Bert."

This was a new name to Susan. Apparently it was not t

Greg, whose eyes flickered rather sharply at Dora. "You mean Bert Prowde?"

Dora nodded negligently, passing one hand over her gleaming, neat blond hair; her orange dress and jacket were precisely the shade of color to bring out the gleams of gold in her hair and the fineness of her white skin. She wore a very faint but alluring touch of green eye shadow, visible as make-up only because the kitchen lights were so bright.

Greg said, "Two strings to your bow, huh? Sensible."

Dora's eyes became veiled and thoughtful for a second, but then she laughed gently, went to Greg and leaned caressingly against him. "Darling, don't be jealous."

Greg looked honestly and completely astounded. Then he laughed, too. "Don't try your tricks on me, Dora. Now then, please go and try to reach Snell. Somebody brought Rose here."

Dora shrugged. "Oh, all right. Be sure you see to those—those animals, Susan. I don't want them wrecking this house as they did the city apartment."

Susan didn't trust herself to reply, not because she might have said too much but in fact because she was afraid she would say too little.

"Go ahead and explode," Greg said, grinning, as the door closed after Dora.

"No, no. She's right. That city apartment—have you been there, Greg?"

"Sure! Rose was no housekeeper."

Susan snorted. "That's putting it mildly. But then—poor thing—Greg, what does G.M. really think? Accident? Or suicide? Or—or murder?"

"I'm not sure what he thinks. But I know what the police are going to think when he's through with them."

"Accident," said Susan flatly.

"Maybe it was."

"You wondered whether Milly could have shot Rose while we were in the kitchen."

"I do wonder. But if the police say accident, then G.M. is in the clear."

"In the clear? You don't think G.M. could have shot her! Greg, he was not the man I saw running. I know he was not."

"I mean G.M. wants to have things put on as even a keel as possible because of the conference next week. He can't call that off now without giving rise to no end of rumors. If faith in G.M. is shaken—it would be, well—" Greg rose, went to the window, stood with his hands shoved in his pockets and said, "It would have a very bad effect. Sometimes it seems as though the whole world is in a peck of trouble all the time about money. One crisis after another. There's no doubt that G.M. has a steady hand—and a genius brain. He's in a self-made position of power and authority whether he likes it or not. The point is there can't be a suggestion of murder in his private life. He's too important to too many people."

Susan thought for a moment. One of the dogs finished eating and went to the water dish. "Tanking up again," Greg said. "Another go at a table leg! Col told me what happened. Dora ought to have known better than to take the dogs in a taxi to the helicopter, hang onto them along the path to the house and then let them go. But watch out. She'll get them to the vets and the happy hunting grounds if she gets a chance."

"She'll not get a chance!"

"Don't be too sure of that. She adores this house. She's spent quite a bit of time here, you know—" He stopped abruptly.

Susan said, "Greg, was she—is she—I mean, she seems ready to take over the house!"

Greg answered her unspoken question promptly. "I really don't know, Susan. She's a very attractive woman. However, to be frank, I was never under the bed. If she is G.M.'s mistress, I don't know."

"I think," Susan said slowly, "she's planning to marry him."

Greg shrugged. "It would be a fine marriage for Dora."

"But then who is this Bert Prowde?"

"I said two strings to her bow just to be mean. She gets under my skin a little. Bossy. Authoritative. I had to say that. I shouldn't have."

"Why not?"

"Mainly because everybody hates the boss. I don't hate G.M. He's done everything for me. But I can't say I like Dora as a kind of straw boss. Anyway, Bert Prowde is a boy friend. Takes Dora around. When G.M. is not available."

"What's he like?"

"Nothing on earth. No, I'll take that back. I've seen him a few times with Dora either when I had to take something to her apartment or—once, I think, at dinner in some restaurant. He's youngish, mid-thirties, fantastically good-looking. I wouldn't trust him with a nickel. That's wrong. I don't have reason to think he's dishonest. I don't know him. He just struck me as one of those handsome, well-mannered, too well-dressed ineffectuals. He may be a very decent fellow. I'm certainly letting myself talk."

"So am I. This whole thing—"

"I understand. See here, it's late and getting later. If my guess is right, G.M. will see to it that the police leave for the present. Everybody is going to be hungry. I'll get some liquor out and we'll—" He glanced around the gleaming kitchen and saw the opened package of hamburger. "We'll broil some hamburgers. Didn't you get some buns?"

It was a sensible and matter-of-fact suggestion; it seemed to put aside the horror of the late afternoon, much as the dogs and her idle but restorative talk with the kind policeman about dogs had done.

Col opened the door and thrust in an inquisitive face and a wooden box which looked heavy. "Dora not here?"

Dora? But of course there was the whole Clanser connection—cousins, a sister, Dora a Clanser by marriage—so all of them were on a first-name basis if they so chose. She didn't think, however, that Dora would like it if Col called her Dora to her face. Certainly not if Dora intended to marry G.M.—and now the way was clear with poor Rose dead.

Col came further into the room. "I just want to say that I've fixed up a sandbox for the cat. Dora was pretty sharp about the dogs and what happened in the library," he said delicately. "She seems to think this house is hers"—there was a deliberate and what seemed an intentional pause while Col eyed Greg, then—"already."

"None of our business, is it, Col?" Greg said coolly. "Where are you going to put the sandbox?"

"I thought out there in the vestibule. Floor is marble. It can be washed. I'll get some kind of blanket for the cat to sleep on. Soon as he gets used to it we'll not have to worry. As for the dogs—"

"I'll see to them," Susan said shortly.

"All right. If Dora says so."

"Let's say if Mr. Manders says so, Col," Greg suggested good-naturedly, yet with a certain command in his voice which caught Col's ear.

"Oh, sure. Whatever G.M. says. Sure—"

He backed away, holding the box awkwardly as he closed the door again.

Greg frowned. Susan said, "I really didn't think there were so many relatives of Rose's."

"Oh, yes. Col really is basically reliable. I'm not so sure about Wilfred. Even Snell is some relative of Rose's. G.M. had some notion about taking care of anybody Rose wanted him to take care of—to employ, anything. And of course they all call one another by their first names, which must have irked G.M. However"—he seemed to think back—"I don't think any of them but Milly ever used his first name. Dora, perhaps, in private only. Dora knows which side her bread is buttered on. Dora—"

"Speaking of me?" Dora said musically, opening the door.

"Yes. Did you get Snell?"

"No, I didn't. I tried and tried. I even went to the other phone and tried some of the bars where I've been able occasionally to find him when G.M. wanted him in a hurry. I didn't find him."

"No news about the helicopter?"

"No, I tried the heliport, too. I got nowhere!"

There was a rather surprised note in her voice as if she seldom got nowhere in anything she proposed to do, which was probably quite accurate. Dora was not a woman to give up easily. She smoothed her shining gold hair and glanced around the room. "What are all those things? Oh, the groceries! Put them away, Susan. And—" She went to the opened package of hamburger. "I see you've been feeding the animals. Broil some hamburgers for us, Susan. There must be enough food in all those packages. I told you to get in provisions for several days. Go on, see to dinner, Susan. Get out some liquor, Greg. G.M. should be returning soon. Put the glasses and ice on the table in the library."

Greg really grinned then, momentarily but wholeheartedly. "Yes, Madam."

Dora's eyes grew very still and opaque. "I'll have no cracks out of you, Greg!"

"I'll say what I want to say," Greg replied cheerfully and departed.

For another moment Dora remained very still; then she said, "Go on with supper, Susan. But don't let those animals out in the house again!"

"Well!" Susan said explosively to herself as the door closed. "Well!"

However, it seemed sensible to arrange for some kind of food. She was experimenting with the broiler when Greg came back. "Here, I'll show you. I know this house." He pushed buttons, waited, and then put the hamburgers under the broiler; then he reached up and found a timer. "They can eat them as they come," he said cheerfully. "Rare or overdone. Milly for one is likely to be in no state to know. She made herself a strong drink and is swigging away. Not that I blame her."

"Neither do I," Susan said honestly.

Greg gave her a quick look, left the kitchen and was back again with a glass in his hand. "If anybody needs this, you do."

She sat down on the edge of a table. "Thank you."

"The policemen looked wistful but aren't drinking. Col and Wilfred are tucking it away as fast as they can."

"We'd better have something more than hamburgers and buns. I think I got some canned mushrooms. And some frozen vegetables."

"The way Milly and Col and Wilfred are drinking they'll not know what they're eating. If, that is, Dora permits them to eat. I poured a drink for Dora and she refused it so nobly that I drank it myself." The timer rang and he drew out the pan. "I'll turn them over just to make sure. I'm handy around the house. Comes of living a bachelor existence. Bear that in mind, will you?" He gave her a natural, flashing twinkle. "In the event I ever get through with my law courses and contrive to set up a practice."

"Law?" Susan had never heard Greg talk of his own affairs. She had known only that he was a kind of aide for G.M.

He looked up at her. "Oh, that's G.M.'s doing. I told you he's been very good to me. I came home from Vietnam. I had a university degree but wanted to go to law school. I also needed money." He turned over a hamburger very carefully before he continued, "One day G.M. told me I was too—well, too good, if you don't mind my bragging, to go on as . . . nothing very much. He asked me what I wanted to do. I told him; he arranged it somehow so I can go to classes and study and yet do whatever chores he wants me to do."

"Oh." It explained Greg's status in G.M.'s office; she had thought of him as a kind of super-secretary, something like an aide-de-camp for G.M. She said, "That's like G.M."

"The great man. He really is great." Greg eyed the hamburgers, sniffed and turned off the broiler. "I think they're done. And barely in time. I think G.M. is coming."

Dora came in first, however, sniffed and said crisply, "Good heavens, Susan, there's a ventilator. The smell of food will be all over the house." She reached for a cord and yanked it.

Greg said mildly, "A good smell if you ask me. Is that G.M.?"

"Yes. The police car has just arrived. Oh, stop that, you two!"

The dogs had leaped for the door, barking, to greet G.M. Dora thrust out a foot at them, which they both adroitly avoided and dashed out into the vestibule.

Somehow Susan had a notion that it was not the first time Dora's neat pump had taken a swipe at the dogs. Then she heard G.M. "Greg—"

Greg sprang out after the dogs. Dora followed. Susan sat on the edge of the table and finished her drink, which did eventually put a little life into her, or at least a little energy, enough so she rose and went out through the vestibule and hall. By then everyone was in the library. The dogs greeted her; she had not only let them outdoors, an exciting experience for both of them, but she had fed and watered them; she was their friend.

But before she could get any idea of what had occurred she realized that the police were leaving, that Col and Wilfred were shambling out after them, passing her as she stood in the drawing room, and that Greg followed like an escort. Dora came to the door, said crisply, "Wilfred, stop in the kitchen and take something to eat to the gate with you. Col, you are going to go home and you're to say nothing except that this was a sad accident. Now then, Susan, what about supper?"

Over Dora's shoulder Susan saw Milly totter to the table where glasses and whiskey stood. G.M. stood thoughtfully before the hearth. He looked up and saw Susan. "Come in, my dear. I'll tell you what the situation is. Dora, if you'll see to something for us to eat, just anything—"

"But . . . Susan—" Dora began and then turned abruptly and started for the kitchen; Milly gave a loud hiccup and waddled after her, carrying a glass in her hand.

G.M. said, "It'll take a derrick to get Milly upstairs if she goes on like this. Susan, I want to tell you how things stand. The police—under some pressure from higher up, which there's no need for anybody to know about—are willing to call it an accident for the time being. They'll continue the investigation but will do it as discreetly as possible. There'll have to be some account in the news, however. It'll be called an accident."

"Wasn't it an accident?"

G.M. shook his head slowly. "Oh, no. Rose knew about guns. It wasn't suicide either. Not Rose."

"But then—"

"Murder, yes." He sat down. For the first time in her knowledge of G.M. he looked exhausted, without any of his usual energy. "Murder. Poor Rose. She was such a pretty thing once. Pink and white and slim. I called her my wild rose. It was long ago," he said, and seemed to look back over the years.

There was something so sad, so regretful in his face—a sort of grief for his lost love—that Susan did something she would never have dreamed of doing in everyday life; she dropped to her knees beside him and then could not think of any words of comfort. The great man understood, however; he put his arm around her and leaned his face over against her head.

He held her closely and tenderly as if the sympathy she could not find words for had somehow reached the hidden depths of his heart. He had spoken of Rose as she once had been, not as she was in recent years, Susan knew that. But she also felt his sense of loss and sorrow for a long-ago time. Dora said from the doorway, "There's some food on the table."

G.M. did not relinquish his hold on Susan at once. He seemed to take a long breath and then patted Susan's shoulder, as if to thank her. Dora said crisply, "Why aren't you helping me, Susan? What on earth are you doing kneeling there?"

Greg had come through the drawing room. Over Dora's shoulder he said quickly, "They've all gone, G.M. For the present."

Susan rose, feeling suddenly and foolishly embarrassed. G.M. rose too. "All right, Greg. Try to keep reporters out as long as you can."

The telephone on the long table rang. Both Dora and Greg

started for it, but G.M. reached it first and said to them, "I'll handle this." He picked up the receiver. "Hello."

All of them listened. At first G.M. looked puzzled. "Who? . . . Oh, it's you. Yes, she's here." He looked at Dora. "It's your husband. I mean Ligon Clanser."

Five

"Ligon!" Susan had never seen Dora discomposed, but she was at that moment. Her eyes were cloudy and angry. With a swift stride she went to the table and took the telephone. "Ligon! What do you want?"

Whatever the man at the other end of the telephone said did not please Dora. "How did you know? . . . I told Col and Wilfred to keep their mouths shut. Do you mean Wilfred actually phoned you from the gatehouse?" Her face tightened in a way which bode ill for Wilfred. "But why should you be told? . . . No, you can't come here. I don't care if you *are* Rose's cousin . . . I said *no*—because I'll not have you—"

"Wait, Dora," G.M. said quietly and took the telephone from her hand. "We must do things quietly. Rose's other relatives will be here for the services. We'll have to arrange—but meantime Ligon has as much right to be here as Col or Milly. Tell him that he can come. He'll not bother you."

Dora hesitated. "But, G.M.—"

G.M. said nothing but apparently said it in a commanding way, for Dora took the receiver back in her white hand. "All right, you can come. But you can't stay in the house. There's no room. It's too full as it is . . . I don't know—nobody knows when the services will be . . . All right, speak to him—if he'll speak to you."

Again she gave the receiver to G.M., who took it and spoke very quietly. "Yes, it was a tragic accident . . . Of course, you are right in wishing to come. I'm sorry the house is full, but there's the Medbury Hills Inn . . . I see . . . Yes . . . Thank you."

He put down the telephone and looked at Dora. "He'll be down from Highbury in the morning. It's only about a thirty-mile drive, isn't it? It is right and kind of him to come, even though he hasn't seen much of Rose for some time. But then nobody has seen much of her—except Milly."

Dora was still angry, trying to conceal it and making a poor effort. "How can he leave his precious business?"

G.M. smiled. "Ligon is past the place where he is unable to leave his office for as long as he wishes. Remember, Dora, he is now a rather—indeed, I'd guess a very wealthy man. He doesn't have to ask permission of anybody for anything. Now we'd better have supper."

He led the way toward the dining room. Dora followed. Greg lingered a moment with Susan, but Dora called her imperatively, "Susan, take those dogs and that cat out to—oh, somewhere, the vestibule, and shut them in. I'm not going to let them run around the dining room while we're eating."

Greg scooped up both dogs and Susan followed him to the vestibule. The cat was nowhere to be seen. Greg said, "Don't mind Dora. I'll find that cat."

The dogs began to explore the vestibule with much interest. There was a long marble bench there. Susan sat down.

She thought of Ligon Clanser, who was, according to the office grapevine, the only Clanser for whom G.M. did not provide. He had been a vice-president in a small upstate bank when Dora had married him. But—again according to interoffice talk—Dora had met G.M. and had found a place in G.M.'s office, and she and Ligon were divorced. In any event Ligon had prospered; long ago he had bought the controlling stock in the bank, long ago he had begun to buy various properties around the state until he was now a well and favorably known figure. "She gave up a certainty for a gamble," one of the girls in the office had said once, tartly. "G.M. will never leave his Rose. Everybody knows that. She"—meaning Dora—"ought to have known it."

G.M. was right in permitting this sole member of the Clansers who did not make any demands upon G.M.'s or Rose's generosity to come in time for the services for Rose. And interoffice gossip was colored by dislike for Dora; everybody hates the boss, even the straw boss, Greg had said.

She didn't want to think of Rose. She couldn't keep from thinking of G.M.'s sad and grave expression when he spoke of his wild rose from long ago.

Murder, G.M. had said. How was it possible that anyone she knew, even so slightly, could be murdered? How was it possible that murder had occurred apparently at the exact moment when she and Greg were approaching the house?

Greg had wondered whether Milly had had an opportunity and time to kill her sister. Milly had a motive.

Murder, she thought again with a feeling of disbelief. It had been a matter of a few hours since she and Greg and Milly had arrived and entered that vestibule; it seemed months. She wouldn't think of Rose, fat and blowzy and tragic, her green dress rucked up over her bulging legs, her eyes open and staring, her face fallen with such ugly and convincing laxity.

Greg came in, the cat wreathed around his shoulders. They left the dogs and cat in the vestibule, closed the doors to the kitchen passage and from the vestibule to the hall, and joined the others. It was like a weirdly nightmarish picnic. Somebody—Greg, it developed—had opened and warmed some baked beans. It struck Susan that probably the magnificent table had never borne such a plebeian but comforting assemblage of food. Greg and Susan ate. Milly was glassy-eyed and spilled beans on her massive bosom. G.M.'s face expressed nothing at all. Dora efficiently laid out the bedroom arrangements. Nobody even suggested sleeping in the room where Rose had died.

There were barely enough bedrooms, all of them furnished with the same almost Spartan simplicity of G.M.'s big room. Greg contrived to hoist Milly up the stairs. He returned to go with Susan and take out the dogs.

The dogs were earning their keep, if only as diversions. G.M. and Dora had vanished into the library. Greg walked along beside Susan down the driveway toward the gatehouse, which now, since it was lighted, she could see, snuggled back into some clusters of pines.

They then walked slowly back to the house, where Greg whistled for the dogs. Greg knew their names. "Beau and Belle. Rose named them. Said every Beau must have a Belle. Poor Rose."

"They've got to go to the vet's and get a trim and a wash."

"All right. I'll try to fix it tomorrow. My little Susan. You look half-dead—I mean—" he caught himself.

"I know." The dogs came racing. The cat was already gracefully curled up on the blanket Col had provided.

The lights were out in the library, and Dora and G.M. had gone to bed. Somebody had brought Susan's suitcase into the tiny bedroom she was to occupy. Greg said, "I'm not far away. Call me if—oh, if anything."

Before she closed the door the dogs came bounding in and leaped on the bed. She hadn't the heart to make them get down or put them out of the room, but she resolved again to see that their curls were properly cut and they had baths. Beau settled down with a satisfied grunt but the female, Belle, watched Susan with bright eyes as she undressed. She left the bed-table light on, she didn't know why. She was too tired, too drained of all energy to think of anything.

Tomorrow certainly Snell and the helicopter would be found. She hoped she wouldn't be asked to identify Snell as the running man. She only knew that the man was not G.M., yet in the dusk, her glimpse of the running figure had been so very swift that she didn't know how she knew that it couldn't have been G.M. Perhaps there was something about the furtive way he glanced over his shoulder toward the house and then slid out of sight as much as any physical property that convinced her that he could not have been G.M.

The bed was narrow but a good bed. The rooms had probably been prepared for those distinguished guests of G.M. who for some reason or other had been obliged to spend a night in the secret house. She wondered, sleepily at last, who had slept there before her.

They found Snell the next morning and brought him to the secret house. The New York police, obliging their fellow policemen of Medbury Hills, had simply gone to Snell's apartment on the West Side and routed him out of sleep and a tremendous hangover. His statement was brief. Yes, he had brought Rose to the secret house. No, he didn't know why she wanted to come. He was shaken, however, when he was asked where he had left the helicopter. He said flatly that he had returned it to the Madilson heliport, but there was something about his response when G.M. told him that the helicopter was not at the heliport, that no one knew where it was, that seemed evasive. Greg and Susan heard the detective and G.M. question him.

Milly had not appeared; she also probably had a gigantic hangover. Dora came into the library while they were talking. There was only a lovely arched and open doorway between the library and the living room, so there was no way to shut a door or hold a confidential conversation there. Not that the inquiry of Snell could have been called confidential. He seemed only too eager to tell them again that he had brought Rose, at Rose's request, to the secret house, that he had taken the helicopter back at once to the heliport. Rose had the key for the gate at the back and the vestibule.

"Did you have a key to the gate?" Lattrice asked.

It was the first time Susan had heard the problem of keys

considered, but it was not the last time; clearly Lattrice had already questioned G.M. about keys. It developed that there were far too many keys.

"No," Snell said. "But Rose had one."

"I told you," G.M. said to Lattrice, "the same key is used for both gate and door."

"You also said that there are a number of keys."

"Yes, there are. Col has a key, Wilfred has a key, I explained that. They have to be able to get into the house whenever necessary. My wife had a key. I have a key."

Dora said, rather impatiently, "You know about this, Sergeant. I have a key, too. There are some duplicates hanging on a hook in the kitchen cupboard."

"Yes, I saw them." He spoke sharply. "It does seem that it would be easy for almost anyone to get a key and enter the gate or the house."

G.M.'s face tightened a little; he continued to be as polite and easy in his manner as always, however. "But you see, Sergeant, that did not occur to me. Either Col or Wilfred was on guard and would have known it if somebody entered the house."

"But they didn't see Mrs. Manders arrive."

Col wriggled. "We can't keep our eyes glued to the house every minute."

Lattrice addressed G.M. "Do you think it likely that some outsider could contrive to enter the house—in someone's company, someone who had a key—and help himself to one of the duplicate keys?"

G.M. had already thought that over; his reply was immediate. "It is possible, yes. But I don't know who, or when that may have occurred."

Lattrice appeared to give up the problem of the keys, at least for the moment, for he turned back to Snell. "You saw Mrs. Manders enter the house."

"Oh, yes," Snell replied. But he had not seen the arrival of Milly, Greg and Susan. He lid not remember looking back at the house as he returned to the airstrip through the gate he and Rose had entered, at the other side of the house.

The detective addressed Susan directly. "Is this the man you saw running away from the house?"

Susan looked doubtfully at Snell. He was only a little more unprepossessing than Col or Wilfred; his eyes were red, his face unshaven; his whole aspect had a kind of shaggy slackness. She tried to make allowances for the hangover which

Snell had, not very shamefacedly, admitted. The detective waited. G.M. waited. Dora was still and poised as a cat at a mousehole. "He wore a hat," Susan said at last. "It was pulled down over his face."

Snell brightened a little. "I never wear a hat. Everybody knows that. And—wait a minute—I wore a leather jacket yesterday."

"Well, Miss Beach?" the detective said.

"No. The man I saw was wearing a dark overcoat. At least—I think it was that. I had such a quick look at him." She shut her eyes, tried to call up an image of the figure she had seen so briefly, and said at a sudden memory, "He wore gloves. I'm sure of that."

There was a little pause. Then the detective turned to Greg. "You say you didn't see him at all."

"That's right. He was gone by the time I got to the window. But we both waited until we heard the helicopter."

There was another pause. At last the detective turned back to Susan. "You are sure that the man you saw was not Snell Clanser?"

"Yes," she said. "At least I don't think so."

"But you'd know the running man positively if you saw him again."

"I think so."

"You're sure there *was* a running man," Dora said with the slightest yet convincing air of skepticism.

"Yes!"

The detective turned to Snell. "You say you did not enter the house."

"Right. Rose—I mean, my cousin unlocked the gate. I saw her use her key again to unlock the door. I had gone that far with her. Then I went back to the copter. I didn't hear anything from the house, no shot, nothing. That's all I know."

"You locked the gate when you left?"

There was a slight pause. Then Snell said, "No. I didn't have a key."

"And it was still unlocked when you arrived?" Lattrice spoke to G.M.

"No, it was locked. I told you. That is, Dora—Mrs. Clanser—actually unlocked it with my key."

Dora spoke definitely, "Sergeant, Mr. Manders had his hands full with the dogs. He told me to take his key from his pocket. I had my own, but it was simpler to use his key. The gate was locked." She finished conclusively as if that settled the question.

"I see." The detective did not look impressed, but then he really didn't look anything; he was merely a smooth, blank but very intelligent face. He turned to Snell again. "Now we find that you signed in at the heliport as usual. The man at the elevator and the dispatcher remember you. One man thinks that a woman was with you."

"I told you. Rose."

"Yes. He also thinks that possibly there was another man with you. He was occupied, it's a busy time, but that's his impression."

"No," Snell said. "Wrong. Nobody with me but Rose."

G.M. leaned across the writing table where he sat. "Snell, you must realize that this is very serious. You must tell anything you know."

"But I have told you—"

"No," G.M. said thoughtfully. "However"—he spoke to the detective—"I really don't think we're going to get any more out of him just now. When he's had a chance to think it over maybe he'll remember something he has not told us."

It was putting it very delicately; G.M. always spoke to Rose's relatives courteously. But Dora's face tightened. "You mean get back his senses after his hangover. Honestly, Snell, I can see why nobody would let you work for him. You may have once been a good pilot—"

"I am a good pilot," Snell said.

"But you've taken to drinking so nobody but G.M. would employ you, and he does that only because you are a cousin of Rose's." Her eyes were like smooth brown velvet, and her words were biting as a whip. Snell wiped a shaky hand over his face.

The detective seemed to give up his inquiry as a bad job, at least for the present. Susan had a notion that he would return to it later. Greg said firmly, "I'd like to use Col's station wagon. He's back at the gate now and it's standing in the drive. I want to take those dogs to the vet's and get them trimmed and washed."

"Of course," G.M. said. Susan said, "I'll go with you."

After a romping chase they cornered the two dogs and got them down the drive to Col's station wagon, which was shiny and new. The gates were closed, and Col came at once into view from behind the cluster of pines and said yes, they could take his station wagon. After they got in, he thrust his sly face in the open window. "I saw them bring Snell. He'd been on a drunk, hadn't he? What did he have to say? Did he bring Rose yesterday?"

"He says so. We may do a little grocery shopping after we take the dogs to the vet's." Before Col could ask more questions Greg started up the station wagon and shot away so swiftly that Col had to jump back. "He's curious," Greg said. "I can't blame him. I feel sorry for Snell; I think that once he really was a good pilot. I looked up the vet in the phone book. He said he could trim and wash the dogs and I must say they need it." Both dogs hung out the windows, their ears flapping, their eyes eager for all these new sights.

"Do you think Snell was telling the truth?"

"Not all the truth," Greg said briefly.

"He seemed—oh, evasive. Unsteady—"

"Hangover. He'd been drinking, sure. But he must have some idea as to where he left the helicopter. Or about the man you saw. You're *sure* it wasn't Snell?"

"I know he didn't wear a leather jacket. It's very hard to describe anybody. But I think I'd recognize him by—oh, just the way you do recognize people. Something about their figures or the way they move or something—"

"A hundred things," Greg said soberly. "I think it would be a good idea for you to pretend or even say flatly that you've thought it over and feel now that you couldn't possibly identify the running man."

"But why? Oh, you mean he may have shot Rose."

"May have certainly."

"So it might be dangerous for me if I insist that I could recognize him."

"No–no. Well, yes. It's just less a danger to you than to say you *can* identify him."

Danger, Susan thought with disbelief. It was a blue and gold October day, the foliage brilliant in all its glowing shades of red and yellow and brown, the clusters of pines along the road standing out vividly alive and green. Danger? She couldn't accept it; but then she could not have accepted Rose's death as it had happened if she had not seen Rose.

Finally she said, "All right, Greg. But I think it's too late."

"We'll try to see to it that it's not too late. Here's the town." He turned along the wider street. "Now for the vet's."

The veterinarian proved to be young and extremely agile, which was a good thing, for once Beau and Belle got a whiff of the kennel smell they were off together, aiming for the high hills. The vet outguessed them, however; he sprang upon them and gathered them in so dexterously that Beau was foiled in a swift attempt to bite. Belle looked at Susan over the young man's shoulder with great sad eyes, as if she wanted to say, "And I thought you were my friend."

"They'll be trimmed and washed and dried by five this afternoon," the vet said and shot the protesting dogs over the lower part of a solid Dutch door. "I'm sorry to hear about Mrs. Manders."

Greg said, "Yes."

"Must have been a terrible shock to her husband. We think a lot of him around here, you know. Not that we see much of him. But he is our prime Medbury Hills celebrity."

"Yes," Greg said again. "Well, thank you. We'll be back for the dogs at five. Now," he said to Susan as he started up and both tried to ignore some reproachful wails from inside the vet's building, "now for groceries. We've got to stock up. Dora gave me a list." He pulled it from his pocket and gave it to Susan, who glanced down it and laughed.

"What?" Greg asked her.

"This list. Caviar, pâté, pheasants—where do you think we can find pheasant?"

"In the woods," Greg said shortly. "Oh, no, we can't. Wrong season. We'll just have to use our heads. Dora can be so damned elegant that it's really funny. Here's a grocery store."

Between them they bought food and did find some red caviar. "It would be good with rye bread," Susan suggested, so they also bought rye bread. Greg paid for the food and took the sacks to the station wagon. "Don't worry," he said. "I'll tell Dora to do the grocery buying herself. I'd like to see her frustrated just once."

"It seems strange. Rose's death yesterday, police inquiry—yet here we are taking dogs to the vet's and buying groceries."

"Life goes on. I wonder if Snell has come to his senses and told the truth by now. He *must* know something about that helicopter. A machine like that simply cannot vanish off the earth."

"But don't helicopters file a—they call it a flight plan, don't they?"

"The airliners, yes. The copters follow a sort of pattern. Never over fifteen hundred feet—even lower close to airports so they can't interfere with a commercial airliner. Taking a helicopter up is not as simple as taking a car from a parking garage, but it isn't very difficult if one knows the drill. Snell's signature must have been Snell's, all right. The men there knew him. G.M.'s copter is small, seats four. That heliport is rather a large one, so there's quite a staff running it. Friday afternoon is a busy one. I've gone with G.M. and Snell; there were never any questions, or anything like a pasesnger manifest. I can see how there could have been a little confusion as to the number of passengers Snell took with him. He just could have had others besides Rose. I don't see how anybody can prove anything unless somebody at the heliport remembers it. The only concrete evidence seems to be the fact that Snell *was* there. What happened later is anybody's guess. But Rose and the helicopter certainly were here. Rose and her murderer."

"Snell?"

He shook his head. "Somehow I don't think so."

After a while she said slowly, "It's better to think it was the running man."

He shot her a swift glance. "Why? Oh, I see—"

"Yes. Not a Clanser. Nobody in the—in the house with us."

"So you don't look at each of them and think, Is this the hand? Is this the face—Yes, I see what you mean. But all the same, there they are. All close to Rose. All with opportunities to get one of those keys."

When they reached the secret house Col came curiously to open the gate and peer into the packages in the back of the car. "What's in them packages?" he asked.

"Bombs," Greg said seriously, and grinned at the look of alarm that leaped onto Col's face.

"Oh, be serious!" Col snapped. "I've been told to look for anything at all. I guess they're just groceries. Looks as if all of you plan to stay here a while. Ligon just got here."

"Oh," Greg said.

Col's little eyes twinkled. "Used to be Dora's husband. That's how she got to be a Clanser. And that's not all. Who is Mr. Prowde?"

"Prowde? What about him?"

"Oh, so you know him?"

"Not really. I'll take the station wagon to the door so we can unload the bombs."

"Dora phoned down from the house and said when Mr. Prowde arrives, I'm to let him go to the house."

"Then do that, by all means. Thanks for the use of your car, Col."

"Do you know Ligon?" Susan asked as they drove between the banks of pines and crowding shrubbery toward the house.

"No. He does appear to have all the financial brains in that family."

"Greg, did Dora leave him because of G.M.?"

He shot a quick glance at her. "No. That is, Dora may have had something in her mind about G.M., but I'll swear G.M. didn't have. She's been very efficient. Really excellent in her job. I have to give her credit for that. Too bad."

As they approached the house, it looked like anything but a secret house. Its red brick shone in the bright sunlight; its windows gleamed brightly; its wrought iron, painted black, seemed only trimming—not very attractive, perhaps, but certainly not intended to keep off intruders.

She had an odd sense of déjà vu when she and Greg again unloaded sacks and boxes of groceries, took them into the house through the vestibule and passage leading to the kitchen, and again plumped them down on the long counter tops. She felt almost as though, if she went to the window and looked out, she would see the running man and they would listen and hear the helicopter take off in its roaring way. She would go upstairs and find Rose. No, no! She thrust that memory away, and Milly wavered in. She had removed the bean-stained dress and wore a green-and-yellow-plaid country suit in which she looked bigger than ever, which didn't seem possible. She eyed them weakly and put her hand to her head. "I've got a frightful headache. I can't imagine why. Susan, fix some coffee for me."

"You need aspirin," Greg said cruelly. "You've got a headache because you were drunk last night. Come on, Susan. She can make her own coffee."

Milly gave a moan and sank down on a chair. Greg pulled Susan out of the kitchen. "I can see you feeling sorry for her. You're not here to cater to Milly. Let's see Ligon. Not that he's likely to be a treat, but Milly is about to work the hell out of you. We'll start her off on the right path."

Ligon was no treat. He seemed to have escaped the general slackness of the Clanser family, however, for he rose promptly; he was medium thin, medium tall, with a long chin and a tweed coat, slacks and heavy country shoes. As Greg and Susan came into the library, G.M. introduced them; there was a polite murmur of how-do-you-do's. G.M. was seated at the long writing table. Snell sat in a corner, watching everyone slyly, and Dora came in, her high heels tapping.

"Bert Prowde has just reached the gate," she said. "Col used the house phone to tell me. Oh"—she glanced at Susan—"I do hope you got all the things on my list."

Greg replied, "Not quite all, Dora. Medbury Hills is not a city, you know. Why is Bert Prowde coming?"

Dora did not even bother to answer. G.M. said, "There's news, Greg. The helicopter has been located, near the edge of the Westchester airport. The police are going over it now for fingerprints!"

"Did anybody see its arrival?" Greg asked.

G.M. shook his head. "Apparently not. It would be fairly simple. Too far away to bother the control tower. Rolling hills, shrubbery, trees. A quick getaway in a car already stationed somewhere, over near Mount Kisco, Greenwich, anywhere. However it was done, the helicopter was reported there."

Dora said, "I'll meet Bert at the door," and walked briskly out of the room.

Six

Snell, like Milly, was still suffering from a hangover. He put his head in his hands and said drearily, "Nobody can say that anybody saw me running away from the house yesterday. I've got to have some coffee." He gave a slight moan, rose and shambled across the room, following Dora.

Ligon's lantern face was puzzled. "What's this about a man running away from the house?"

G.M. sighed. "Susan—that is, Miss Beach here—saw a man running toward our airstrip."

Greg said a little too firmly, "But she cannot possibly identify him. No question of that. She had only a glimpse of him. What about this conference, G.M.? Did you decide?"

"Yes," said G.M. reluctantly. "Nothing else to do in the circumstances. I'll get busy on the direct lines downstairs. Dora can help me."

"You mean you're going to postpone it?"

"I don't know. I can catch one of our friends in London, I think. Another in Paris. The meeting was scheduled for next Wednesday. Perhaps by then—Well, we'll see."

Ligon's face could not conceal a flicker of curiosity. "One of your decision-making economic conferences?"

"I wouldn't call it that precisely. It is only intended as a discussion." G.M. rose wearily as Dora's heels returned swiftly across the living room. A man followed her and looked very much as if he wished he were elsewhere. Greg had given a very good description of him.

He was remarkably handsome, with dark wavy hair, regular features, large blue eyes, and an ingratiating smile on his mobile lips. He passed a hand over his hair and adjusted his tie, which needed no adjusting; Dora introduced him. "This is my friend Bert Prowde. Mr. Manders, Mr. Cameron, Miss Beach—oh yes, and my former husband, Ligon Clanser."

Ligon had risen again, politely but giving a rather chilly glance at handsome Bert, who also bowed in a flustered way here and there and adjusted his tie again. Dora sat down composedly. "Now, Bert, will you tell everybody here just where I was yesterday between—oh, five o'clock and half-past six?"

"Well, I'm not sure of the time, you know, Dora," said Mr. Prowde, "but it was about that time we were having cocktails."

"Tell them where," said Dora.

"In—in my apartment, of course." Mr. Prowde swallowed hard.

Ligon looked at G.M. "What is all this? What does it matter where Dora was when the accident occurred?"

Dora replied cuttingly, "Surely even you, Ligon, must have guessed that it was no accident."

"But then *what?*" Ligon's long chin seemed to lengthen further.

"Murder probably."

"But—murder!" Indignation and dignity struggled in Ligon's voice. "Nobody told me! The police—"

"Oh, the police have been here and will be here again," Dora replied coolly. "That's why I wanted Bert to come and tell you what my alibi is."

"A—alibi," said Ligon.

G.M. took a long breath. "It isn't in the papers yet, Ligon. It is—so far—called an accident."

"But Dora said murder! She said the police—"

"The police are investigating and will continue to investigate."

"But I—but the police—but—" Ligon seemed to pull himself together. "If I'd known this—" he began, and Dora cut in, "You can leave any time you want to, Ligon. Remember it was you who insisted on coming."

"But Wilfred didn't say—he only said an accident—"

"That is what it is just now," G.M. said shortly. "You didn't need to ask Mr. Prowde to come here, Dora. I don't think the police have got around to requiring alibis yet."

"But they will," Dora said. "And I for one have an alibi, haven't I, Bert?"

"What?" Mr. Prowde started, twisted his shoulders nervously and said, "Oh, yes. Yes, indeed. You were with me exactly when you said you were with me. I didn't really notice the time, of course, but I'm sure you did."

"I'm perfectly sure I did." Dora's eyes were cloudy. "And you'll stay here, won't you, Bert, until you see the police?

The house is full, but there's a very good country inn. Ligon will stay there too."

Ligon paid no attention to Dora. "And you—" he said to Susan. "You actually saw someone running from the house?"

"Barely a glimpse," Greg said quickly again. "She couldn't possibly identify him."

"Not so sure of that," Snell said, appearing suddenly in the doorway. He looked refreshed and carried a bottle in one hand. "She's got sharp eyes. Said right away it wasn't me she saw."

"Snell!" Milly surged into view beside him. "Give me that bottle."

"Sure," Snell said cordially. "Have some, old lady. Hair of the dog, you know."

"Oh, my God!" For an instant it looked as if Dora might leap at Snell's throat. Greg, however, good-naturedly but quickly got across to Snell, removed the bottle firmly, ignored a kind of squeal from Milly, and went across the living room and out of sight.

Ligon got out a handkerchief and mopped his forehead. "But I thought—I mean—well, of course, I can't possibly stay if—"

"You said you wished to come," G.M. said.

"Well, naturally, yes. But I didn't know—" Ligon gave his forehead another swipe. "G.M., you're a big bug. I'm not in a class with you. But I'm respected in my own bailiwick. I think I can say that I'm fairly well known. At least it has been suggested that I run for Congress. I do have my connections and . . . the point is if it's murder—"

G.M. nodded. "You want to have nothing to do with it."

"But—well, the newspapers and all that and—"

Bert Prowde offered his first voluntary remark. He pulled a newspaper from his pocket. "It's in this morning's papers. It says accident. It's not prominent." He hesitated, giving G.M. a worried look, and then handed the paper to Dora. Dora didn't hesitate for an instant. She tore open the paper, glanced down it and then went swiftly to G.M. "Here it is. It's really not too bad, G.M."

She leaned over his shoulder while he read. Greg returned, took in the situation and went to stand at G.M.'s other shoulder and read. He and Dora looked like two well-trained and devoted aides standing beside their commanding officer, ready to help. Snell and Milly engaged in some sort of mumbled talk of which Susan caught a few words, "Greg has the keys

. . . Yes, it's locked up," referring she supposed to the liquor cabinet, for Snell said clearly, "But there's more down in the cellar. Quantities." "That's locked up too," Milly said, adding virtuously, "Not that I am interested in drinking anything."

"Huh," said Snell, adopting what appeared to be the Clanser grunt, copyrighted by Col.

Dora said almost absently, "The paper isn't bad, G.M. Maybe the police will keep on calling it an accident."

Apparently Ligon made up his mind. "Whatever they call it, I really am afraid I can't stay. I'm very sorry and all that, but I—"

"Running out?" Dora said.

Ligon paused, seemed to think it over and then resumed his seat. "Certainly not. I can see that in the event—that is, in the circumstances it looks much better for Rose's family to show our support for G.M." He glanced at Bert Prowde. "I'm sure you need not stay."

Dora laughed. "Stay right here, Bert."

Bert, looking very handsome and very miserable, sat down and carefully adjusted the legs of his trousers.

G.M. said soberly, "We'll have to get to work, Dora. You can help us at the phones, Greg, if you will."

Dora hesitated. "G.M., I've been thinking—perhaps you might call in your lawyers—"

G.M. shook his head. "No. Not as things are." He dropped the newspaper in a wastebasket, said absently to Ligon, "Milly will see that you have lunch. I hope you'll be comfortable at the inn," and walked out of the room.

Dora and Greg followed, marching after him again like two efficient aides. Ligon shifted his weight uneasily. Bert Prowde still looked very handsome, very miserable and very embarrassed.

Milly put a lavish lunch on the table, buffet style, so they helped themselves. It was a hearty but rather plebeian lunch which probably, Susan thought again, had never before appeared in that elegant room. Peanut butter and bologna sandwiches and coffee. She remembered Greg's large and sensible purchases of both, and was thankful.

After some thought she filled a plate with sandwiches and rather hesitantly took it downstairs to the basement room. G.M., Greg and Dora sat together, Dora at the telephones, Greg taking notes and G.M. sitting with earphones on. He nodded as she put the plate down on a table. Dora said, "I've got your man in London."

It was a small, curiously unbusinesslike room except for the switchboard; it was concrete-enclosed; there were doors leading, Susan supposed, to the wine cellars and the furnace room; there were several card tables, paper and pencils and a few kitchen chairs. As G.M. began to speak she went hurriedly back upstairs to her room.

It had been a long morning. It was a short afternoon. She tried to sleep and couldn't and wondered among other things if Ligon and Bert were together. It was not likely.

The shadows were growing long in the woods when G.M. knocked at her door. "Susan?"

She bounced up hurriedly and opened the door. He said, "I've done as much as I can do just now. I need some fresh air. Want to come with me?"

"Oh, yes."

"Better get your jacket. It's turning cooler."

She snatched her jacket and paused to brush her rumpled hair. G.M. liked his women to look neat. After Rose, who wouldn't like neatness, she thought suddenly, and was ashamed of thinking so of Rose. Poor Rose, nobody except G.M. seemed to grieve for her, yet even G.M.'s grief seemed more for his past years and his pink-and-white Rose than for the present time and the present shocking fact of—well, murder. Call it that, she said to herself; they'll prove it's murder; get accustomed to it.

G.M. led her out of the front door. She glanced at her watch. Soon she and Greg must go for the dogs. G.M. said, "Let's walk down into the woods. To tell you the truth, I've had about all I can take just now. Why Dora wanted to bring that Prowde here—but of course"—he was always reasonable—"I do understand it. Dora is a realist. She knows it was murder. She knows that—" he hesitated and then continued, "that all the people close to me or close to Rose will be under some suspicion. She's quite right in taking steps to establish her alibi."

They turned toward the path that led to the airstrip. The green pines began to close around them. Just about here, Susan thought, she had seen the running man. The brick wall was almost six feet high, with a rustic-appearing but very solid gate. G.M. took a key from his pocket and unlocked and opened the gate.

Almost at once they passed into heavily wooded country. G.M. shoved his hands in the pockets of his heavy country jacket; he wore a brown turtleneck sweater and slacks and seemed very different, younger than the man she had known only in his office. His hair was barely touched with gray, his face was sober, but gradually, as they walked, he seemed to regain some of his usual resiliency and command of any situation.

"Well, I've done what I had to do. I couldn't keep Rose's death quiet even if it had been right to try. I did still call it an accident, but I had to say that the police were investigating. Couldn't do anything else."

"You mean you told the—the men who are coming here next week about Rose?"

"Oh, yes. As I said, I had to. I've always played things straight. Besides, it's only a matter of time till the police say it's murder."

"What about the conference?"

"There's nothing much I can do about that. I left the decision to the others. Of course, the men I was to see can't come here now. I only wish I could know just what's going on everywhere. A money crises can sweep up as fast as a hurricane, but it can die down as fast too."

"But you are needed."

He looked down at her, half smiling. "I'm not indispensable, Susan. I've only studied and worked very hard since I was young. I suppose I either had or developed a certain instinct about money. A country rests upon its economy. There are times of something like crisis . . ." He paused, thought and went on, "There is a crisis, it seems to me, almost every day. The problem is that a crisis can involve not only my own business interests but the whole national economy."

"You work very hard."

"It doesn't seem like work. It's more—oh, a debt I owe to something. My own interests, of course. But also my country's. I don't want to sound pretentious. But if anyone relies on what judgment or skill I may possess, then it's right for me to do my best."

"You've never taken public office."

"Oh, no." G.M. shook his head decisively. "I couldn't possibly do that! I've always steered clear of politics. I do better working as I do, behind the scenes. I'm not ambitious in a political way. I want to keep out of the limelight and out of feuds."

"Yes, I understard that."

He gave her a swift look. "I think you do understand. I'm not the only man trying in as quiet a way as he can contrive to do what seems the right and wise thing. We can get all snarled up, Susan. Like cats in a bag. Trade relations don't happen by themselves. People work on seeing the other fellow's viewpoint." They walked on until they came out in the clearing that had been made for the helicopter landing. G.M. said suddenly, "Dear Rose, she was so ambitious, you know, in her way."

"Rose!" Susan could not have kept the astonishment from her voice.

"Oh, yes. In the early days of our marriage she wanted to be a senator's wife or a cabinet member's wife. Something like that. I disappointed her. Probably that was why she fell into the family habit."

"Family—"

"You've seen Snell and Milly. Dora keeps a tight rein on Col and Wilfred. But she also sees to it that the liquor in the house is locked up. No need to tempt them."

"Rose drank? I can't believe—"

"You would believe it if you had—never mind. She was such a pretty thing once. However, if I search my conscience, as I have many times, I must be honest and say that if she hadn't had all that money her first husband left her and I hadn't known it, I might not have been so precipitate about our marriage. I rather think I rushed her off her feet. She was five years older than I was but seemed childish. She had only Milly to advise her, and Milly really is a fool—sometimes a malicious fool. At any rate, there you have the story of my life. Can you bear it?"

She looked up at him, but there was not the usual twinkle in his eyes, nothing but serious thoughtfulness.

"You must have been very young."

"Old enough to persuade Rose to marry me and to let me use her money. Oh yes, I was old enough for that. I did pay it back. I tried to give Rose everything she wanted. I failed miserably." She looked back at what they could see of the red brick house. "Funny," he said almost to himself. "All this nonsense about armed guards and a secret house. The private lines on my own switchboard that cost like the devil. As if anybody in Medbury Hills or in fact anyone along the phone line is hanging on to hear whatever I say."

"But I thought that was your idea. I mean, all that care to protect whatever you and—your guests might talk of."

He laughed shortly. "It wasn't my idea."
"Then whose idea was it?"
"It was Rose's idea," he said rather dryly.
"Rose!"

Seven

"It's due to an accident, really. I was mugged one night walking through Central Park on my way to the apartment. I wasn't really hurt, just mauled about. But when I got home, Rose—she'd been drinking, you see, but was sober enough to see that I had been knocked on the head. I had to call a doctor to stitch it up. She got the truth out of me before I thought of its effect on her. She said it was an enemy agent or an industrial spy—flattering to me, I must say."

"She may have been right."

"I really don't think anybody in the world would bother with me. But there had been those tragic assassinations. The upshot of it all was that I finally gave in, and, to be honest, by that time I had begun to see that there could be a real use for a kind of home away from home."

"Oh." Susan thought of the Fifth Avenue apartment as she had seen it. G.M. guessed her thought.

"Naturally I couldn't depend on Rose to act as my hostess. I couldn't depend on a dinner, say, being properly served or arranged in the big apartment. My hotel apartment is really tiny, merely a place to sleep in. Once I decided, I went whole hog, so to speak. Everything that was suggested by the contractors was done."

"Soundproofing? A man at the gate all the time?"

He nodded. "But that actually was to give employment to two of Rose's relatives, Col and Wilfred. I had some decorators work on the inside of the house. All I did was choose—oh, colors, rugs, a good picture or two. I can't say that I ever much liked the outside of the house, but I do like the arrangement of the inside. It's beautiful, I think. And very comfortable. Also, I must say the private phone lines do give me more freedom in reaching people I want to talk to and in saying whatever I have to say. The only thing I objected to was a suggested scheme of electrical gadgets. I didn't want the Medbury Hills police to have to come dashing to the rescue whenever Col or Wilfred forgot the alarm and opened some bugged door or window. The big front gate has an electrical switch, but that's all and it is controlled from the gatehouse, that little shed where Col and Wilfred spend as much of their time as Dora allows them. They see to keeping the place in order. Mainly I began to see the advantages of having the house, set off here in the country."

He sighed. "I suppose now it'll be in the newspapers, all sorts of nonsense."

"Perhaps you can stop that."

"You can't stop news. But I've liked the house. Dora has been a great help to me in running it. I did nothing. And it has been a very pleasant spot to wine and dine people I want to see or who want to see me. I've had a sense of freedom here. Oh, I've made excuses to people about it—all the secrecy, I mean, the guards. Everything. But the fact is it became extremely convenient to me."

They walked on slowly. The dusk was growing blue under the trees. At last Susan said, "Did Rose like the house?"

He laughed shortly. "By the time the house was built and finished she had lost interest in it. But by then she was drinking more heavily and had got it into her head that any attempt to assassinate me would be dangerous to her. She scarcely left the big apartment. She holed herself in, afraid of everyone but Milly. In a sense she was right. Somebody killed her. I'll find out who it was, believe me."

She did believe him. There was a cold resolution in his voice and in his face that made her pity anyone who ran afoul of him.

He said presently, "Rose came here only once or twice. She didn't like it. She never wanted to live here, and to tell the plain truth, that relieved me. I never knew what state she might be in at any time. I've got to find out why she came here yesterday, what she intended to do. She did not intend to kill herself. I know that. Besides, oh, long ago, I taught her to use a gun. She was always nervous, even before I became—through her money, I have to say again—rich enough to invite thieves or prowlers. No, she'd never have killed herself. She'd never have come here yesterday without some pressing reason. But she did come and she was shot and I've got to find that man you saw running from the house."

"G.M.," Susan said hesitantly, "is there anybody at all who had some reason to hate Rose that much?"

He frowned. "I've thought of that. I've thought of everything, but none of her relatives would have killed her. For one thing, she meant too much to them, money-wise."

He turned abruptly to her. "I'm the kind of man who looks ahead. That's been my only talent. I couldn't see ahead when Rose and I were married. We ought to have gotten to know one another better."

"She must have been very pretty."

"She was. She listened to everything I said, every opinion I had. It wasn't long before I discovered that she didn't really take in anything. Finally I had to acknowledge to myself that she didn't talk because she had nothing to say. Her prettiness began to go—so fast. Milly was never a good influence for her. None of the Clansers was a good influence, for all of them played on her weakness. She liked to do things for them, not as a Lady Bountiful, but I think out of real affection; they knew that if they managed to get to her when she'd been drinking they could get anything they wanted out of her. Milly will now have most of Rose's money. She will come into about three million. The rest of it is divided equally among the others—except for Dora. Rose would never accept Dora as a Clanser, as of course she is not. I don't know exactly what the Clansers will get. I should say about thirty thousand each. It won't last them long. To Col or Snell or Wilfred, thirty thousand will seem like a fortune. Ligon will know better. I did my best for Rose. I really did. But I couldn't fight—her drinking. I couldn't get on the right terms with her."

It was the old story, Susan thought, watching G.M.'s strong but now sad face. A man may marry when he's young; he may marry a pretty face and figure only to discover that as he advances in life the pretty face and figure leave and there's nothing left, no way for his wife to accompany him.

"Rose was so credulous, you see," G.M. said. "Her first marriage was a boon to her family. He was much older than Rose and, as you know, had money which must have seemed to them an enormous fortune. It seemed so to me when I married her. I've told you that. They all looked on me as a fortune hunter, as in a way I was. I can't let myself forget that." He looked directly down at her through the darkening twilight. "I've talked a great deal about myself. You must forgive me."

"I'm so sorry," Susan said.

His face was very grave. As if at an impulse he put his arms around her and held her. "I believe you are sorry for me. I believe you've listened to all I've said—" He paused, seemed to think of his own words, and continued, "—out of the kindness of your heart. I've never talked to anyone like this before."

She stood for a moment in the warm, hard circle of his arms. His arms, the great man's arms holding her as if she had done him some tremendous favor—as if, she thought amazed, he liked her for being a woman to whom he could talk.

Something frisked around her ankles. A dog gave a happy little yelp. G.M. released her and both looked down at Belle, who was dancing around them as if she had been away for a very long time. Beau also joined in the romping circles which Belle had begun. Greg stood at the entrance to the airstrip, with the dark woods behind him.

She wondered confusedly what he had seen, and knew that he had seen her in G.M.'s arms. There was no way of telling whether or not he had heard what G.M. had said. But there was nothing at all in what G.M. had said to bring that rather set look into Greg's face. He said, "I couldn't find you at the house, Susan, so I went to get the dogs. I was afraid the vet would close up shop."

G.M. glanced at the dogs, amused by their wild cavorting. "Dear me, they do look elegant."

They did indeed look elegant, clipped and handsomely trimmed, with pompadours brushed up, legs looking as if they wore pantaloons and bright eyes dancing as they whirled around ecstatically. "Fifth Avenue poodles," Greg said dryly.

"If they're going to sleep on my bed," Susan said, "I hope they've been thoroughly washed."

There was still an unnatural air about Greg; he behaved as though he were some stranger on very formal terms. Dora emerged from the path behind him. She was so lovely, even in the twilight, that Susan didn't see how any man could resist her appeal. She didn't even glance at Susan. She came directly to G.M. and put her white hands on his arm. "I can't get a word more out of Snell. He insists that he doesn't know why Rose came here. He keeps saying the same thing over and over again. Rose phoned him, she asked him to bring her here, she said she'd meet him at the heliport. He said he brought her here; she had a key to the gate and the front door. He said he didn't hear anything or see anybody. He says he doesn't know how or why the helicopter was left near the Westchester airfield. But of course I can guess why."

"I can guess too," G.M. said. "He managed to get some whiskey into himself and luckily brought the chopper down without crashing. Somehow he got himself back to town and to his apartment, where he slept off his drunk. But I can't help thinking that Snell knows something he's not telling."

Dora nodded, her beautiful face very thoughtful. "But I don't see any way just now to make him tell it—if there really is something he knows. Susan—" She seemed to be aware of Susan's presence for the first time, but of course she had been perfectly aware of her the instant she entered the clearing. "Are you *sure* he was not the man you say you saw running toward the gate?"

This time Greg did not step forward with a firm statement to the effect that Susan could not possibly identify the man she had seen. But G.M. said, "You heard her, Dora. She's only sure that it was not Snell."

"It does seem to me, Susan, that you could have retained some kind of description even if, as you say, you saw him for such a brief time." Dora's voice was sharp. She came closer to Susan. "Now listen, my dear. We all know you would do anything you could to keep an inquiry about Rose's murder from involving anybody—well, to be honest, from involving G.M. Wouldn't you?"

"It wasn't G.M.; I'd have recognized him."

"Of course." Dora's flexible voice, one of her charms, was suddenly coaxing. "But if you really did see someone, surely you could identify him."

"I saw a man running," Susan said, and G.M. broke in, "It's late. Let's get back to the house. Always chilly these autumn evenings." He whistled for the dogs, who came joyfully, frisking their brushed-up legs. Dora asked, "Are you really going to keep those dogs, G.M.?"

"Certainly," G.M. replied rather shortly and fell in beside Dora as they entered the narrow path through the woods toward the house. Susan followed. Dora took G.M.'s arm in a confident and accustomed way.

Greg, walking a little behind Susan, said nothing at all. The dogs leaped around them, and as they emerged from the woods, lights shone from the house windows. The kitchen window from which Susan had seen the running man was clearly visible. So was Milly bending over something on a table. G.M. locked the gate and they walked toward the house.

Snell came into view in the kitchen and appeared to expostulate with Milly, who shrugged her vast shoulders.

Dora said clearly into the twilight, "Snell wants the key to the liquor cabinet or the wine cellar. He asked me for one of them. I wouldn't give him either."

They rounded the corner of the house. It struck Susan for the first time that there appeared to be no back entrance. She said, "The man I saw must have come from the front door. It's the only door, isn't it?"

Dora replied, "Oh, yes. G.M. didn't want back doors for servants' use; the hall from the kitchen to the vestibule is sufficient for disposing of trash. Col or Wilfred takes everything to a trash burner near the garage. You are quite right. The man you say you saw had to come from the vestibule door."

"Unless," Greg said shortly, "he wasn't in the house at all. Snell says he left Rose at the door."

"Somebody had to be in the house," Dora said with conclusive logic.

G.M. opened the door to the vestibule.

"We'll not change," Dora said. "No sense in it. God knows what Milly is getting for our dinner. She says that miserable cat got the steak."

"There'll be something," G.M. said mildly. "Greg, you have a key for the liquor closet. Please get out something for us to drink."

Greg nodded and started for the kitchen passage. G.M. strolled across the enchantingly beautiful living room and down the steps into the equally enchanting library, where Ligon and Bert Prowde sat and looked at each other. Neither seemed to like what he saw.

Bert Prowde sat in a corner on the edge of a chair. Ligon sat at ease in a big comfortable chair.

Ligon spoke. "Snell is helping Milly get dinner."

"Good," G.M. said. "Now we'd better have something to drink."

Nobody's eyes brightened. If anything, Bert looked more miserable. Ligon lifted his eyebrows slightly. "As you know, I'm not a drinking man, G.M. However, on this sad occasion—"

"All right, Ligon, all right." G.M. went over to the writing table. Dora eyed Ligon and said sharply, "No, you never had any minor vices, Ligon. I've often thought that you really must have and conceal some major vice."

"Really, Dora!" Ligon's face turned so red that Susan instinctively thought of a stroke. Having thrust at him in a telling way, however, Dora said almost happily, "Oh, I don't mean I think you've embezzled anybody's money. I know you too well for that. You are as tight as the paper on the wall, but you employ one of the best firms of accountants in the country and your books are gone over with their microscopes. No, you haven't stolen from anybody. Besides, you'd be afraid to. What do you get out of life, Ligon? Besides making money?"

G.M. rubbed his hands over his forehead; Bert Prowde seemed to shrink back in his chair. Luckily there was the tinkling sound of glasses and ice approaching across the living room. Ligon regained his self-control, gave Dora a half-amused glance and settled back into his chair as Greg appeared with bottles. Milly came after him with ice and Snell with glasses and water, quite as if the Clansers were drawn by the magnet of bottles.

As they proved to be. Snell took it upon himself to pour and poured very stiff drinks for everybody. Dora served them, thrusting a glass at Lignon as if she'd have liked to follow it with her fingernails.

Greg put aside a glass which looked very strongly supplied with whiskey, poured another one with a decidedly lighter color and brought it to Susan. He didn't look at her; he merely handed it to her so their fingers didn't so much as touch.

The Clansers were on their second strong drinks when Lattrice arrived. Snell, still clutching his glass, went to answer the bell, and returned with Lattrice. G.M.'s face tightened as if he had known that it would be Lattrice and also as if he knew what Lattrice intended to say. Lattrice gave everyone a kind of general nod and looked at G.M.

"I'm afraid we can't do more, Mr. Manders. The medical examiner says there's no doubt it was murder. There are no powder burns on her dress and apparently whoever shot her stood some feet away. He says"—Lattrice walked over to stand before the writing table—"I—we—have to investigate."

"I know," G.M. said quietly. "I was sure that this had to come. At first I did hope that we might be able to postpone your inquiry."

"We've been told to keep things as quiet as possible," Lattrice said unhappily. "But I don't know, when it's murder things do get out in spite of everything. What about this conference you were to have next week?"

"I don't really know. I had to inform some of my associates of my wife's death. The papers so far call it accident. However, you'll have to use every means at your disposal to find out why my wife was murdered and who did it." G.M. didn't sigh; he only straightened his shoulders as if to meet a problem. "How much publicity will this thing bring about?"

"We'll try to keep the publicity at a minimum, sir. But we can't stop news."

"No, of course not."

"As long as we could assume it to be an accident—" Lattrice began; G.M. interrupted him, saying, "Yes, I know. Nobody could have been more helpful to me than you and the Medbury Hills police. But after I had thought about it I came to the conclusion that it couldn't possibly have been an accident and that my wife would never have killed herself. Now the medical examiner leaves no doubt that it was murder. I'm sure that everybody here will cooperate with you in your investigation."

Dora came over to the writing table and put her hand on it possessively. "I know—at least I've been told—that the husband is a suspect always. Well, I can tell you that Mr. Manders would never have killed his wife. It's true that she was a drunk and a slattern, but he wouldn't have killed her."

Ligon put down his glass with a sharp thump. "You must not speak of Rose like that, Dora. She had her weakness, but she loved her family."

Eight

G.M. said, "Sit down, Lattrice. A drink?"

Lattrice looked as if he'd very much like a drink. Duty overpowered him, however, and he shook his head. "No, thank you. It's a nasty business, Mr. Manders. We can't find out who brought that helicopter so close to Westchester field and left it there. I—we—are unable to discover why your wife came here." There was a shade of evasion in his manner which Susan did not understand, but G.M. apparently did, for there was a look of comprehension in his shrewd eyes; he nodded and Lattrice went on, "Your wife would have come, of course, if you asked her to come."

"I told you. I didn't know she had come here."

"Then, Mr. Snell Clanser, you were the pilot. You are sure that she said nothing at all to indicate her purpose in coming here?"

Snell's face emerged briefly from his glass. He shook his head. "Not a word. I've told you everything I know."

"Weren't you surprised when she asked you to bring her here?"

"Surprised?" Snell seemed to weigh the word carefully as if it concealed a trap. Then he shook his head again. "Nope. Nothing Rose did ever surprised me. I mean, she had her little notions, you know."

"Notions?" Lattrice said sharply.

"Nothing—I mean—well, really I didn't mean anything. But when she phoned me and told me she wanted to come here and wanted me to bring her in the helicopter, what could I say? She was G.M.'s wife. She had a right to come here if she wanted to." He upended his glass, draining it to the last drop and added, "Of course, Rose left Milly a bundle."

Milly also drained her glass swiftly; Susan had never seen anything like the Clansers for swigging; they seemed to pour liquor down without so much as swallowing; it was too bad, she thought in a detached way, that Col and Wilfred were not there to get their handouts.

Milly didn't put down the glass; she rose, waddled over to the table where Greg had deposited the bottles, poured herself another drink and said, over her shoulder, "How did you know that, Snell?"

"How did I know that!" Snell sneered. "You told me. You said if anything ever happened to Rose it would do me no good because you were to have her money. You said she had told you."

Milly came back to a deep and easy chair; she settled down, fat ankles protruding below a remarkable purple garment which somewhat resembled a caftan. "Well, and if she did tell me, what of it! You're surely not trying to tell the police that I shot Rose. My sister. My best friend on earth. Besides"—she took another long swallow—"I have an alibi. Susan and Greg both know where I was all afternoon."

Lattrice addressed Greg. "I'm sure that's true."

"Well—" Greg's face still had a taut look which seemed to Susan to have intensified. "Not every moment. As you know, Susan—Miss Beach—and I were putting groceries in the kitchen. She saw a man running. I went to look. We waited for some time until we heard the helicopter leave."

"Forgive me if I seem to repeat my inquiries," Lattrice said politely. "It's only because sometimes people have second thoughts, remember something which they'd forgotten. Now, do you think, Miss Beach, that the man you saw could recognize you? That is, did he get a clear enough look at you to, say, know who you are? Or as I said, know you if he saw you again?"

Something in the whole room seemed to turn a little cold and still. "Why, I—I don't know," Susan said at last slowly. "I suppose he could have seen me. Yes."

Greg said, "She had only a glimpse of him."

"Yes, yes," Lattrice went on. "Now, I keep thinking of the length of time in which you stood in the kitchen and waited to hear the helicopter leave."

"As I told you, I don't know. Not long. Long enough perhaps for someone to enter the house and shoot Rose."

"Why, Greg, you liar!" Milly fortified herself with another prodigious gulp and glared at him. "You know that I—I—couldn't possibly have come into the house without your knowing it and shot Rose. How dare you suggest such a thing! G.M., you must get rid of this upstart, this liar, this—this—"

"Milly," said G.M. peaceably, "nobody is accusing you."

"He did. That is, not in so many words, but he accused me!"

Snell giggled. "You had a motive, Milly. A big motive. And it seems you had opportunity."

Lattrice sighed; his dark face was troubled. He said, "I don't believe—" and looked at Ligon and then at Bert Prowde. Bert Prowde seemed to make every effort to sink himself into invisibility. Ligon rose. "I am Ligon Clanser. My name may be unfamiliar to you, but—"

"How do you do," Lattrice said politely and turned to Bert Prowde. Dora hastily introduced him. "A dear friend of mine, Mr. Prowde. We were having cocktails in his apartment at the time of the accident—that is, murder."

Bert Prowde straightened a little and crossed one leg over the other. Lattrice nodded. "One of the state police will be here tomorrow to take fingerprints. Not"—as Milly squealed—"not that that is anything but a matter of form. As a rule," he added honestly but rather ominously.

Milly said, "My fingerprints are on that gun! I picked it up! I've told everybody!"

Ligon said to Lattrice, "But surely you took fingerprints yesterday when you were called here!"

Lattrice eyed him coolly. "We hoped that her death would prove accidental. Besides, nobody has run away. The state police have their hands full. There's no reason to trouble all of you tonight." He turned to Susan. "Miss Beach, may I speak to you alone? That is, I must remind you, if you are perfectly willing to be questioned. It is your right to refuse to talk to me or to have your own lawyer if you want him."

Susan glanced at G.M., who nodded. She rose and went with Lattrice into the living room just as Col, Wilfred and two policemen entered it from the vestibule. One of the policemen was the man with the setters who had spoken so kindly to her the night before, and she said, "Good evening," as he gave her a kind and rather pitying glance. Col and Wilfred seemed a little depressed but also thirsty, for they headed for the library as if they too possessed a kind of instinct for a supply of drinks.

Lattrice paused. "It's all so—so open," he said, looking at the lovely arch of the doorway from the living room to the dining room. "No place to talk privately."

"There's the kitchen," Susan began and also thought of the disorder which almost certainly now prevailed since Milly had prepared dinner. "If you don't mind, there's my room."

"If *you* don't mind," Lattrice said politely and followed her up the stairs. Once in her room he looked around rather blankly. "Kind of surprising, isn't it?" he said. "I mean—well, everybody around here knows about this house, you know. Beautiful downstairs. We know of course that some very important men come here—really from all over the world. Even the President sometimes, they say."

"I don't—I really don't think so. I don't know who G.M.'s guests are. I only know that he finds this house a convenience."

"He must have got outside help in building it. Soundproofing and even a private switchboard. Costs the earth but he's got money. Well, it's not my business. I'd better get to the point. Now—" He leaned against a chair. "I've talked to the district attorney. I believe he talked to the state's attorney and the governor. I believe that Mr. Manders talked to one of them—maybe all of them last night. He was using a public phone booth. The district attorney was the one who phoned me and said to call it an accident unless or until it was proven to be murder. Now then, once more, you saw a man running from the house."

"Yes."

He had not closed the door; he shook his head as if annoyed at his carelessness, went to the door and closed it. Again he eyed the room with something like surprise. "The rest of the house is so luxurious," he said as if apologizing for his own surprise. "However, I expect not many people stayed overnight, and it's none of my business. Now, I want to make sure—again—whether or not you would recognize this man."

"I just don't know. Really. I've told you—"

He nodded. "You seem very sure that it was not Mr. Manders himself."

"I am sure of that."

"Or the pilot—Snell?"

"I don't think so."

He thought that over, his dark eyes alert. He's good-looking, Susan thought absently. Not as good-looking as G.M., no air of command. But she had a notion that he was intelligent and observant and also tenacious.

"But it is possible that he might have seen you."

"I don't know!"

"Perhaps he didn't. Now, you told me about finding Mrs. Manders last night. Will you please tell me again, everything you can remember?"

It was a long interview, but nothing was brought up that Susan thought could possibly be new to Lattrice. Perhaps the mere hammering of the few facts she knew was designed by him to uncover some small item which might have meaning. He asked her about the gun, where it had been when Milly picked it up; she thought it was on the floor, along with Rose's fur wrap and her handbag. He nodded at that.

"The key to the front door and the gate leading to the landing strip was not in her handbag. Did her sister Milly remove it?"

"I don't think so. She only picked up the fur wrap."

He went on. How did it happen that they had brought such a supply of groceries to the house? Was that to last until the conference next week?

"They were for our use. But the dinner itself was to be supplied by caterers."

He thought for a moment about that. "But it does seem a long time for you and Miss—you call her Milly—to prepare for what was merely a business dinner. Why were you two and also Greg Cameron sent here so far ahead of time?"

"I don't think there was any special reason. Dora—that is, Mrs. Clanser—only told me she couldn't come herself owing to pressure of business and that she wanted to make sure that the house was in perfect order and to give me time to get acquainted with things. She said that sometimes G.M.'s guests desired some particular thing and I must know how to get it. I mean—oh, one of them has to have some kind of bottled water. Another is allergic to strawberries. That kind of thing."

"I see. Yes, that sounds reasonable. Mrs. Clanser must be extremely efficient."

"Yes, she is."

He eyed the polished toe of one oxford. Then he said, "Miss Beach, does it seem possible to you that Mrs. Manders—that is, you all call her Rose—knew herself to be in danger, opened the safe, got the gun—and then her murderer wrested it away from her, shot her, and got out of the house before you and young Cameron arrived?"

"I don't know. I never thought of that."

"Seems far-fetched. Still, murder itself is out of the ordinary. Certainly her sister Milly has a motive." Without pausing he got to his feet and crossed the room as lightly as the cat could have done, noiselessly opened the door, and listened. Presently he closed it again. "Don't mind me. I thought I heard something at the door. Is there anything else at all, Miss Beach?"

For an instant a wild thought of repeating what G.M. had told her, his real reasons for the secret house, crossed her mind, but she dismissed it. She had a strong sense of having been told those reasons in confidence. If he felt like telling them to the police then it was his business to reveal them, not hers. She took her head. "Nothing."

"I see. Yes. Now let's just go over the whole thing again, if you please."

Wearily she went over it again; he prompted her when she faltered or omitted some detail. She told nothing she had not told before. She had a notion that time was passing, a great deal of time. She began to feel very tired and wished that she had brought the whiskey and soda Greg had poured for her upstairs. The Clansers, she thought in a kind of parenthesis, were undoubtedly making full use of G.M.'s supply of liquor.

At last Lattrice thanked her and went for the door. "Is that all?" she asked, not quite believing it.

"You've been most patient and obliging. Once more, however: is it possible that given the right circumstances, the right light, everything, you could identify the running man you talk of?"

"I might be able to. In the dusk and if he wore the same clothes—"

"Dark coat. Hat over his face—"

"Y—yes."

"Keep that to yourself. Good night," said Lattrice and disappeared.

She sat for a moment, too drained of energy to rise. When she did at last get up, go to the simple chest of drawers which seemed to serve as a dressing table, brush her hair and look at herself, she was astonished to see how pale she was. Even her lips looked unwontedly white. She touched them with lipstick and at last went down the stairs to the hall, clinging to the velvet-covered banister. She had been both right and wrong about the Clansers; they were still drinking—at least Milly, Snell and Col had glasses. But they were in the dining room and had apparently finished whatever dinner Milly had provided. Bert Prowde was there, too, looking as unhappy as usual; and Lignon Clanser looking as if he wished he were elsewhere.

Dora was not there. G.M. was not there. Greg was not there.

She started for the library, and before she had stepped off the rug, so her footsteps had not tapped on the parquet floor, she heard Dora's voice, clear and musical against the babble of Clansers in the dining room. Dora said, "—so after what I told you that Thursday night, you killed her. You knew there was only one way. I'll never tell, of course."

Susan couldn't have moved if her life depended on it. She heard Dora continue, in that clear and musical voice. "So now there's no obstacle. Rose is gone. We can be married as soon as—"

"Dora, you'll remember what I told you Thursday night."

Dora laughed. "Oh that! Saying you had no idea of marriage to me! You didn't mean it. Thursday night I told you that you would have to choose between me and Rose. Friday, Rose was shot."

"That was a tragic coincidence."

"Call it whatever you like. But you chose me—"

"Dora, I did not kill Rose in order to marry you or for any other reason. Go and see if Greg has got his call though."

"You've got to do what I want you to do—"

Susan made herself move, hurry. Certainly the secret house was no place for a private dialogue. She ran lightly across the drawing room. She didn't care to hear the babble of the assembled Clansers. She went into the vestibule, where the cat opened a lazy blue eye and the dogs leaped upon her, asking to go out. She took it as an excuse to get out herself.

No police car stood now in the driveway. Lattrice and the policemen must have gone.

The air was cold and infinitely refreshing. The dogs dashed ahead of her and disappeared into the heavy shadows of the pines.

It was a cloudy night, no moon, no stars. There were lights from the house behind her, and as she rounded a curve, she thought there was a light showing in the shed where by now the night man, Wilfred, was presumably sitting on guard with his gun at his ample waist. Probably almost, if not entirely drunk.

Eavesdropping is not a pretty thing, she thought, yet she couldn't have forced herself to move once she had heard Dora's words. "So after what I told you that Thursday night you killed her. You knew there was only one way. I'll never tell—" It was remarkably revealing. Susan had not paid much attention to office gossip to the effect that Dora was G.M.'s longstanding mistress. It was nevertheless almost a confirmation of gossip to hear that Dora, according to her own words, had given an ultimatum. She had certainly told him—Thursday night, she had said—it had to be either Dora or Rose.

G.M. had rejected the idea.

Yet Friday Rose had been killed.

It struck Susan in a dreadful way that somehow, some way, a hired assassin might have been the running man she had seen. Hired by whom?

A tragic coincidence, G.M. had called it. It was a coincidence that could interest the police far too deeply.

She walked on, scarcely hearing her own footsteps on the driveway. The dogs were somewhere in the shadows.

A grave and, it occurred to her, immediate danger struck her. If Dora chose to go to the police and tell them what Susan had heard, they would say—wouldn't they?—that G.M. had a motive for killing Rose. They were not likely to swallow completely a notion of coincidence.

But if Dora did that, she would automatically give up forever her plan to marry G.M. He was not the kind of man to forgive.

In an odd way Susan felt childishly hurt, as if a treasured illusion had been shattered. It was almost as if she herself were in love with G.M. She wasn't, of course; she was simply very grateful to him and admired him wholeheartedly. Only that evening he had seemed to take her into a confidence he had shared with no one else. He had seemed to rely upon her, little Susan Beach. She had had for a moment a kind of Cinderella feeling; the great man had talked to her in a close and confidential way, almost as if he wished to turn to her with his grief, regrets and trouble.

She was quite near the gates, which to her surprise were open. The night was dark, but she could see that the driveway stretched ahead, with no barrier, toward the public road. She wondered whether she ought to tell Wilfred, and then concluded that for some reason he had been told to open the gates; perhaps someone might be coming. Lattrice? Surely not again so soon.

There were faint lights coming from behind the enormous

clumps of pines which shielded the small gatehouse. Thinking, she waited for a long time before she turned back.

The dogs must be very near her, somewhere in the shrubbery. She could hear faint rustling and something almost like the patter of feet, but they did not come out into the driveway. Let them run, she thought, remembering the stuffy, big apartment on Fifth Avenue where Rose had apparently kept them far too confined.

Strangely they seemed to keep pace with her as she walked back toward the house. They were so near it was as if they walked purposefully, making little yet detectable sounds.

The slight rustle came closer, almost as if someone were stealthily following her, watching her from the shadows, like an animal waiting its chance to pounce.

Nine

This is preposterous, she told herself. She *must* not let her fancy run wild. But she had to hurry now.

There was a deep patch of shadow from the thickets of pines and then a curve. If she could get past that, she would defeat that stalking and furtive accompaniment. Oh, this is preposterous, she said to herself again and began to run.

Her footsteps thudded along the driveway, yet she was sure she could hear an increased rustle and motion going along with her, running faster than she could run.

A light sprang up somewhere behind her. At the same time a man's footsteps pounded along the driveway from the house toward her. The light was a giant flashlight, and Wilfred called to her, "Anything the matter? Wait! Anything the matter?"

A man's figure came from the shadows ahead; it was Greg. "What's wrong?"

She seized his arms, clung to him and tried to catch her breath; and still her heart thumped too rapidly.

Wilfred came up beside them; his flashlight and an aura of whiskey fell upon them. "What's happened?" Greg asked. "Why was she running like that? I could hear her."

"Darned if I know," Wilfred said behind the glaring curtain of light which shielded his face.

"It wasn't anything," Susan cried. "Silly—nothing!"

Greg tilted his head. "You don't run from nothing. What was it?"

"The dogs—I thought it was the dogs, I know it was the dogs—but then I was afraid. No reason. The dogs were running along beside me in the shrubbery and pines and I—thought—Oh, it was nothing!"

"All right," Greg said, but he did not seem satisfied. "Wilfred, have you closed the gates?"

"Oh, my God!" Wilfred jerked around. He went thumping back toward the gates, his flashlight jerking, leaving only the alcoholic aroma behind him. Greg took her arm. "Now then, we'll get back to the house. You've had a scare."

"I scared myself. I do feel like a fool."

"All right," Greg said again. They emerged from the deep patch of shadow. The light from the vestibule streamed out. Two patient little figures were waiting at the door to be lct in.

Could the dogs have run ahead of her, toward the house? Yes, of course they could. But she moved closer to Greg. He said, "You've got to go away from here," and opened the door. The dogs frisked in and ran for the library. As Greg turned to close the door she saw that Wilfred had shambled rapidly after them. "Please, Greg, don't tell G.M. I left the gates open. He'll have my hide."

He gave a startled kind of yell as something streaked in the open door and made for the blanket on the floor It was Toby, eyes glittering red, indignant and fur on end.

"Wow," said Wilfred. "I was really afraid for a moment that I—well, that I'd maybe had a little too much to drink—"

"You had," Greg said shortly. "Susan, did you let the cat out?"

"No. He was sleeping on the blanket when I took the dogs out."

"Then somebody came out of the house after you went out. Let's see who it was. And what he was doing."

The house, though, was curiously silent. There was no mingled chatter from the Clansers, no sound at all. Greg went through the kitchen passage, looked in the kitchen and came back. "Nothing there but dishes and cooking things. All stacked up hit or miss."

"I'll see to them," Wilfred said eagerly. "I don't have to be at the gate all the time. I can hear the buzzer. I'll see to the dishes."

It was clearly meant as an ingratiating gesture. Greg said, "Suit yourself. I'll just lock up the liquor cupboard."

Wilfred bit his lip in a disappointed way. Greg disappeared toward the kitchen again and came back. "Now then, go ahead, Wilfred, and clear things up. Susan, come with me."

The door opened again and both Greg and Susan turned to see Dora coming in. "Oh," Greg said, "it's you. Been out for a stroll?"

Dora had an orange coat flung over her shoulders; her face was resolute. "Certainly. With Bert." Bert Prowde appeared behind her, his coat collar turned up. Dora said, smiling,

"Where have you two been, Greg? Out for a stroll, too? I didn't see you."

Greg said shortly, "We were out with the dogs. Did you let the cat out?"

"Of course. I see he's back again. I hoped he'd get lost."

Bert uttered one of the few observations which Susan had heard from him; it was something rather diffident to the effect that it was hard to lose a cat. Dora paid no attention, Wilfred peered out from the passage to the kitchen. G.M. came up the basement stairs.

All of them waited for him to speak as if he were royalty. He nodded at them and went on into the library. Greg hesitated, then followed him. Susan sat down on the bench as if her knees wouldn't support her.

"What on earth is the matter with you?" Dora asked sharply.

Susan shook her head. "Nothing, really."

Bert again offered an observation. "Looks upset."

Greg called them. "Susan, G.M. wants to speak to you."

Susan started for the library. Dora came with her, swiftly. Bert followed as far as a chair in the living room where he hovered.

G.M. was at the writing table. "Now, what's all this? Greg tells me you had a scare."

"There!" Dora said. "I knew something was wrong! What happened?"

G.M. said, "Tell me about it, Susan."

"I was silly. I got a notion that someone was following me—that's all really. I'm sorry."

G.M. waited a minute. Then he said, "Greg, Wilfred had left the gates open?"

"Yes. He's closed them now."

"It's not the first time he has done that," G.M. said. "Usually it didn't matter but now—where is Wilfred?"

"In the kitchen," Greg said, "washing dishes."

A kind of flicker touched G.M.'s lips. "Serves him right. I'll have a word with him later. Now then, Dora, where are Milly and—oh, all of them?"

"I haven't the faintest idea," Dora said coolly. "The last I saw Ligon and Snell they were trying to boost Milly up the stairs. My advice would be to lock up all the liquor as long as the Clansers are here."

G.M. lifted his eyebrows. "Not bad advice. Now—Dora, will you go to the switchboard and get hold of our man in

California. I'm leaving at the end of the week. The place of the conference will be changed."

"What about the services for Rose?"

Dora was questioning him as alertly as if his business were also her business—as indeed in a way it had always been. G.M. rubbed his eyes wearily. "That must be postponed. The police have to continue their investigations, but they hope to do it quietly. The point is—oh, it's nonsense—but you'll remember that Rose once got it into her head that some enemy agent or some industrial enemy might attack me. There seems to be a notion that someone just might have shot Rose in the hope of discrediting me."

Greg said suddenly, "You're ex officio but needed. You're like a diplomat portfolio."

G.M. smiled. "I'll tell you one thing. If I had any sort of government post, duly elected or duly appointed, I really think I could live my own life more freely. Sounds contradictory. But when anything is put to me as an authority, in a way, and as a friendly and trusted colleague, what can I do? I'm bound by every thread there is."

Dora said, "G.M., *could* they be right? Could some enemy have done this in the hope of discrediting you, in the hope of your being suspected of your wife's murder?"

"No," G.M. said positively. "There's not the slightest chance of it. I'm no threat to anybody in the world."

"You're a very famous man. You won't admit it. You've refused every government commission offered you. You say you've no time for that. You never want your picture in the papers. You never want your name to be used in any way—yet the man in the street, everyone knows about you."

G.M. shook his head again. "No—"

"I know what I'm talking about. Greg, do you agree with me?"

"Yes, I do in a way. G.M. is a great man. No matter how hard he tries to keep out of the public eye, he's there, right in the middle of important affairs. But I don't see what an enemy could hope to gain."

"Postponement!" Dora snapped. "Cancellation—or simply G.M.'s failure to attend. I know more of the infinitely entangling interests of business economics than you do, Greg."

"I'm sure you do," Greg said calmly.

"And there's another thing none of you can understand. A great man *is* a target. All you have to do is think back to recent history."

"There are always crack-brains," Greg said.

"And crack-brains can use guns," Dora said. "I'll get at the switchboard, G.M." Her heels clicked on the parquet floor and then were silenced by the thick rug.

G.M. said, "Now then, Susan, I believe we ought to tell Lattrice that someone might have been in the pines, following you."

Susan said firmly, "G.M., please don't. I'm sure that I just—scared myself."

G.M. shook his head. "You're not the hysterical type."

"I was this time," she said with bitter truth. "Greg didn't see anybody. Wilfred didn't see anybody."

"He might have," G.M. said calmly, "if there was a Clanser following you; you never know with a Clanser. They are loyal to one another. I'll say that for them. But they do unexpected things. Poor Rose. She was loyal to her family. They were loyal to her in a way. They gave her a sense of security that I didn't give her. I neglected her, but I didn't realize that I did. I studied hard when I was young. I tried to learn everything about money and markets that I could learn. I worked over industrial reports as I had worked over calculus in my school days but much harder. I was using Rose's money to back up what I could learn. Well, so I did. I was the boy wonder," he said dryly. "I had made a fortune—starting with Rose's money—when I was very young. Oddly"—he looked down at his sensitive, folded hands—"sometimes I still think of myself as the boy wonder. I'm getting into my fifties now. I feel like a hundred. And probably if I should reach an old age I'd still feel myself the boy wonder. It's a good thing to be lucky when you're young, but in another way it's a handicap. You have so much so early. You feel a compulsion to keep on going, becoming greater and greater in your field, whatever it is . . . I'm sorry. I'm giving you both quite a lecture."

Greg said, "I think I'll just check the Clansers. It's too late for Lattrice and the police to find any—any intruder in the woods now."

But as he turned toward the living room Dora came running to the door. "G.M., a call came through just as I got down to the switchboard. You'll have to change your plans again. It was put very delicately, very tactfully. It was put on the basis of your wife's having died so recently, but the fact is—"

G.M. said, "The fact is my presence is no longer desired."

Dora nodded.

"Yes. I expected that, really. I had reported it, as you know, as much as I knew of it, at once. But there's been time for second thoughts—also time for a rather indefinite notice to get in the newspapers. I can quite understand it. I expected it before this."

Greg cried, "They can't do that to you!"

"Oh, yes. I'm not welcome in an inner counsel when I am suspected of murder," G.M. said equably.

"But you didn't kill her!" Greg said angrily.

"I can't prove that. Not as things stand now. Why, I haven't even an alibi. In a big hotel nobody is likely to remember or notice when some accustomed figure comes or goes. No"—he thought for a moment—"I didn't stop at the desk for anything. A number of people were in the elevator when I arrived there. Nobody particularly noticed me."

"But, G.M."—Dora leaned her lovely hands on the desk, her head was bent as if she could force his attention by looking at him—"but, G.M., when I first tried to reach you by phone you were not in the office. You were not in your hotel!"

G.M. waited a moment. "I stopped in at the bar for perhaps an hour or so."

"You didn't tell the police that," Dora cried almost accusingly.

"Why should I?"

Greg came across to stand at the writing table, too. "Then you suspected even then that Rose had been killed in an attempt to frame you, discredit you. Get you accused of murder."

G.M. looked suddenly very tired yet very honest. "My dear young man, in my life I have learned to suspect everybody of everything, almost all the time. You see, you've got to know or be able to guess what the other fellow is up to. Usually it's a plan to cut your throat. Always it's a plan to advance the other fellow. Suspicion is part of my life. I try to conceal it. Naturally I had to report her death and the possibility that it was not accident, merely in honesty. I did think it was better to keep what we knew of her death out of the news, at least for the present. It was a compromise. My clear duty lay both ways. I had to think of my responsibility.. My instinct was to get the truth out at once, give the police all possible aid. In a way they've been tied by the lack of publicity. Yes, Ligon?"

Ligon Clanser stood in the doorway. "I'm sorry. Am I interrupting something? I was only waiting for Dora and young—that is, Mr. Prowde to come back into the house. I understand that he and I are to stay at the inn. I thought perhaps Dora would phone for a taxi for us. In the meantime I went to sleep."

"Where?" Dora asked sharply

"Why, in a vacant room upstairs. That is, there are no suitcases or anything like that around. It's got a safe set into the wall."

There was a complete silence for a moment. Then G.M. said, "Of course. Phone for a taxi, will you, Dora?"

Greg said to Ligon, "You haven't been outside the house tonight at all?"

Ligon eyed him and shrugged. "No."

"Dora, where did you and Mr. Prowde stroll?" G.M. asked.

"Around toward the other side of the house. You see"—Dora did not hesitate as she dropped the bomb—"we were planning our marriage, dates and all. Weren't we, Bert?"

A rather reluctant voice came from the living room. "Yes, yes, certainly."

"Why, Dora!" There was actually a gleam of amusement in G.M.'s eyes. "This *is* a surprise. I thought you were going to marry me."

Dora's lovely face stiffened. Susan had a notion that the world had subtly altered somehow; only a short time before that she had heard Dora urging marriage with G.M. Now practically in an instant she had turned around and become engaged to marry Bert Prowde.

G.M. rose and put out his hand. "My dear Dora, I wish you every happiness."

Dora looked rather as if she might bite the hand with those firm teeth; instead, she took it with grace and poise.

Ligon, however, said abruptly, "You're up to some game, Dora."

Ten

Dora did not reply, for there was a rapid surge of motion through the living room and Milly appeared in the doorway; she was wearing what resembled a salmon silk tent; her hair was wildly disheveled, her face blotchy and her hand gripped the door casing as if she might fall. "G.M.," she gasped, "I've just remembered something. I heard the phone ring."

Snell, still in slacks, turtleneck shirt and leather jacket, came up behind her. "Honestly, Milly, once we get you to bed I wish you'd stay there. I heard you on the stairs. It's no easy job to get you back again."

"Sit down, Milly," G.M. said. "What phone are you talking about?"

"Your own phone. In your apartment. It rang just as I was leaving. Just as I was going down to meet Greg and—her." She tossed her head toward Susan.

"Who was it?"

"I don't know," Rose answered. "We were out of servants just then, as you know. Or would have known if you had come home more often."

Snell took her by the arm and propelled her into a chair. He then gave the table on which the bottles and ice bucket stood a glance, went over to it and eyed the completely empty bottles wistfully.

G.M. said, "Who telephoned Rose?"

"I tell you, I don't know. She just answered and I took it that it was someone she knew and then the elevator came, so I shut the door. But somebody did phone her."

Susan only happened to be watching Snell; she saw him glance over his shoulder at Milly and he looked frightened.

He *was* frightened, she thought; she was sure of it. Yet why? He turned back quickly to the table.

"Milly," G.M. said patiently, "what did Rose say at the phone?"

"She said hello."

"Was that all?"

"It was all I heard."

"What made you think it was someone Rose knew?"

Milly rubbed her glassy eyes. "Something about the way she spoke, you can always tell. I mean it wasn't a stranger."

"You're sure of that?"

"I—why, yes. I guess so. Now that I think about it, I believe she said something like, 'Oh, it's you.' "

"Aren't you sure of that?"

Milly blinked, then nodded violently. "Oh, I'm sure. I guess."

G.M. waited a moment. Then he said, "I see. You were right to tell me. Snell, will you get Milly back to bed again?"

"No! You won't touch me!" Milly clasped the arms of her chair defiantly. "You think because Rose is dead you'll all fasten yourselves on me and get her money. But I won't let you. It's my money now—or will be."

"Milly," G.M. began peaceably but Milly turned on him.

"And you are going to kick out every Clanser as soon as you can. I knew it the minute I knew Rose was dead. You never wanted to have anything to do with us. You gave Snell over there and Col and Wilfred jobs only to please Rose. You felt indebted to her and you ought to feel that way."

G.M. nodded at Snell, who grasped Milly hard above the elbow. She gave a shrill yip and the cat, who had apparently wandered into the room, leaped up on the table where the empty bottles and ice bucket stood. For a wild instant it struck Susan that even the cat must have caught the Clanser affection for strong drink. She was mistaken, however. Snell had removed the lid of the ice bucket and the cat stretched down his aristocratic neck and lapped thirstily. She felt justly rebuked, for she had forgotten to make sure of a supply of fresh water for what Milly called the menagerie.

There was a bit of a struggle but Snell firmly and muscularly got Milly up the two steps into the living room. Ligon wiped his forehead with a snowy handkerchief, and said, "Dora, will you please phone for the taxi?"

"Gladly," Dora said, looking again as if she'd like to bite somebody. She took up the telephone on the writing table. It was like her, Susan thought in an absent way, to know the Medbury Hills telephone number for a taxi. "They'll be here right away. You'd better tell Wilfred to open the gate. Or walk down to the gate yourself. Do you good."

Bert Prowde appeared in the doorway, gave a rather scared glance around and said, "A good idea. Good night."

Ligon didn't even say good night. He marched out without looking back. As if he didn't know what else to do, Bert followed him.

G.M. smiled. "You might have said good night to your fiancé, Dora."

"It doesn't matter," Dora said coolly. "Poor darling! Thrust into such a shocking affair. Not his fault. Nor mine, if I may say so. Good night, G.M."

She walked gracefully and quickly out of the room. G.M. waited a moment and then said in a low voice, "Greg, do you think Milly could have been right?"

"When she said somebody phoned Rose just as Milly was leaving? Yes, I think so."

"She ought to have mentioned it sooner."

"Milly?" Greg said.

"Yes, well, she's like that. But she's not really stupid. She's sharp enough about her own interests when she's not drinking. I believe she really didn't think of that phone call before now."

"Maybe."

"It *could* be that the phone call sent Rose to the heliport and out here."

Greg nodded. "And the man Susan saw might have been waiting for her here. But I do feel that Snell is lying about something."

Susan said, "He's afraid."

There was a moment's surprised silence. Then G.M. said, "Why do you think that?"

"Something in his face. It was when Milly talked about that phone call."

Greg saw the cat, absently took him off the table and replaced the lid to the ice bucket. G.M. as absently fiddled with a paper cutter. The cat—not absently at all, but with single-minded purpose—sprang to the writing table, sat down and washed his black face as hard as if he could wash off the black.

"Think it was Snell himself who phoned Rose, Greg?" G.M. said at last.

Greg shook his head. "It could have been anybody. I wish Milly had heard more." Greg came across to the table and said earnestly, "G.M., I'm sorry about that conference."

"You think it's a blow to my prestige? I'll survive." G.M.

gave the cat's long black tail a light tweak, which surprisingly evoked a hoarse purr from the cat. "I must change the plans for the services for Rose."

"Yes," said Greg. "I'll see to things for you. Let me know what you want."

"Thank you, Greg. It wasn't very respectful to Rose to try to put off the services. I didn't like doing it. Yet there again I was torn between two pressing duties. I make my mistakes, don't think I don't. I've made them in the past and I'll make them again. One mistake, perhaps, was in letting you talk me out of calling the police tonight, Susan, as soon as you came in. If you heard an outsider and the gate was open, it would have been easy enough for him to enter the grounds. It would be easy enough to leave. The switch that controls the gate is in the little place Wilfred and Col use. Anybody could have turned off the current any time. But it hasn't happened since Wilfred closed the gate. If it was a Clanser—"

Susan said firmly again, "I don't think it was anybody. Please believe me."

G.M. looked at Greg, who looked at nothing.

She caught a brief blue glance from the cat which seemed to reproach her. She said, "I'll get water for the cat and dogs," and went to the kitchen. Here Wilfred was cleaning up, apparently in deep thought. She got bowls from the cupboard, filled one, set it in the vestibule and went upstairs with another. G.M. and Greg were still in the library; she could hear the murmur of their voices.

No matter what G.M. said, his personal prestige would suffer until it was definitely proved that he had not murdered his wife—and thus that someone else had and who that was. The dogs bounced companionably after her. There was a tiny bathroom adjoining her room, so Spartan again in its arrangements and space that it proclaimed the fact that visitors were not expected to make a long stay in the secret house. She filled the bowl she carried with water and put it on the floor and was again rebuked when both dogs shoved their newly clipped noses into the bowl and lapped furiously. Of course, she thought ruefully, drawing on her experience with dogs, that continued lapping would require getting them out at an early hour in the morning. She didn't really want to go out of the house alone, even in the morning light.

The door had no key but there was a bolt. Half ashamed of her own uneasiness she slid the bolt.

She had got into bed and the dogs had had their fill of

water and taken up their places at the foot of the bed when someone knocked at the door. She had not yet turned off the bedside lamp. She sat up. "Who is it?"

"Greg. I want to talk to you."

"All right. In a minute." She slid out of bed and into a dressing gown. Greg came in quietly and with a swift and guarded look over his shoulder he closed the door behind him. "All right now, Susan. I've talked it over with G.M. You're to leave this place tomorrow. We'll find a place in town where you can hide."

"Leave here?" Susan said blankly.

"Of course. Somebody is afraid of you."

"Me?"

"Don't be a dolt," Greg said angrily. "You saw the running man. I think you were right tonight. I think there *was* somebody in the woods, waiting for a chance to—to— Don't look like that."

"You can't mean to murder me! Because I might identify—"

"Certainly I mean that. But I don't intend to let it happen."

"You are trying to frighten me."

"I am indeed. I want you to get out of this house, go to the city, go anywhere, but hide."

She sat down on the bed. Beau wriggled into an easier position. Belle came over and put her head on Susan's arm.

"No," Susan said, "no, I can't do that."

"For heavens' sake, why not?"

"Where could I hide?"

He made an impatient gesture. "A hundred places. A million places. But you've got to get away from here. You must believe me. I am sure that you made no mistake tonight. I am sure—I've told you this before—that if whoever killed Rose thinks you can identify him—the running man—then your life is in danger. Can't you see that?"

"But I'm not sure I can identify him. And I'm not sure the running man is the murderer."

"We know you saw somebody."

"It wasn't G.M."

"So you said. But—this thing tonight. You didn't imagine that. You've got to leave."

She smoothed Belle's pretty head and tugged gently at her silken ears. "No."

"Why not?"

"Where could I hide? No, don't say again there are a million places. I suppose I'd go to my apartment. Anybody could find me there. If anybody wanted to—to kill me then there are more opportunities in the city than here. Crossing a street, going down for the mail, going to the corner drugstore anywhere. I can't hole up in my apartment and refuse to answer the door bell or the phone or—"

"You can. But if you won't do that—" He frowned at the floor a moment. "You could go to a hotel. And let nobody know where you are."

"If somebody is determined to—to kill me, he'll find a way."

"That's not like you, Susan. There is some other reason why you don't want to leave. Is it G.M.?"

She looked at him directly. "Greg, who do you think killed Rose?"

"I don't believe it was G.M. But there are motives for some other people here."

"Milly?"

"Milly had time, I think. She's enormous, but she can move quickly when she wants to. She inherits from Rose. But Milly could not possibly have been the running man. What was he doing here? Why was he running for the airfield? Of course Ligon Clanser might be thought to have a motive."

"Ligon?"

"Revenge. Dora left him. You know the gossip."

"I think it may be true."

His eyes narrowed. "Why do you think that?"

"Because I heard G.M. and Dora talking."

"What did they say?"

She pulled up Belle's ears and smoothed them to Belle's great satisfaction, for she looked up at Susan with bright, pleased eyes. "Dora said that Thursday she had told G.M. he had to choose between her and Rose. She said that now Rose was dead there was no obstacle. She said they could be married."

"What did G.M. say?"

"He told her to remember what he had said to her on Thursday night."

"What was that? Did you hear?"

"He said that he had told her he had no intention of marrying her. Something like that."

"Dear me! Dora didn't like that."

"She said that she knew he hadn't meant it. And that Rose

had been shot the next day. He said that that was a tragic coincidence. She said to call it coincidence, but that he had chosen Dora. He said he hadn't killed Rose for her or any other reason. Oh, yes, and in the beginning Dora said that G.M. knew she'd never tell."

"You heard a great deal," Greg said dryly.

"They were talking in the library. They didn't hear me cross the living room. I couldn't possibly have failed to listen for a moment or two."

"I'd have listened to the whole thing if I'd been there. Well, it could look bad for G.M. Dora still doesn't take his refusal seriously."

"But she said right away that she was going to marry Bert Prowde."

"I doubt if she means it. She's got her head set on marrying G.M. Always had, I think. And that's why Ligon might have a motive. Suppose she left him because of G.M. Suppose Ligon had been just waiting to damage G.M. one way or another. This way, framing him as neatly as he could, getting him suspected of killing his wife and thus finishing G.M.'s career as a respected authority—"

"Greg, we keep assuming that G.M. was the target. Suppose it *was* Rose."

"We did think of that. Milly had time and the chance to do it and Milly profits. The Clansers will not profit so much individually. And according to Milly's outburst tonight, they'll not be permitted to bleed her. But nobody can count on a Clanser, really."

"Who else? There must be somebody."

"The running man. Now then, why did you evade me when I asked you if it is because of G.M. that you don't want to leave this house?"

She waited a moment, thinking hard, and finally replied, "I don't know."

"Don't know!" Greg had been sitting in the one chair the room provided. He rose and crossed to her quickly, with a suggestion of such anger that she expected him to shake her. "Listen, Susan. Are you in love with him? Is everybody in love with him? I don't think it's his money you want. It's got to be G.M."

"Don't talk to me like that, Greg. But I—no, I don't want to leave him now. He's in trouble. He's in for a bad time. It's like desertion for either of us to leave him."

Then he did put his hands hard on her shoulders and give

her a hard and exasperated shake. "But he's not in danger of his life! You are. You've got to leave this place if I have to drag you out by your pretty hair."

"You wouldn't leave him!"

"That's different. I owe him loyalty and—"

"So do I."

"But you're determined to stay here because you think you're in love with him. Isn't that the truth?"

"Greg, let me go. You're hurting me!"

Someone tapped lightly on the door and opened it. G.M. came in.

His extremely alert and intelligent eyes took in their posture in one glance. He smiled the little, rather enigmatic smile which often accompanied some very shrewd guess on his part. He closed the door, sat down on the bed beside Susan and said softly, "You were shouting, both of you. I couldn't hear what you said, but naturally I knew you were quarreling. Not nice of you, Greg." He put his arm around Susan.

She leaned back against it thankfully. With G.M. she felt safe and protected. Greg's face had flushed.

"I talked to you about it. I want Susan to leave."

"And she won't go?" G.M. said softly.

"She's going," Greg said stubbornly.

"I think you'll have to let Susan decide things for herself. What I was thinking about before I heard such remarkably loud voices coming from this room"—his eyes actually twinkled—"was something I want you to do for me."

"Dora would do anything you want done, better than I can." Greg was still angry and flushed.

G.M. drew Susan a little closer to his lean, trim body. He claimed to be getting into his fifties; he looked scarcely over thirty. He seemed scarcely over thirty, yet he knew more than a man of thirty can possible know.

"I can't send Dora. You heard her say that she's about to marry this young Prowde."

"I don't think she really means it," Greg said.

"We must see that she does mean it. This is the chore I want you and Susan to do for me tomorrow. No, that's Sunday. Monday then. But take the car tomorrow and go to the city—I'll fix it with Lattrice. On Monday select the handsomest engagement ring you can find for Dora. You see," G.M. said quietly, "young Prowde hasn't any money to speak of. Dora deserves a handsome ring. All women want that."

Eleven

Greg looked stunned and disbelieving. He sank down into the chair again. G.M. gave a little chuckle. "Any reason why I shouldn't give her that?"

Probably there was every reason why he should, but as an engagement ring in view of Dora's marriage to himself. Susan could almost see the words form on Greg's lips and the effort he made to stop them. Finally, looking as if he were about to burst into anger again, he said sharply, "Wouldn't money make a handsome wedding present? If Bort Prowde is so short of money—"

"No, no, Dora wouldn't want that."

Dora wants to marry you; again Susan could almost see the words in Greg's mind. Again he managed to restrain them. He said instead, "But would Dora accept an engagement ring from you? Would Prowde accept it?"

"Oh, I think so," G.M. said mildly. "Now there are some things I want you to do for me on Sunday, Greg. I'll explain." G.M. rose but still kept a hand on Susan's shoulder. "Let's let this child get some rest."

Greg's face clouded again. "But, G.M., she's got to be made to stay in the city. Or somewhere safe."

"How about it, Susan?" G.M. asked.

"No! I'd be in more danger in the city than here."

"But you can keep your whereabouts a secret. You needn't tell even me or Greg. Indeed, if you are in any danger from anybody, you must not tell anyone where you are. I believe you are right, Greg. When you and Susan go to the city tomorrow, take Susan to her apartment so she can gather up a few clothes and then—then let her go. She's got sense enough to find a hiding place and stick to it until we can get this thing cleared up. How about that, Susan? You'll be doing the right thing for yourself and for me, too. God knows I don't want you to be frightened or hurt. So pick your own hiding place and stay there."

"I won't," Susan said.

Greg interjected harshly, "You're a wily scoundrel, G.M.!"

"Why, Greg!" G.M. smiled.

"You know perfectly well that that was the best way to get her to stay here. Tell her to go. Tell her to leave you. Tell her you don't want her to be hurt."

"But I don't want her to be hurt," G.M. said mildly.

Susan put her head down against Belle's silky curls. She knew that she was going to cry from sheer nervous exasperation. "Will you both just get out of here and leave me alone!" she snapped. Her voice, however, wavered so betrayingly that apparently it affected both men. One of them said "Good night, Susan." That was G.M. Greg said nothing. But they both left rather hurriedly and when she heard the door close she put Belle off her lap and went to bolt the door.

There is nothing, she thought, that frightens a man as much as a weeping woman. And she was going to cry. She was going to get her head down on the pillow and cry as hard as she wanted to.

Nerves, she thought: too frightening, too revealing a night too much conflict; decidedly too many Clansers. She was going to cry her heart out.

She was very hungry, but she didn't intend to creep down to the kitchen and find food. By the time she settled herself she was too hungry and tired even to cry. Sleep fell upon her like a cloud.

Greg woke her the next morning. He tapped lightly at the door again, and it was a moment or two before she remembered the errands with which G.M. had entrusted them. She got into her dressing gown, went to the door and opened it Greg had coffee for her. "We'd better get off," he said. "All the Clansers are asleep. I'll take the dogs out." The dogs bounced out happily.

"Thank you."

She took the coffee. He had thoughtfully provided a plate of toast. Fifteen minutes later she went downstairs, quietly as she had no wish to encounter a blowzy and hung-over Clanser. Greg was waiting in the vestibule. "G.M. isn't down yet You didn't bring your suitcase."

"No."

The big car was waiting; the dogs were back in the vestibule and wished to go with them, but Greg closed the door firmly.

Col was at the gate. "I don't know when we'll be back," Greg told him. "G.M. will know."

Col peered at them curiously as he had Friday evening when they arrived.

"We'll have lunch in town." Greg started up the car again, leaving Col watching after them. "There are things G.M. wants me to do. He told me last night after you threw us out."

"I didn't throw you out."

"Sounded like it to me. However, he wants me to see to private services for Rose in the city. That can be arranged on Sunday. Then you'll spend the night in my apartment."

"Oh, no."

"You said yourself you wouldn't feel safe in your apartment. I assure you," said Greg with a touch of sarcasm, "you'll be quite safe in mine." He looked in the rear-view mirror; he looked several times. Finally he said, "Good old Lattrice. He's letting us go without police on our trail. G.M. said he would talk to him. There's another thing G.M. wants me to do. He gave me a key and a note to the superintendent in the event that I need it. He wants me to take a look through his apartment."

"Why?"

"For anything that might help, I suppose. Anything Rose might have left. Specifically, she just might have left some note relating to that phone call Milly heard as she left the apartment. He also wants me to talk to the elevator man and the doorman and try to find out whether anyone was with Rose when she left Friday afternoon. Lattrice told G.M. that he had talked to them yesterday, but they didn't talk much."

So that, Susan thought parenthetically, accounted for the evasiveness of Lattrice's manner the previous night, and for the swift look of comprehension in G.M.'s shrewd eyes, when Lattrice said he was unable to discover why Rose had come to the secret house.

"Didn't like the idea of being questioned by police perhaps," Greg went on. "Didn't know just how G.M. would take anything they happened to say. They know me, however. I've been at the apartment often enough for them to know that I'm in G.M.'s employ. He thinks they just might give me some hint that they didn't give the police. I don't know. I can try."

It was a strange and subtly ominous day. The skies were gray and heavy. The Manhattan streets were all but deserted. Susan sat in the car on Madison Avenue and waited while

Greg discharged the first of his chores. He came out of the building, gave himself a kind of shake as if he had found his task a heavy one, and then took Susan to lunch at the Plaza where they sat near a window and watched the gold and brown park foliage and the little groups of strolling people and had, as a matter of fact, an extremely good luncheon. "Better than Milly cooks," Greg said. "But we can't blame her really. We chose the groceries."

Susan's cocktail had restored her spirts a little; she was by then ravenously hungry and the good food restored her too. But, too soon, they drove up Madison and then across to Fifth Avenue and the big apartment that had been Rose's home.

"We'll take a look through the apartment first," Greg said as he parked the car at the nearest corner.

No one stopped them. No superintendent appeared. The doorman knew Greg, for he nodded and called him "Mr. Cameron." The elevator man was a little more talkative but not much. He had read the papers. He said it was dreadful about Mrs. Manders, wasn't it? He supposed Mr. Cameron had come on some business for Mr. Manders. Greg said yes, but the man still stood at the door of the cage and watched until Greg drew out the key to the apartment and opened the door.

The first thing that struck Susan was the mustiness of the apartment, with again the underlying smell of cat and the overlying smell of heavily perfumed room deodorizers.

Greg sniffed, made a face and went to one of the big windows. "We'll have to get some fresh air. Now then, where do we begin?" He looked around helplessly at the overdecorated living room, the flounces, the cushions, the scattered stacks of magazines, the several used glasses on the tables. Without a word he gathered up the glasses, made another face at the smell from them and took them out through a dining room; in a few seconds Susan heard him turn on water and vigorously rinse glasses.

When he came back he looked very sober again. "Poor old Rose. She did drink. I can't blame G.M. for avoiding his home as much as he could. There was always Rose, wandering around in some kind of messy negligee, drinking. Milly wandering around with her—also drinking. Sometimes Snell. Sometimes *any* Clanser, I suppose. They were a close family, all of them battening on Rose—and thus on G.M. I should have said they *are* a close family."

"Milly didn't sound very close to any of them last night."

"Milly was drunk. She'll change her mind. Now then, where's the phone Milly must have heard? I'd say it's the extension here. There's an extension in Rose's room, I think. I know there's one in the kitchen. I saw it just now. And there's one in what was called G.M.'s library. But the one Rose answered must have been near enough the door for Milly to hear. So let's look around the table first."

It stood near enough the door to allow for Milly's hearing Rose answer its ring and say, "Hello . . . Oh, it's you." It was a low table with a pink marble top and ornately curved legs; again Susan felt sure that no decorator would have permitted its presence in what was orginally designed to be a beautiful room. The telephone was pink and stood on the table amid scraps of memo pads, clippings from newspapers and full ashtrays. One of the empty glasses had stood there, too. There were several pencils, pink, with "Rose Manders" printed in gold on them. All of them were either broken or looked as if they had been chewed. The table alone could have given evidence as to the state of the entire apartment and was as different from G.M.'s neat and elegant office, the beautiful orderliness of the secret house, as night from day.

Greg looked at the mess of loose papers, pulled up a tiny chair with gilded frail legs which apparently was intended to harmonize with the dreadful table, and began to go through the papers carefully, one at a time.

"I don't see anything here," he said finally. "Advertisements about everything from hairdressers to auctions. Lists of food—cat food, dog food. Gin. Gin. Gin. You wouldn't think a Clanser would need to be reminded about ordering gin. G.M. gave Lattrice the key to the place yesterday and Lattrice must have gone through everything here. If there was anything that interested him he'd have taken it away. But G.M. told me that there might be something which I'd know might have some sort of significance and Lattrice wouldn't know. There isn't. Now then, G.M. told me to take a look in Rose's bedroom, especially around her phone there. He thought she just might have made a note of—oh, a phone number, anything. Do you mind very much helping me?"

She did mind. Indeed, there was a still kind of horror in the apartment. But she did go with him, and she minded it even more when she saw Rose's bedroom. There was an enormous dressing table, ruffled with pink silk. The bed had soiled-looking silk sheets and the bed had not been made. A lacy negligee lay on the floor along with a wrinkled-up girdle.

An empty gin bottle stood on the floor. Greg went to the door of the adjoining bathroom, looked inside and said, "It can't be!"

Susan looked over his shoulder. It couldn't be but it *was* unbelievably splashed and dirty: towels lay on the floor; a pair of stockings dangled from the towel rail, obviously unwashed. A ribbon of toothpaste had emerged from its uncapped tube. A hairbrush lay on the floor, still with Rose's dyed blond hair in it. Susan began to feel slightly sick. The flowery odor of the room was stifling. A lipstick without its cap lay on the edge of the pink wash basin. Both bathroom and bedroom were altogether too intimate and ugly a revelation of Rose's character. Only too clearly Susan remembered Rose as she lay on the floor. Rose had indeed been a pathetic figure. Perhaps she had been drunk when she left the apartment; it seemed a reasonable view.

"Let's get out of here. How G.M. could stand it—well, you go and sit in the living room. I'll take a quick look through the rest of the place."

Susan was only too thankful to leave that task to Greg. She sat in one of the preposterously bogus French armchairs near the door and thought of Rose. Once pretty, slim Rose, "my wild rose," G.M. had said he called her. She wondered how and when Rose had so deteriorated; was it due to an innate lack of character? Had it occurred during her long and constant drinking? Was it in any way due to the influence of the Clansers, particularly Milly?

Was it, as G.M. had seemed to reproach himself, at least partially due to what Rose might have considered neglect of her?

Whatever it was, it was tragic and sad.

Greg returned. "Gosh! If you didn't like Rose's room you ought to see Milly's. What a home G.M. had here! There's no use looking further. I'll get hold of the elevator man and the doorman."

It was not as simple as it seemed; first he had to make sure he had the elevator man who had been on duty Friday afternoon, and when he did, the man was not particularly communicative.

Yes, he had been on duty Friday afternoon. Yes, he had seen Mrs. Manders leave; she had a fur wrap of some kind over her arm. No, she hadn't told him where she was going, naturally. She rarely spoke to any of the staff. Yes, she was alone.

"Had anyone called on her that afternoon?" Greg asked.

The man hesitated, fidgeted in his neat uniform and said, "There was a man—that is, I brought him up here."

"A man?" Susan was sure that Greg was trying not to scare off the elevator man by showing too much interest. "Calling on Mrs. Manders?"

"He rang. I waited a moment and she opened the door. But then my bell rang. I work two elevators, you see. I brought him down a few minutes later. I brought Mrs. Manders down about twenty minutes later. She was alone."

"What about this man who called on her? Can you describe him?"

The elevator man passed a worried hand over his lips. "I don't know. If Mr. Manders sent you—I mean he wouldn't have wanted any of us to talk to the police. There were police here yesterday, two of them. In plain clothes, but police. So I thought Mr. Manders wouldn't like me to tell about this man. Besides, I had never seen him before."

"But you'd know him if you saw him again."

"I'm not sure. It was a busy time of day. I don't know that I paid much attention to him."

"You know that Mr. Manders sent me. I'm on his office staff. He asked me to talk to you. Is there anything at all that you remember about this man?"

Again the elevator man nervously rubbed his mouth, eyeing Greg in a troubled way. "Mr. Cameron," he blurted suddenly, "the paper said accident. I don't know why there'd be so much inquiry if it was only accident."

"Oh, that's the police way," Greg said as calmly, Susan was sure, as he could. "You know! They have to do something to earn their salaries."

The elevator man's face cleared slightly. "I guess that's right. Now this man—as I say, I didn't pay much attention to him. He was just a man, sort of medium height as I remember it, nothing remarkable about him. Plain dark suit, hat. Come to think of it, he kept looking in the mirror of my cage so his back was turned toward me. I didn't take a very good look at his face. I had to watch my floors and signals. No, that's all I remember about him."

"But Mrs. Manders opened the door for him?"

"Oh, yes."

"Did she say anything? 'How do you do,' or call him by name, or anything?"

"N-no. She just opened the door. She had on a kind of

green dress. Her hair—well, it looked kind of tousled. But then she was never neat like our other ladies. Chic," said the elevator man, pronouncing it to rhyme with *click*. "Not that she didn't buy plenty of clothes and things. So the package room always said."

Greg turned away and walked to a window where he stood, hands in his pockets, looking out at the gray sky. The elevator man gave a nervous look in the direction of the hall. Greg turned at last and said, very seriously, "I have to ask you a delicate question. I am acting as Mr. Manders asked me to do. Was Mrs. Manders a little drunk when she opened the door? Or when she left the apartment house?"

A wary look came into the man's eyes. He shook his head but not very decisively. "Not really drunk."

"Just a little—tiddly?"

"I—now you'll have to excuse me to Mr. Manders. Everybody in the place likes him."

"So you felt she had been drinking."

"She was always drinking," said the man and then clapped his hand over his mouth. "That's a terrible thing to say. We always protect our ladies here and our gentlemen. I didn't mean—"

"That's all right. Is there anything at all you can tell me about her departure, about—oh, anything?"

"No, no! Excuse me. I'm sure that's my bell—excuse me." He hustled out of the door. The elevator began its dignified, barely rumbling descent.

"Ran like a rabbit," Greg said. "I can't say that I blame him. Tomorrow the papers are very likely to say it's murder. He'll wish he hadn't said a word, poor duck. Now for the doorman. Let's see him downstairs. I can't stand this stinking place another minute."

"Better close the window you opened. It might rain."

"Do the place good," Greg said crossly, but he closed the window.

Susan rose from the bogus armchair near the door and started ahead. Greg said, "Good heavens! You ought to see your back!"

"My back!"

She was wearing her brown tweed suit; she had rather treated herself to more than she could afford in buying the suit, but it was well tailored and a good design. She twisted around. "What's the matter with my back?"

Greg gave a half laugh, half groan. "Cat hairs. All over you. Wait, I'll see if I can find a brush in this hell hole."

He found a brush in G.M.'s room. "Only place in the house with a semblance of order," he grumbled, returning. "Turn around."

He brushed at her skirt and jacket. "Damn things stick like glue. There, that's better. Come on." He flung down the brush, went out into the hall with her and rang for the elevator.

The doorman was not even as helpful as the elevator man but he was worried. "Is there anything—well, *wrong* about Mrs. Manders' accident?" he asked with a perceptible pause before the word "accident." "You see, some men—some policemen were here yesterday just when I came on duty. They qustioned me too, asked if I had seen anybody going to Mrs. Manders' apartment, asked if I had seen her leave. I had. She was walking toward that corner, but that's all I know. I didn't see any stranger, but it's a busy time of day. Around four or a little earlier. Is there anything really wrong?"

"Oh, the inquiry is only police routine," Greg said. "You think Mrs. Manders was meeting anyone?"

"How could I tell? I just remember that she was walking and she went around that corner. Of course, nobody can park in front of the place unless he's coming from the north. Anybody coming from downtown has to come up Madison and park on a cross street, and then walk around to our apartment house. So if—I can't say she did, but if she was going to meet someone in a car, she'd have walked to a cross street from Madison where a car could have been parked."

"I know," Greg said. "That's where I'm parked now. Is there nothing else you remember about Mrs. Manders' leaving?"

"That's all. I am sorry about the—accident. You tell Mr. Manders for me, will you? All of us here like Mr. Manders."

But if the doorman had seen the mysterious visitor to the Manders' apartment Greg was obviously convinced that he could never have recognized or identified him.

They walked slowly back around the corner to the Manders' car. Once in it, Greg drove without speaking to a parking garage in the seventies where he left the car and hailed a taxi, which took a sedate way through the sparse Sunday traffic. When they reached the number on Sixty-third Street which Greg had given to the taxi driver, Greg got out, paid and took Susan by the wrist.

"Tell him to keep his flag up—" Susan began.

"You're coming with me. I promised G.M. not to let you out of my sight."

"But I—why, I can't stay all night!"

Greg's face changed, became young and lively; he laughed so hard that the taxi driver turned around to eye him.

"What's the joke, friend?" said the cabdriver.

"This girl. In this day and age. Come on, Susan, or I'll pull you out by main strength and give everybody in the neighborhood something to see. And probably report to the police. Do you want the police to nab me for mugging or assault or anything? I'll do it, I promise you. Come on."

The taxi driver was grinning. "Better go, Miss. I think he means it."

With a cold unease Susan realized that he did mean it. And if he were right in his conjecture, then certainly she'd be safer with Greg than alone in her own apartment. She crawled out of the taxi with sudden docility. Once in the self-service elevator, Greg said dryly, "Don't worry. You can sleep in my bed and I'll take the living-room sofa. It's miserably uncomfortable, as a matter of fact. An aunt sent it to me when I first rented the apartment and I haven't had the heart to get rid of it. So call sleeping on it a measure of my devotion."

Susan was only grateful. "I'm not a fool."

"Sometimes you act like one," Greg said cheerfully. "Here we are."

He led her into a smallish but comfortable living room; it was obviously a man's room, easy chairs, books, the sofa which did indeed look adamant, a plain rug, ashtrays.

"That door leads to a bedroom. The other one to the bath." Greg waved his hand. "What they call a kitchen is over there. I want a drink and I'm going to give you one."

He paused for a moment, in a puzzled way. "Do you think it can be that some of the Clanser affection for drink is rubbing off on me? You can't imagine the number of times yesterday I had to stop myself from getting absolutely pie-eyed."

Susan sat down. "Me, too."

He went into the kitchen. There were sounds of ice and the clatter of glasses. He called thoughtfully now, "The man who called on Rose Friday afternoon could have been the running man. Certainly he was somebody she knew and probably was expecting after that phone call."

Twelve

He came back and thrust a glass into Susan's hand. "I wish I knew just what he must have said to Rose. I wish the elevator man had heard even a few words. Whatever he said, it looks as if he induced Rose to go to the house and came to take her there. Well, here's to—no, not crime—to us."

She settled back in her chair. "Greg, did that apartment seem to you—horrible?"

"You should have seen the kitchen. It would have put you off your food for a month. Rose was not a housekeeper."

"It gave me the creeps."

"It gave me the creeps, too. Always did. I don't see how G.M. stood it even as little as he did."

"It would have been so easy for Rose to be the kind of wife G.M. needs."

Greg considered it, moved an ashtray, and shook his head. "Nope. She had no will power. Not much in the way of brains either. She just drifted any easy way."

"The apartment must have been beautiful once."

"I didn't see it when he first bought it. Only after Rose had had her way with it, Rose and Milly."

"Do you suppose we'd get anywhere if we could get pictures of everybody close to Rose—or to G.M.—and show them to the doorman and the elevator man?"

"If Rose was killed because she was Rose, I mean, if she was the target—as she certainly was in a literal sense—then it would be reasonably simple, I should think, to get pictures of everyone who was close to her. There's got to be a certain intimacy between the murderer and the murdered person. That is, as a rule. I can't imagine Rose having the strength of mind to make an enemy of anybody. Yet she did have money and her relatives do inherit."

"Especially Milly."

"Especially Milly. Even the stuffy Ligon might have some need for money. I think Lattrice will investigate that possibility. A busy little man is Lattrice. Rose was killed Friday afternoon late. This is Sunday. He's already gotten G.M.'s key and called at G.M.'s apartment and asked questions. I imagine he has also tried to establish for certain the alibi that Dora claims—Dora and her Bert. Of course, in my opinion Bertie would say anything Dora told him to say. She's a powerful woman. But I may be doing him an injustice."

"He doesn't look very happy."

"Who would in that atmosphere? I think they could get photographs easily enough of people close to Rose. Apparently she never went out, she just holed up in that ghastly place. Seems too bad, as you say. But if G.M. was the target, the field is wide. Hard to find out what enemies he may have made. He may not know himself. Impossible to get pictures of everybody he has ever known. But I think that the man who phoned Rose that afternoon called on Rose. Then he went down to the street, avoiding being seen in her company, slipped around the corner and waited for her in a car. I think she came later and he took her to the helicopter."

"He'd have to know how to run the helicopter."

"Oh, yes. I was in the Air Force in Vietnam. G.M. was in the Air Force in World War II. I do wish," Greg said irritably, "we'd stop calling it World War II as if there was an absolute certainty of engaging in a third world war. In any number of world wars."

"There can't be," Susan said.

"I know. If anybody starts using the big bomb, then everybody starts in with big bombs and all at once there won't be anybody left to slaughter. Fine thought, I must say. Are you hungry?"

"Not yet really."

"It's later than it seems. Took us a long time in that apartment." He looked at his watch. "Time for another drink." He took her glass and brought it back refilled. He brought another for himself, sat down on the sofa and stared at nothing. "Dora—Ligon—Milly—each has a motive, yes. Ligon, jealousy; that's more likely than a need for the money Rose had left him. Dora's motive would be to take Rose's place and marry G.M. Against that notion there really was not time for Dora to get back to the city when I reached her by phone. As to Milly, she certainly has a motive, Rose's money. But the time when she was left alone and you and I were in the kitchen was very short. She'd have had to move like lightning—maybe she did and she can on occasion. But that idea leaves out Rose's afternoon caller and the running man. They may be the same. It also leaves us wondering what, if anything, her caller told Rose to set her off to the secret house."

The room was growing darker. Greg rose absently, turned on several lamps and sat down again. "It's no use wondering about things. We've got to get at some facts—what's the matter?"

"Why, nothing."

"You sort of sighed."

"Oh, that was—well, it must have been because I'm so comfortable. This place is so—so clean," she said with a burst. "So neat and normal and—and everything."

"After Rose's apartment? Well, I hope so. A woman comes in twice a week and cleans for me. Usually she leaves something cooked in the freezer."

"What's that?" Susan sat up. Greg was on his feet instantly. Someone was pressing the door buzzer over and over. Then the doorknob turned, its polished brass glimmering in tho lights. There came then the sound of a key in the lock, and Greg relaxed. "It's all right. It's my aunt. She lives near here. Come in, Aunt Lalie." He opened the door.

A woman came in, glanced around the room, looked at Greg and said, "Hello."

She was a little woman, feminine, neatly clad in a black dress, a short fur wrap, white gloves and no hat on her shining gray hair. "This is my aunt," Greg said to Susan. "My friend, Susan Beach. She's staying with me."

Aunt Lalie did not turn one of those neat gray hairs. "Really, Greg? What good taste you have!" She put out a small but, Susan discovered, a very strong little hand. "I'm glad to see you. I don't meet many of Greg's friends. Is that a drink you have there, Greg?"

Greg chucked. "Want one?"

"Certainly." Aunt Lalie sat down on the sofa, rose at once and said, "You know that sofa was your uncle's favorite."

"He must have had an elastic spine," Greg said cheerfully and went off to the kitchen.

His aunt chose a chair, sat down, tossed her fur wrap onto the unpopular sofa, took off her white gloves, and looked at Susan. Her eyes were a very bright, intelligent, gray. In spite of being so very feminine and delicate in appearance, there was something about her eyes or the modeling of her face that proclaimed her as Greg's relative. "Now then," she said composedly, "I don't for a moment believe that you are living here with Greg. In fact I know you're not. I've read the papers. Both of you were at Gilbert Manders' country place when his poor wife was shot—or shot herself."

Greg, in the kitchen, heard. "She's staying here, all right. It's safer."

His aunt's eyes sharpened. "Safer?"

Greg appeared with another glass in his hand which he gave to his aunt. She sipped her drink and said, "Was Mrs. Manders' death murder?"

Greg nodded. "And unfortunately Susan caught a glimpse of a man running from the house just after Rose was killed."

Apparently his aunt did not need to have things spelled out. "I see. It's not very nice to be in a position of possibly being able to identify—anybody." She sipped again and said, "Well, now you've told me that much, you may as well tell me the whole thing."

"You mean that's why you came?"

"Not at all. I saw your lights, I was walking past. I thought your cleaning woman must have left them on. I was trying to save you money on your electric bill by turning them off."

"That's very kind of you, Auntie. So I'll not talk of anything about Mrs. Manders—"

Their little bout of bickering was comfortable and friendly. But Aunt Lalie put her glass down and said soberly, "Of course, I want to hear. I did see your lights and I thought you'd be here and—the fact is—I'm not a suspicious woman but there was something about the newspaper account that made me—"

"Smell a rat?"

His aunt nodded. "I don't know why. It was only a little too careful. Guarded. As if there was more. I found it hard to believe that Mrs. Manders would go to that house, where you had told me she almost never went, get out a gun and have an accident with it. You may as well tell me the whole thing."

"And you'll not stop till you get it out of me. But it's rather a muddle."

His aunt proved herself direct. "Who killed her?"

"We don't know. There are a number of possibilities, but—no, we don't know. The police don't know. Susan and I have been doing a little detective work this afternoon. It came to nothing."

"Tell me the whole story."

Susan leaned back, listening and not listening, as Greg began with their arrival at the secret house. But in the middle of his tale she sat up abruptly. "Greg!"

"Did I forget something?" he asked.

"No. That is, yes. The dogs. The cat."

"Oh, that's all right. I told Col to see to them. He's good-hearted—when he's not drunk."

"Col?" his aunt said. "Oh, the gate man, Columbine Clanser."

Greg stared. "Columbine?"

"It was in the paper. Although how any Christian man can let himself be named Columbine I can't see."

Greg rubbed one ear and then the other. "Well, of course he wasn't a Christian *man* when he was named. But—Columbine!"

"I tell you it was in my paper, all spelled out. The gate man, one of the Clansers. Just possibly the murderer?"

"I don't think so," Greg said. "No."

"Go on," his aunt said. "You'd got to the arrival of the cat and the dogs and G.M. and Dora Clanser."

Greg went on. By the time he arrived at Susan's fright on the previous night, when she had felt so sure that someone was following her in the woods and yet, later, so sure that she had let her imagination gallop at full speed, his aunt's face set itself.

"You were right to bring her here. Greg, go on. What was the apartment like?"

Greg gave a slight shudder. "I'll spare you that. Gin. Empty glasses. Full ashtrays. Even cat hairs everywhere. On the chairs, all over Susan's skirt when we left. Listen, Aunt Lalie, we can't eat if we talk of that apartment. Come on, let's see if there's anything in the freezer."

The three of them crowded into a tiny but sparkling clean kitchen. They found a casserole in the freezer. Aunt Lalie put it in the oven.

Susan moved about, setting up trays at Aunt Lalie's suggestion, finding silver and china and napkins, only half listening now as Greg and his aunt talked.

"But if one of the Clansers killed her," his aunt said finally, "then Susan is in no danger here in town. None of them would dare leave this country house of Manders'. If it was someone else—the man you call the running man—he might be anybody. Mr. Manders must have made some enemies in his life. He made such an enormous fortune, apparently when he was still very young. He controls heaven knows how many companies. He must have stepped on somebody's toes somewhere along the line, perhaps without knowing it. I met your G.M. a time or two."

Greg looked surprised. "You did?"

"Oh, yes. That hospital I serve as a board member for got into financial troubles. Somebody on the board knew your G.M. and got him to come and advise us. He did. And I must say everything he told us to do, every investment, every money problem, straightened out. He's a kind of genius, I think. Not that a genius is always very level-headed about anything outside his special field. You're *sure* he didn't manage to get his wife out there, shoot her and get back to town?"

"Susan says she is sure that he was not the running man."

"*Are* you sure?" Aunt Lalie asked Susan.

"I *was* sure. I'm still sure, but I've thought of it so much that honestly I can't be sure of anything."

"Oh, you're only tired and shocked. If the opportunity came to identify this man, you'd be completely sure. Of course that wouldn't necessarily mean that the running man killed Rose Manders."

"You needn't put things so clearly," Greg said.

"I don't think I'm at all clear. But your G.M.—I don't impress easily but I did find him very impressive. Attractive, too. Handsome as all get out. This Dora must have had some sound reason for believing that G.M. would marry her."

"Let's eat," said Greg.

They put the food on trays and took them to the living room, where Greg turned on the television. "There should be some news about now."

There was news, but there was nothing at all about G.M. When the news program was over, Aunt Lalie got her gloves and her fur wrap, looked at it thoughtfully and said in an odd tone, as if addressing nobody, "Cat hair is so very adherent, isn't it? Good night, Susan." She put up her cheek for Greg to kiss as he did, stooping over the neat little figure. Then she went away, leaving a sense of comfort and safety behind her.

Greg fussed with the lock for a moment. Then he said, "All right. My bedroom is in there. I'll have to get out a pillow and some blankets or something. What did she mean by saying cat hair adheres?"

"Well, it does." Unexpectedly Susan yawned.

"Bed for you."

She *was* tired. She slept in Greg's big bed and in some handsome red silk pajamas he said his aunt had given him for Christmas and he hadn't had the courage to wear. In the middle of the night, however, a loud crash and thud and some muttered words which sounded like swearing woke her. She stumbled sleepily to open the door to the living room, and Greg angrily was picking himself, blankets and a lamp off the rug. "I fell off," he said savagely. "That damned sofa!"

"Oh."

He shoveled blankets back on the sofa and muttered something about pigs. "That bed of mine is plenty wide for two!"

Hastily she went back to the big bed and roused thoroughly only when Greg called her. There was a fragrance of coffee and bacon. By the time she got to the tiny kitchen Greg had a hearty breakfast ready. "I told you I'm a good cook. What a husband I'll make for some happy girl!"

He had the morning newspapers. "Is the murder—" Susan began.

"Yep. Very delicate handling. But it's there."

She read the newspaper account carefully; Greg drank more coffee. "It's almost time for Cartier's to open."

"This newspaper account really isn't as bad as it might have been. It said murder but there was a kind of suggestion that there was a burglar."

Greg nodded. "Oh, sure. But the story will grow. Now then, got your handbag, gloves, jacket, everything? We'll taxi to Cartier's and then taxi back uptown and pick up G.M.'s car."

In the taxi he said abruptly, "What kind of ring would she like, do you think? Or rather what would G.M. like?"

"A star sapphire," Susan said instantly.

Greg turned to her, surprised. "You sound as if you'd been drooling for a star sapphire all your life."

"Not that I've much chance of getting it. But somehow I don't think G.M. would care for just a big plain diamond."

He looked dubious. "Dora might. But we'll settle for a star sapphire."

Cartier's was as still and somehow solemn as a church at a time so near the opening hour. A solemn and neat young man who looked as if he might be about to usher them to the right pew came forward.

"Star sapphires," Greg said.

The young man's eyes took in Susan swiftly; they also took in Greg. "Any—er—price range?" he asked delicately.

"I rather think the sky is the limit," Greg said. "However, show us some."

"For your—your fiancée, no doubt."

"Certainly," Greg replied with aplomb. "She'll choose the one she likes."

"If you'll come this way—"

Greg pressed Susan's arm in a loving way as they followed the precise young man, who got a gleam in his eyes as he began to show them the gems which were already set in rings. "You might try this one," he said to Susan, and Greg, again with a most loving manner, took her left hand and tried the ring on her third finger.

"Do you like it, darling?" he asked her.

"I loathe it, darling," Susan said sweetly. "Still, if there's nothing better I suppose it will have to do."

The clerk was hurt. "But it's a perfect star, as you see. The diamond setting is good too. Simple but perfect stones. I think the little lady will like it once she wears it."

"She'd jolly well better like it," Greg said, suddenly less loving and probably thinking of Dora. "All right. That will do."

"Good. Er—charge or—"

"A check," said Greg, took out his wallet and presented a check. Susan glanced at it as it lay on the counter and could not fail to see that it was made out to cash with the amount left blank and signed by Gilbert Manders.

"Good heavens! Have you been carrying around a blank check, a signed check, just like that in your wallet? Why, suppose something happened!"

"Nothing did," Greg said shortly, asked for the amount of sales tax, added it to the price of the ring and handed it to the pop-eyed clerk.

"But I thought Mr. Manders—I mean I thought he'd be older than you—" The clerk began to stammer.

"He is," Greg said. "You'd better phone his office for identification."

"I—er—that isn't necessary. However—just a moment," said the clerk and went away rather swiftly.

Greg tapped on the glass counter. "You know, he's so upset I could walk away with this ring and no questions asked."

"I think there'd be a good many questions asked before

you got as far as the door. Really, Greg, did you have to put on such an act?"

"Why not? Give the guy a little pleasure on Monday morning, a glimpse of romance."

The clerk came back, all smiles. "Thank you. I wish you happiness. I always say that we may not go to the wedding, but the real marriage takes place here when the bridegroom puts the engagement ring on her finger—I mean the prospective bridegroom. Do you—"

"Put it in a box," Greg said. "I'm sure my fiancée will prefer getting it on her finger when we are alone."

"I could choke you, Greg," Susan said, not so sweetly this time.

The clerk was perhaps excusably and certainly visibly startled. Greg said, "She doesn't mean it. My sweetheart! It's only her loving way of speech."

The clerk swallowed hard. However, he put the ring in a box, put that box in another box, escorted them all the way to the door, and had so far recovered as to say, "Good wishes to you both," as he bowed them out.

"We'd better walk over to Madison and get a taxi uptown to collect the car," Greg said pleasantly.

"You didn't have to make such a fool of me."

"No, you can do that for yourself."

It didn't deserve an answer even if Susan could have thought of a sufficiently crushing response. They were swallowed up in the sudden influx of traffic. The taxi took them to the parking garage; Greg got out G.M.'s big car. They arrived at the gate of the secret house and found the driveway jammed with cars.

Col—Columbine? Susan thought with incredulity—came to meet them and couldn't wait to gasp out his news. "They've murdered Snell."

Thirteen

Greg stopped the car with a jolt. *"Who* murdered him? *How?"*

Col looked flabby and slightly green. "He was in my station wagon. I don't know as I'll ever be able to drive it again."

"You'll not be able to drive anything," Greg said in a dangerously soft voice, "unless you tell me what you're talking about."

"I did tell you, Snell was murdered. Head stove in, they say, probably with a rock."

"Where was he?"

"On the road from Medbury Hills, coming back here. He had borrowed my car."

"Go on."

"I was late going off duty because I had to see to the cat and the dogs, like you told me to do. Wilfred had just got here for night duty. So I told Snell, sure, he could take me home and then bring the station wagon back here. So he did. And this morning they found him. Just parked alongside the road."

"Who found him?"

"Ligon and that Prowde fellow Dora says she's going to marry. They were coming back by taxi. They saw the car and pulled up and there was Snell. Head bashed in. Dead as a doornail!"

"What did they do?"

"Stayed there with Snell and sent the taxi driver back for the police. Then one of the policemen, Charlie, he lives in Medbury Hills, keeps dogs—"

"Don't maunder," Greg said sharply. "What did he do?"

"Brought my station wagon back here. Town policemen and state troopers and state detectives came too." Col wiped his forehead with the back of his hand. "Questions, questions, questions. That Lattrice fellow going around like a hound on the scent. Not"—a cunning look came into his little eyes—"not that he's found a scent. At least I don't think so."

Greg waited a moment. "I suppose Wilfred left the gate open last night."

"He says he didn't." The cunning look was still in Col's eyes. "But I wouldn't be too sure. There was an empty bottle in the shed. I got rid of it. But I wouldn't be too sure that he closed the gate." He squinted at the road behind them. "Huh! Looks like reporters. With cameras. I've got to get the gate shut and ask Dora what to do about them."

He shambled with the uncanny rapidity of a crab to the switch that controlled the gates. He barely got them closed in time, for there was a squeal of brakes and angry voices coming from the road.

Greg started up G.M.'s car quickly. "I ought to have left you in the city. At Aunt Lalie's, anywhere. It looks as if our murderer is getting desperate. Snell did know something—so what? There's Col's station wagon."

They had rounded the curve and there indeed was Col's station wagon. It was apparently the focus of a swarm of police, state troopers, and men in plain clothes.

"Fingerprints, everything," Greg said. "We'll go on into the house if they'll let us."

One of the state troopers, however, detached himself from the busy men around the station wagon and came briskly toward them. "You are Mr. Cameron?"

Greg nodded. The state trooper said, "And Miss Beach? Mr. Manders told us to expect you."

"Is it all right if we go into the house?"

"Oh, certainly."

The dogs came bouncing from somewhere in the house and leaped upon both of them with rapture as if they had been away from months. Even Toby sauntered out to greet them, but then sat down and licked a stray hair into shape.

G.M. was in the library with Lattrice. "You've heard," G.M. said.

"Oh, yes. When I got to the gate, Col told me."

"We tried to get you by phone earlier when we heard about Snell."

"We are doing that errand for you. Here it is."

Greg took the Cartier box from a pocket and gave it to G.M., who dropped it in a drawer of the writing table as casually as if it were a matchbook. "You had no trouble with the check?"

"I have an honest face," Greg said. "No."

"Did you get any information Sergeant Lattrice didn't get from the elevator man or the doorman at the apartment?"

Greg sat down. Susan sat down, too, wishing she had stayed in the city with Greg's aunt or with anybody. The cat promptly got into her lap, foiling Belle's effort to do so. Belle sat down sadly. Susan listened as Greg told of the man who had called on Rose that afternoon of her death. Lattrice's face didn't change. Greg went on, "They hadn't wanted to talk much to you, Mr. Lattrice—"

"Detective sergeant," Lattrice said softly. "Please go on."

"They said they didn't want to offend Mr. Manders. They seemed to think that Mrs. Manders left the apartment shortly after her caller had left and walked around the corner to where—possibly—he had parked his car. That's not certain."

G.M. linked his fine hands together. "Let's have it all in detail."

Greg told him in detail—*almost* in detail: he omitted the dirty glasses and the gin bottle in Rose's bedroom.

"We might try them with photographs," Lattrice said when Greg had finished.

"We might," G.M. agreed.

"However, if this is some enemy of yours, Mr. Manders, I really don't know where to look."

"Neither do I," said G.M. slowly. "Oh, I've made some enemies. Perhaps I crossed somebody up and never was aware of it. But Snell—"

"Snell knew who came with him and Rose," Greg said

"If Snell was here at all," Lattrice said gently.

"But he must have been here. The helicopter—" G.M. began and stopped. "I see what you mean. The man who called on my wife could have brought her here. Snell could have lied when he said that he brought her and saw her turning the key in the door before he left. But in that event—"

Lattrice nodded. "Yes. We'll have to check on Snell's afternoon and evening in New York more closely than we've been able to do so far."

Belle put a beseeching paw on Greg's knee, and absently he lifted her to his lap. "That would mean Snell knew all along who came here with Rose and therefore could have known the murderer and could have determined to blackmail him and—Did Snell get his cigarettes?"

"No," Lattrice said, "but don't jump to the conclusion that he had borrowed Col's station wagon in order to keep some appointment. We've checked that out. There are only three places in Medbury Hills where Snell could have got the brand of cigarettes he wanted, and he asked for them at every place. There are phone booths in every drugstore, however; obviously there must have been a time agreed upon when he and his murderer met. We've tried to check everybody in the house, also Ligon Clanser and Prowde. The people at the inn only know that the two, Clanser and Prowde, came in last night and as far as they know they did not come out. That can't be proved. It also cannot be proved whether or not Snell had an appointment. But he must have had."

"To meet on the road," Greg said.

"I think so. Wilfred says he had locked the gates for the night."

"Col will kill me for telling you this," Greg said. "But Col wasn't too sure about that. It seems he found an empty bottle in the shed. He got rid of it to protect Wilfred."

Lattrice's face stiffened, but he said quietly, "Clansers do seem to protect one another, don't they?"

"They do," G.M. said. "All the same—I feel that there could come a time when they would turn against each other rather violently. Certainly nobody really has an alibi for the time when Snell was killed."

There was a pause. Then Greg said abruptly, "If we're on the hunt for alibis again, I can give Susan a perfect one. She spent the night in my apartment."

Lattrice didn't lift an eyebrow but looked as if he wanted to.

"Dear me," said G.M.

"And furthermore, she can give me an alibi because I fell off a sofa in my living room and knocked over a table and she heard me."

There was a faraway twinkle in G.M.'s eyes. "My dear child," he said to Susan, "nobody thinks you came out here in the middle of the night—or at least early in the evening, as a matter of fact, some time after seven when Snell borrowed Col's station wagon—waylaid Snell, and—"

"Bashed him over the head," said Lattrice with what Susan felt was in fact an assumed professional detachment.

She began again to feel a little sick. "Where is Dora?" she asked. "Where are the rest of them?"

"Dora and Ligon are downstairs. Dora is trying to do what she can to stop—well, she can't stop the news stories but perhaps she can soften them. Ligon is helping her. I don't know where young Prowde is. He took some aspirin and disappeared. I'm afraid he wishes he had never come here."

Don't we all, Susan thought, and choked back the words. Greg said, "Where's Milly?"

Again there was actually a faraway twinkle in G.M.'s eyes. "In shock. She says."

Oddly, at that instant a kind of liking for the Clansers seemed to seed itself in Susan's heart like an unwelcome but stubborn weed. There was nothing likable about them. There was indeed a latent danger in Milly. She couldn't find a reason for liking any of them. There *was* no reason, she told herself.

"May I go upstairs?" she asked Lattrice, who instantly rose, made a polite little bow and said, "Certainly. We need your fingerprints but there's no need to question you further just now."

"My fingerprints? You said the police—"

"Oh yes, of course. I'll get the man in—"

It was a rather grim little ceremony; Susan stared at the little black lines her fingers had made and wiped them off in something with which Lattrice obligingly provided her. She watched while Greg's fingerprints were taken.

"Of course," Lattrice said pleasantly, "these will check with your fingerprints, Miss Beach. They are all over the place. Easily identified. And of course on the gun that killed Mrs. Manders."

"Oh!" Susan felt flat.

Greg said, "Go on, Susan. See to Milly."

She put down the cat, who resisted but allowed himself to be detached, leaving a cloud of beige-white hair on her brown skirt. G.M. stopped her. "Wait a minute, Susan." He took the jeweler's box from the drawer and handed it to her. "Just put this in the safe, will you? It's open. When you close it all you have to do is whirl the dial around a few times. Thank you."

He hadn't even looked at the ring which, whatever else it represented, certainly represented what to Susan was a great deal of money. She took the package and went upstairs, where she entered the room with the safe.

She couldn't bring herself to approach the chalk lines drawn around the area where she had found Rose. She went around them carefully, trying not to remember how she had found Rose and failing. The safe was open.

She placed the box within it, closed the door firmly and twirled the dial. She had the unnerving notion that if the room could talk, if any of the objects in the room could talk, the facts of Rose's murder would no longer be a secret. She went out hurriedly and then had a twinge of pity and knocked at the door of Milly's room. Milly answered with a groan and she went in.

Milly had already reduced that Spartan, simple room to a shambles. Clothes were strewn everywhere; shoes, stockings and paper tissues littered the room, and Milly herself was in bed with a wet towel over her forehead. A bottle of whiskey stood beside the bed.

From the appearances of the city apartment Milly's and Rose's favorite drink had been gin. But then perhaps the Clansers had wide tastes; so long as it was alcoholic, anything suited them.

Yet in a curious way they were like rather backward and certainly wayward children. Milly could be dangerous. Perhaps all of them could be dangerous.

Susan asked Milly if she could do anything for her.

"Have they told you about Snell?"

"Yes."

"Poor Snell! My favorite cousin. Oh, poor Snell." Milly hoisted herself on one elbow and peered glassily at Susan. "He must have known who murdered Rose."

Susan had no answer to that. Milly collapsed again, mumbled along for a time, saying over and over again, "Poor Snell," and then reached for the bottle. Susan left her to it. In the room that had been allotted to her, she found Bert Prowde, also prostrate on the bed.

He looked up as she came in, groaned much as Milly had done, and shut his eyes.

"You're in my room. You'll have to get out," Susan said pitilessly.

He groaned again and seemed to shut his eyes tighter. Even that way he was startlingly handsome, a John Barrymore profile, hair which kept its glossy waves even then and a surprising heavy hand dangling limply from the bed.

"I said you have to get out!"

"Please don't talk!"

Susan advanced to the bed and—perhaps not oversuspicious, surrounded as she was by Clansers—sniffed. There was not the faintest whiff of whiskey. He opened his large, blue eyes. "You don't know how terrible it was. There in the car—he looked awful."

"So do you," she said brutally. "Come on, now. Get up."

He shut his eyes. "I'll never get over it."

She thought for a moment. "Where's Dora?"

"Down in the basement room with the phones. Ligon is with her." There was a slight pause; then he opened his eyes again. It seemed to Susan that there was a faint gleam of hope in them. "Ligon doesn't want her to marry me. Maybe he'll talk her out of it."

Susan stared at him. "Don't you care?"

He gave another slight moan. "But there's not a chance of it. Dora is a very powerful woman."

Susan stared again. He relaxed helplessly against the pillow and looked sick.

"Well, you'll have to get out of this room," she said at last.

"Can't," said Dora's husband-to-be.

"Oh, can't you?" She took him by his shoulders, which proved to be remarkably muscular below the shoulders of his jacket, and jerked him up. When he gave evidence of collapsing again, she seized his feet and dragged him around so his feet were on the floor. He looked at her reproachfully. "How can you treat me like this?"

"Because I'm a shrew at heart," Susan said and meant it. But if the recent events couldn't turn a woman into a shrew, nothing could, she told herself, and gave him a push. "Now, go on! Get out!"

He did waver to his feet but then said, "Where shall I go?"

"Go down to the basement room and talk to Ligon and Dora. Go anywhere. Just get out." She gave him a shove toward the door and he went, shambling along like Col but not as rapidly.

She closed the door after him and turned the bolt.

"He's a fool," she thought. "He's what Greg thought he is. A handsome weakling. Why on earth would Dora get herself engaged to him?"

That was Dora's business, however. But if she had thought to hurt G.M. she had certainly failed.

She took off her jacket and hung it up. Her jacket still bore some stray beige hairs from Toby; doesn't he ever stop shedding? she thought crossly.

She got into a blue wool dress, simple and straight, which she had bought—it seemed a long time ago—from the city for country wear during the time she and Milly were expected to stay in the secret house.

Somebody had to see to lunch. She had a sinking notion who that somebody had to be.

She was mistaken. When she got down to the kitchen Ligon and Dora were there. Dora gave her a swift look. "Oh, so you're back. High time. I suppose you know about Snell."

"Yes."

"Well, help me. Ligon will do the hamburgers. Good heavens! Couldn't you and Greg think up anything to eat except hamburgers?"

"Why didn't you go yourself to get the food?" Susan said.

"Why, really"—Dora's lovely eyes turned dreamy but fixed themselves upon her—"you are getting a little above yourself, aren't you? Just because I'm going to marry Bert and leave G.M.'s office you needn't think you are going to take over. Nobody," said Dora with utter conviction, "can take my place."

"Where's your Bert?" Susan asked.

"I have not the faintest idea." Dora handed a broiler to Ligon. "Make yourself useful, Ligon."

"He didn't seem very well," Susan said.

"You saw him?"

"He was in my bedroom. I helped him out."

"Well . . ." Dora did hesitate. "Of course he had a frightful shock. He's very sensitive."

"I'm sensitive too," Susan said shortly.

"And I'm sensitive," Ligon said. "But I hope I've got more guts than that weakling you say you're going to marry, Dora."

"I wouldn't really call him a weakling." Dora smiled. "I may marry him and I may not," she added airily and walked out of the kitchen, leaving Ligon and Susan.

Ligon began to shape hamburgers and put them on the broiler. Susan opened cans almost at random, got baked beans again and resolved never to eat hamburgers or baked beans again. Ligon said dourly, "If Dora marries that guy, she'll never stay with him, and the first thing I know I'll have her back on my hands again."

"Don't you want her?" Susan said carefully, thinking of the motive of jealousy which she and Geg had considered.

Ligon slapped down a hamburger. "Hell, no. She's pure poison. Bossy, unbearable! She'd do far better to marry G.M. If you have any influence with her or with G.M.—"

"I haven't," Susan said definitely. It didn't seem wise to tell Ligon that G.M. had refused to marry Dora.

"You can try," Ligon said gloomily and slapped down another hamburger.

They were broiling and Susan was beginning to think hungrily that she had denigrated hamburgers in resolving never to eat them again when the door opened and Milly came in. She wore the preposterous purple garment and had not combed her hair, but she did seem to have recovered a semblance of sobriety. That or the odor of food had brought her forth; a woman as fat as Milly likes to eat, Greg had said.

Somehow, higgledy-piggledy they got food on the table in the big and stately dining room. "We may as well eat," Ligon said, still gloomily. "I don't know what the rest of them are doing and I don't want to know. The grilling the police put me through this morning, you wouldn't believe it."

"Well," said Milly, "you did find dear Snell."

Ligon turned pasty white. "Would you just as soon not talk about it!"

With Milly's first gulps of food her curiosity, no less gluttonous than her appetite, returned. "Why did you go to New York?" she asked Susan. "You and Greg? And stayed overnight, too. Why?"

"Chores for G.M.," Susan said shortly.

"What kind of chores?"

"Let him tell you if he wants to." Susan was learning to defend herself—yet at the same time that unwelcome little weed of liking for the Clansers seemed to have taken a firmer hold. She poured more coffee for Milly.

Dora came in, walking swiftly but very gracefully, as was her habit. "I got Lattrice to take Bert back to the inn in Medbury Hills." She sat down. "Good heavens, couldn't you find anything else to eat?"

"Be thankful you have this," Milly said with unexpected spirit.

Greg and G.M. appeared in the doorway and came to the table, where G.M. sat down, glanced at the food and helped himself calmly. Greg sat down, too. Dora said, "I did everything I could do, G.M. As you know, I know most of the newsmen and have always been on good terms with them. There'll be news, of course. But they'll try to soften it—I think. There's a notion that it must have been a burglar and that Snell saw him—something like that."

"A notion you gave them, I'm sure, Dora," said G.M. mildly.

"I did my best. I also pulled every string I knew you had to pull, G.M."

"I'm sure of that, too." G.M. reached for another hamburger, which he ate heartily.

"Have all the police gone?" Milly asked.

G.M. nodded. "For the moment. They've done what they could do now. They've taken Col's station wagon with them. He'll not like that. However"—G.M. shrugged—"can't be helped. By the way, Snell didn't bring Rose here Friday afternoon."

Fourteen

This was a real bombshell. Dora sat up as if a wire had jerked her. Even Milly emerged from a mouthful of beans on which she had poured catsup so it streaked down her chin. "What!" she cried.

G.M. was as cool as ever. "Lattrice had the aid of some detectives of the New York police force. It didn't take them long to run down Snell's favorite bars. It seems that he was in one bar from about four o'clock Friday afternoon until close to six-thirty, when—thoroughly tanked—they were told he staggered out and apparently went to his apartment, where he slept it off."

"So he couldn't have brought Rose here!" Milly cried through beans and catsup.

"But—but he must have been at the heliport!" Susan said.

"Oh, yes." G.M. reached for another hamburger. "Snell was there, all right. But after considerable questioning it develops that nobody knew quite who was with him, except for—a lady in a green dress."

"Rose!" Milly squealed.

G.M. went on, "And a mechanic thinks he saw Snell leave the heliport. He's not sure, but of course that would mean that someone else brought Rose here, someone who knows how to run a copter."

"Then"—Dora thought it over—"then perhaps Susan really did see the murderer running back toward the copter."

"I saw someone," Susan said firmly.

"So," Dora went on, "if that man brought Rose here he could have shot her and left. In a hurry."

Greg shot her one look. "In a hurry, naturally. Susan didn't get a good enough look at him to identify him."

Everyone looked at Susan. Even G.M. had a certain question in his eyes.

But Milly cried, "If you *did* see a man and *refuse* to identify him, my girl, you'll be an asses-acsech—"

"Accessory," Dora said coldly.

"That's what I said." Milly began to cry, tears mingling with the catsup and dropping into her vast purple bosom. "Poor Snell! Some wicked man got him drunk and then got Rose to the copter and brought her here and killed her. Poor Rose. I need a drink."

"You've had too much already," Dora said. "Eat your food."

Milly sobbed. "First Rose. Then Snell. Now there's only me and Col and Wilfred. Oh, and Ligon, but he never seemed so much a Clanser."

"You mean he doesn't drink like a fish," Dora said. "It might do him some good if he did."

"Dora," Ligon said stung. "A man in my position—"

"Oh, shut up," sobbed Milly. "As if you've done anything remarkable."

"I make a living," Ligon said. "I've made a position for myself. In spite of Clanser relatives."

"You're a stuffed shirt, and you're another," Milly said to Dora. "You two really belong to each other, you and Ligon. Ambitious. Just alike."

"Not at all alike," Dora snapped.

Ligon said, "Milly is drunk. Pay no attention to her, Dora. We are divorced, that's true. But I've always had great respect for you and your good judgment."

"Then stop giving me advice," Dora said. "And if there are only four Clansers left, that's four too many for me!"

Susan was fascinated in one way; in another, more pressing, way she felt she couldn't stand the Clansers' bickering any longer. Fortunately at that point Col came to the door. "The police have all gone," he told G.M., "and I've got rid of the reporters. I'm afraid some of them took pictures of the gate and of me, but I couldn't help that."

"No," G.M. said equably. "Have you had lunch?"

"Oh, my lunch is down at the gate." Col turned to Susan. "Do you want to take the dogs out, Miss, or shall I? I didn't let them out while the police were here and—"

"I'll go." Susan got up quickly and went with Col out to the vestibule. The dogs happily accompanied her and Col outside, where they disappeared into the pines and shrubbery with an effect of joyously kicking up their heels. Col trudged along beside her. "You know, I've got a terrible feeling that somebody wants to do away with the whole Clanser family," he said miserably.

"Oh, I don't think so."

"You don't know a thing about it. Or do you?" He peered at her suspiciously.

"No, I don't know anything about it. But I don't think it is likely that somebody started out on a blood feud to kill the entire Clanser family."

He trudged on for a while. "Maybe not," he said at last. "I'm sure I hope not. I'm in kind of an exposed position there at the gate all day, so far from the house."

"Wilfred's job is worse. He's there at night."

Col seemed to cheer a little. "That's right. But then the gate is almost never opened at night. Unless, of course, he forgets to close it, as he did last night," he added lapsing into gloom again.

They walked together as far as the gate, which was now closed. Col disappeared into the shed behind the pines. Susan, taking some relief in getting out of the secret house and all its clashing elements, thought with envy of Bert, who had managed to do so. She also thought of his surprisingly muscular shoulders and the rather smug and secretive smile on Dora's face when she said Bert was no weakling.

She turned through the woods, finding her way among shrubbery and pines, following the high brick wall. The dogs intermittently joined her, as if to check on her presence, and then dashed off on their own pursuits in the woods, pretending they were chasing rabbits or squirrels probably, although she was sure that neither of them had ever seen a rabbit or a squirrel in his life. She followed the wall, catching glimpses of the red brick of the house until she came to the gate leading to the airstrip. It was closed, too, and locked. The dogs came leaping toward her and Greg came after them.

"So here you are," he said. "I wasn't sure you hadn't followed Dora's Bert into Medbury Hills. And a good thing. I'd like to do that, too."

"Oh, Greg they really are terrible."

He nodded.

"And yet you know I seem to have a sneaking kind of liking for the Clansers. But I can't have! Can I?"

He laughed. "I suppose you can. But it'd be hard." He shoved his hands in his pockets and leaned back against the gate looking up at the glazed red brick of the secret house. He wasn't handsome as Bert was handsome but he had the kind of face she liked and trusted.

He said thoughtfully, "The man who brought Rose here in

the copter must have been the running man. He must have known how to run a helicopter. He must have had some sort of experience. That fact ought to limit the police inquiry a little. Not much perhaps. But a copter is not really as easy to maneuver as some people seem to think. I'll not say it's extra hard to learn, not if you've had flying experience. But it's not so simple either."

"So all the police have to do is find somebody who knows how to run a helicopter."

"And that's not as simple as it seems either. I do think that Snell's murderer was afraid of Snell's knowledge, whatever it was. It does seem likely that Snell not only knew who brought Rose here but was prepared to—blackmail, I suppose. In any event, it does seem likely that that was the reason for Snell's murder."

The dogs chased another imaginary squirrel. Susan said at last slowly, "Milly didn't run that helicopter. She was with us. Dora was in Bert's apartment—"

"So she says. So Bert says. Susan, *could* that man you saw running have been actually a woman in—what do you call it—a pants suit?"

She considered it and gave up. "It was a man's hat, I'm sure of that. And a dark coat. But honestly I've tried so hard to remember details, anything, everything about him, that I'm reaching the place where I'm not sure of anything. I only know that somebody ran toward the gates here, stopped and looked back at the house sort of—oh, slyly. I can't describe it—and then ran through the gate and was gone before you got to the window. We waited. We both heard the helicopter. That's just all I know."

"Could it have been Bert?"

"Bert! I don't know. If I saw him again, in the same clothes, the same light, the same—oh, I *don't* know. But I don't think Bert would have the nerve to just walk up and shoot somebody."

"I'm not sure of that," Greg said slowly. "I asked G.M. about him. G.M. knew, he would know. I was altogether mistaken about his abilities. The fact is that Bert was a union official—"

"Bert!"

"He got into trouble recently by knocking out a colleague who didn't agree with him. Nearly killed the other guy."

"Bert!" she said again.

"That's not all. The reason he got into trouble is because he was once a prizefighter."

She stared at him. "I simply don't believe it."

"G.M. knew. You see, that makes Bert's hands lethal weapons, under the law. It's forbidden for him to hit anybody ever. That's why he had so much trouble about the fight with the other guy. He's no longer a union official."

"But his face! His perfect nose—"

"It seems he even had an obvious nickname, 'Pretty Boy.' In any event he retired from his fighting. Wasn't extra good at it perhaps."

She thought of the unexpectedly muscular shoulders again and the heavy hands. "That's what Dora meant, then. She told Ligon that Bert was no weakling. And oh, Greg, I had to push him out of my room—"

"What was he doing in your room?"

"Just lying on the bed. Saying how terrible he felt. But I took hold of his shoulders and they were like a—a football player's. A truck driver's."

Greg smiled. "You know all about those shoulders?"

"Oh, shut up! I'm trying to tell you—but Greg, if he did that to one of his—his colleagues or anybody, he's capable of violence."

Greg replied absently, thinking, "I suppose almost anybody is, given enough provocation. Motive. Anything."

"All the same, Dora has tremendous influence over him."

"So did Delilah over Samson. Ligon seems to have escaped Dora's influence, but—I don't know. He could hide the fact that he's jealous of G.M. He still could have a motive for making trouble for G.M."

"No, he hasn't. He told me and I'm sure he meant it. He doesn't want Dora to marry Bert. He says if she does he'll have Dora back on his hands and he doesn't want her. Pure poison, he called her. He wants her to marry G.M. I'm sure he meant it."

"I wonder when G.M. is going to give Dora her sapphire."

"I wonder if she'll take it."

"Oh, she'll take it. Dora knows the value of a penny—let alone a magnificent piece of jewelry."

"I think there'll be sparks."

"Oh, sure. A certain amount of hell to pay when she discovers that G.M. intends to take her word for it that she's to marry Bert. She probably counted on G.M. to regret his own decision—something like that. Ligon was right. Dora is pure poison."

"Oh, not that bad! Really—"

"Quite that bad. If there were any possible way for her to shoot Rose I believe she'd have done it without a qualm. If, that is, she could do it safely."

"We know she didn't."

"There's always the possibility of a hired killer. I've never much believed in that notion, yet there have been hired killers. We all know that."

"This hired killer, we think, would have to know how to get Rose to talk to him, get her to come here with him, and know how to operate a helicopter."

"He'd also have to know about the gun in the safe. Dora could have told him that."

"Anybody could have told him that," Susan said dismally.

"There are two important considerations. Rose would not be likely to accompany a stranger via helicopter to this house. She might have, but it's not likely. The other is a question: Why did she come without telling anyone of her purpose? I mean without telling G.M. or Milly or anybody."

"Greg," Susan said slowly, "we think of Col as rather a good-natured fool. He did seem perfectly self-possessed when we arrived at the gate, Friday. But he had an opportunity to shoot Rose and then get back to the gate."

"Yes. I've thought of that."

"And G.M. seems to think that nobody in all his business connections would try to damage him."

Greg nodded. "G.M. knows what he's talking about. I really think that's not likely. For one reason most of the men are highly responsible people. Even the board members of the various companies, including the overall Manders company, may be rubber-stamp boards in some cases, but no—I don't know as much as Dora knows about the entire connections but I wouldn't think for an instant that G.M. has not gone over every possible source of enmity. Of course he may have injured somebody without knowing it, but I think he'd be more likely to know it and guard against anything in the way of—" Greg smiled. "Call it reprisal. Hard on Rose."

He turned abruptly and tried the lock in the gate. It was a solid lock set into the redwood crosspiece at the top. "There are too many damn keys. Anybody almost could have got one of them. Oh—hello, G.M."

G.M. came strolling around the corner of the house toward them. "Am I interrupting?" he asked, smiling.

"Yes," Greg said.

"No," Susan said.

"Seems to be a difference of opinion here. Don't differ, please. I've had too much of the Clanser motif in these past days. I really don't think I can stand much more of it."

The dogs heard him and came running, their ears streaming back with their gleeful speed.

He leaned over and patted them. "The balloon will go up tonight. All the news media. Dora is very good at public relations and at pulling all available strings but—" He stood up straight and looked sadly and rather wistfully at the secret house. "I grew to like this place. I felt free in it. Now it will be turned into God knows what! A secret house, where probably skulduggery to no end goes on. Secret meetings with money men to manipulate money affairs in a way the public doesn't know about. Secret orgies, me and my harem. Secret anything. Oh, they'll be careful of the law. And of trying a case before it comes to court—not that the police yet have anybody to arrest and arraign. But tonight the balloon goes up. I think I'll get drunk along with Milly."

"Go ahead," Greg said. "I'll join you."

"So will I," Susan said with such determination that both men looked at her surprised.

Greg recovered first. "I trust not on Milly's scale. I'd have to carry you upstairs tonight."

As it worked out, however, there was only the usual Clanser drinking that evening; Ligon was there and was doing his modest share; Dora was always moderate, but both Wilfred and Col contrived to leave the gate and join the other Clansers. Bert Prowde, it developed, was still suffering from what Dora called a nervous headache and did not come to the house.

The balloon did go up; it was, however, a most cautiously controlled balloon. G.M. had his importance, and apparently there was an extra effort made not to offend or suggest any implication of guilt to anybody at all.

They watched the television in the library; there was a handsome but unobtrusive cabinet in one corner which Susan really had not noticed before; its doors opened and the news of Rose's murder (and now Snell's murder) were the first items which appeared, along with extremely diplomatic but factual and thus provocative comments. G.M.'s career was sketched out: "the wonder boy of Wall Street," the man who had amassed a fortune while still in his twenties, the man who had become—this last was very cautious indeed—"an adviser and counselor concerning finance." It was at first thought his wife had been killed by accident; later it was proved to be murder, thought to have been done by a burglar surprised in the act of looting a safe. But then the great man's helicopter pilot had been most brutally murdered on the road leading from Medbury Hills to what was already called the secret house.

Rather a story was made of the secret house and its armed guards night and day. It was more than suggested as a secret meeting place for giants of industry. It was said that Mr. Manders had direct wires installed in the house at great expense so he could reach a number of important persons at any time without the fear of being overheard by anybody. Something, not too much, was made of this.

There was a report, brief by now, for the announcer was running out of time for this particular news story, of the people present in the house when Mrs. Manders had been found—Miss Susan Beach, a secretary; Miss Ludmilla Clanser, a sister of Mrs. Manders; Mr. Greg Cameron, an aide in Mr. Manders' New York office.

Nothing was said of the running man; nothing was said of the soundproofing in the house. But enough was said to stir any inquiring and inquisitive mind to explore and try to get at the truth behind all these cautious statements.

There were pictures of the house flashed on the screen, not very good pictures because they had been taken through the wrought-iron gates and consisted mainly of clumps of pines and shrubbery with only the peaked roof of the house and Col's foolish face peering through the gates. There were clearer pictures of the apartment house on Fifth Avenue, and G.M.'s apartment was called "luxurious," as once it certainly had been.

The New York price were cooperating with the Medbury Hills police and the state police. They would now have the sports report and the weather.

Dora snapped off the television. There was silence except for the accustomed gurgle from Milly's direction.

Finally G.M. said, "Not as bad as I expected."

There was another rather dubious silence. Then Wilfred, gurgling from a glass, too, said, "I suppose this means you'll sell this place and Col and I will be out of jobs."

G.M. eyed them. "You'll have enough money from Rose's estate."

"Are you going to sell the house, G.M.?" Col asked flatly.

"Too soon to decide. Besides, it would not be an easy house to sell after—all this."

Milly tottered back to a chair with a freshly filled glass. "Col and Wilfred will run through their inheritance in a year. And when you do"—she gave Col and Wilfred glassy-eyed but threatening stares—"you needn't come to me for help. I've told you that. I mean it."

Ligon leaned back, putting his fingers together like a neatly manicured tent. "No need to get in a hurry about anything. Take your time, that's what I'd advise, G.M. This is a good house and a very convenient one. Dora does run it beautifully, no question of that."

Col and Wilfred spluttered indignantly; Col won. "But who does the work? You, Wilfred, and me!"

"Speaking of work," Dora said to Col, "why are you here? It's Wilfred's turn at the gate. Come to think of it, why aren't you at the gate, Wilfred?"

Col was heard to mutter something about rallying around, guessing that the news reports would have reached television; it was confused and so was Col. Wilfred merely looked at Dora and said he was there because he wanted to hear the news and that he had locked the gates and she needn't complain.

Ligon examined his linked fingers and said that of course all Rose's relatives were deeply sympathetic with G.M. and, again, he was sure that Dora would do her utmost to help him at any time.

Another plug for Dora, Susan thought waspily.

G.M. rose. "The show's over." There was an unusual edge to his voice. "Dora, will you send for a taxi for Ligon? After he has gone, Wilfred, make sure the gates are closed as usual."

Dora picked up the telephone; her gaze fell on the table which held bottles, ice and glasses. "Greg, please lock up all that liquor," she said and began to dial.

Wilfred didn't pick up a chair and brain Dora, but he looked as if he wanted to. And indeed there were two or three half-full bottles left on the table. Milly surged up and seized one of them by the neck. Dora groaned into the telephone. Greg made an abortive attempt to wrest the bottle from Milly, who waved it at him menacingly. "My nightcap!" she cried. "I have to have my nightcap."

"Let her have it," G.M. said. "Maybe you'd better stay here, Wilfred, long enough to help her up to bed."

He said a polite good night to the room at large, avoided Toby who chose that moment to stroll into the room, and went toward the stairs.

"But he hates all this just the same," Milly said shrewdly.

"He likes his privacy." Ligon rose. "I don't blame him. So do I."

"Then why are you hanging around here?" Milly demanded.

Ligon seemed to feel he need not reply to that. "Good night. I'll wait for the taxi down at the gate," he said to Dora and walked out.

Col and Wilfred converged on Milly, or more accurately on the bottle she clutched. Feeling that another Clanser fight was in the making, Susan all but fled up the stairs and into her own small room. She was pleased but not surprised to find both dogs at her heels and settling themselves at once on the bed. Belle looked smug and pleased with herself, Beau very sleepy.

Susan bolted her door. She wouldn't think of Snell and she wouldn't think of Rose and she wouldn't think of the news reports, which would certainly grow more and more dramatic as the investigation went on. She wouldn't think of G.M., whose treasured privacy was to be invaded so ruthlessly and cruelly and whose dignity and standing so ruthlessly assailed.

She wondered when he would give Dora the sapphire and what Dora would say. But probably Greg was right; she would take the ring. She's pure poison, Ligon had said. But Ligon didn't want her to marry Bert; he wanted her to marry G.M.

That could be reasonably explained; if Dora married G.M., then Ligon himself, in a left-handed way, would have some kind of connection with G.M.

She looked at the bolt to make sure that it was firmly in place and that night for the first time had the courage to turn out her bedside lamp.

She put up the window and paused for a moment. Her window overlooked the gate leading to the airstrip, and again she raked her memory for the smallest identifying mark of the running man and could not remember one. Yet it was possible that if she saw him again—in the same light, the same position, she would recognize him.

The night was dark and cloudy, so no stars showed. The brick wall, the gate, the clumps of pines could not be seen in that all-enveloping darkness, but there was the barest, slightest breath of wind which seemed to whisper and sift through her room.

No, she wouldn't think of anything, anything at all. Certainly not Snell in his leather jacket. Not Rose, no, not Rose.

She slipped into bed, whereupon Belle came up to snuggle close to her arm and began to snore very gently. She felt grateful for the dog's presence and warmth. The house was as still as the night.

But in a dream the night suddenly turned stormy. She roused, thinking hazily she had heard faraway thunder.

It wasn't thunder. It was Belle, growling softly beside her. Beau woke and growled, too.

Susan sat up with a jerk. She fumbled for the lamp on the beside table and turned it on. She blinked, trying to focus her sleep-laden eyes. Both dogs suddenly jumped down off the bed and plunged to the door. Susan cried out sharply, "Who's there?"

There was no answer. She told herself, it must be Greg. Or G.M. Or, it occurred to her, the running man, who had locked the gate behind him and still might have the key.

Fifteen

The dogs would not growl nor would they surge menacingly toward the door if Greg or G.M. stood there. They wouldn't growl at Milly or Dora. Wilfred could have entered the house but was supposed to be at the gate.

Was Wilfred the running man?

There was no sound whatever in the house. She could hear the whisper of the light breeze in the blackness of the night outside, but in the house not even a footstep echoed anywhere—at least if there was a footstep, she could not hear it. She did not have the courage to take off the bolt and open the door. She did not have the courage to go exploring through that house, not even to find Greg or G.M. and tell them—tell them what? Tell them that the dogs had growled—well, at what? Somebody?

She settled back after a long time; the dogs remained at the door, not growling but very still—their bright eyes alert, their ears perked up—sitting down at last but suggesting a watchful guard.

They're such good dogs, she thought with a rush of gratitude. Dora doesn't want G.M. to keep them. If G.M. decided not to keep them, she'd keep them herself and the cat too, although it would mean a different apartment for her.

That was looking too far ahead. She couldn't go back to sleep. After a still longer time she got out of bed and went to a stack of books, apparently left on a table by some previous brief occupant of the room. Every one of them had something to say about money and its uses; she riffled through one, took it back to bed with her, and in spite of her certainty that she would not sleep, did go to sleep over a possibly thrilling chapter about the wisdom or folly of deficit spending; she hadn't quite made out what the author felt when sheer weariness overcame her.

Morning was as bright and glittering as the night before had been dark and overcast. Greg came, knocked, and said he would take the dogs out. They went happily with him. They certainly had not growled at him the previous night. Now in the bright light of day their behavior in the night seemed like a confused sort of dream on her part.

Milly was in the kitchen cooking with one hand and clutching an aspirin bottle with the other. Over her coffee—which Milly made extremely well, as a matter of fact—Susan debated about telling Greg or G.M. or both of her experience during the night. On the other hand, if she told Greg he was quite capable of carting her off to the city again. G.M. would be more reasonable about it.

There were only herself, G.M., Dora, Milly and Greg in the house. At least there were supposed to be only those people. How could anyone else have entered the house and crept to the door of her bedroom and stayed there until the dogs and Susan herself alarmed him and he crept away again? By using one of those too numerous keys, which were far too easily available to anyone who at any time had visited the secret house. By getting past Wilfred at the gate, and that could be done if Wilfred had forgotten to lock the gate. As a matter of fact, if anyone chose to make his way through the woods and get to the gate in the wall, it would have been simple to enter the house. And pause at the door of her room.

And if anybody had been there, then why?

Greg—and G.M.—had supplied too reasonable an answer. She might be able to identify the running man.

The coffee gave her courage, so she decided not to tell Greg of what after all was half imagination and so promptly told him the moment she had a chance.

The chance did not come until late afternoon. A messenger from the New York office arrived, was permitted into the house by Col and brought with him a briefcase full of mail and reports. He went away, eyeing the place and everybody he saw with curiosity. After that Dora, Greg and G.M. retired to the basement room, which was becoming a kind of makeshift office for G.M., and stayed there until a late lunch which Milly again prepared, aided by Susan.

Ligon and the ex-prizefighter turned up after lunch. The ex-prizefighter still looked as if he wished he were elsewhere. Susan looked at his hands, remembering with a kind of nervous twinge that they were, by law, lethal weapons. They looked merely rather large and clean and he looked as handsome as ever, no cauliflower ears, no broken nose. Milly told them both that G.M. and Dora were busy; Ligon went for a stroll around the place. Bert settled himself in the library with a book which he did not seem to be reading with much zest.

The police did not return. Reporters did return after a fracas with Col at the gate, which Col reported to G.M.; G.M. admitted all of them. They crowded the library. They too were curious, examining the interior of the house not only for news notes but, Susan thought, from their own natural human inquisitiveness. It was clearly the first time any reporter had been allowed to see the house. They were brought into the library by Dora, who with Greg stood on either side of G.M. at the writing table and again looked as if they were very efficient aides to G.M. as he talked to the reporters.

He was affable, seemed candid and told them almost nothing. No, he had not known that his wife had intended to come to their country house. No, he did not know who had accompanied her. Yes, he had sent one of his secretaries—he nodded at Susan—and another one of his office staff—he nodded at Greg—and his wife's sister ahead of him to the country house.

An alert reporter asked why. He answered that it was simply because he was expecting some friends from the financial world to have dinner with him and to talk over present economic affairs; some of them might wish to stay overnight; his wife's sister, his secretary and Mr. Cameron were there merely to see to domestic arrangements in preparation for that conference.

A torrent of questions shot out. What was the conference to be about? What were they coming to discuss? Who were to be there? G.M. fielded them all neatly. He shrugged, said nonchalantly that there were always things to talk about and that he couldn't tell them in detail, and went smoothly on. He and Mrs. Clanser—it was Dora's turn for a nod in her direction—had come after they had heard the news of what they first believed to be accident. Yes, the New York police were cooperating with the Medbury Hills police and the State police. No, he did not know why Snell Clanser had been murdered.

No, he did not know when the inquest would take place. The police could inform them of that; he believed that all the evidence of murder was a matter of record prepared for a later inquest. This was a new item to Susan; she had not so much as thought of an inquest.

She noted too that G.M. always referred to the house as "their" country home or country house. None of the reporters called it the secret house, and all of them, she felt sure, would so refer to it in their news dispatches. A secret house suggested, as G.M. had said, all kinds of secret business and was of more interest than merely a country house.

When the fact was brought up that there was an armed guard on the place at all times, G.M. merely shrugged again and said that the house was isolated and that both guards were relatives of his wife's. When a persistent reporter asked him about the various companies which he controlled either outright or by a stock majority, G.M. became both dignified and curt; all that was a matter of record; if the reporter wanted to know these various business interests he could certainly discover them for himself. Just now—G.M. was courteous but resolute—just now they would understand that he could tell them no more than he had already told them; he regretted it, but he had many things to see to and they would understand that. With which he rose, nodded affably again, and was out of the room and gone. His dignity was such that none of the reporters tried to stop him, a feat in itself. Dora efficiently and Greg with determination accompanied the reporters out of the house and as far as the gates. Susan gathered up used flashlight bulbs which had been popping constantly and then again took out the dogs. Both of them had been prudently shut in the kitchen by somebody, Dora perhaps. It would do news stories no good if old Beau had decided to take a nip at anybody's heels, and Susan wouldn't have put it past him. Or for that matter Belle would have been quite capable of attack if she had taken such a notion into her coquettish little head.

So Susan was outside again as on the previous afternoon when Greg came to find her. He was wiping his forehead. "You've got to hand it to G.M. Nobody could have managed that interview better. I don't see how he does it. Where's Ligon? Where's Bert?"

"I don't know. Greg, I think somebody was just outside the door to my room last night."

He stared at her. "You *what?*"

"Both dogs growled. They growled and growled."

"Why didn't you yell?"

"I—I don't know."

"Who was it?"

"I don't know."

"Don't you know anything?" He looked angry, exasperated, but also alarmed.

"I listened. I couldn't hear anybody leave."

They had almost reached the gate to the landing strip; Greg walked on, frowning, his hands jammed into his pockets. "All right," he said at last. "That settles it. You're to go to town and stay there. Hidden. Whether you like it or not."

"I knew you'd say that. I won't."

"Susan, it's so silly of you to take chances."

"Who could have been at the door?"

"Anybody."

"No, that's wrong. If Wilfred had the gates locked—"

"Suppose he didn't. They weren't locked the night Snell was killed."

"Even a Clanser can't get drunk every night."

"Why not?" Greg said savagely.

"The supply would run out, for one thing."

"They can have hidden talents for nosing out liquor. This—whoever it was was either already in the house or had a key to open the door. I locked it myself."

"You said yourself there are too many keys. Almost anybody could have got hold of the key at some time."

"You are determined to get some outsider into this, aren't you? Somebody with access to the keys, somebody who could induce Rose to come here? Somebody who could bring her here in a helicopter, somebody who could induce her to go upstairs to the room with the safe, get that gun, kill her and run?"

"Oh, Greg, I don't know what I think."

"Well, I know what you are going to do. I'm going to ask G.M. for the big car and take you to town."

"I won't go."

He took her by the shoulders and swung her around not very gently to face him. "Susan, tell me the truth. Is it G.M.? Are you that much—I'll not say in love with him but do you like him so much?"

"That has nothing to do with it. We've talked of this before—"

"I can't stand a mulish woman!"

"You don't have to. There's Ligon. And Bert."

And there were Ligon and Bert, coming in through the gate to the landing strip. "One of them has a key," Greg said.

Ligon turned to look at them. Bert—ex-prizefighter whose face was beautiful and whose hands were lethal weapons—

also looked at them, his big blue eyes merely blank and lovely.

She wouldn't have wanted to face him some dark night, say in Central Park, if he had been an enemy.

Yet he seemed mild enough, tame enough for Dora to lead by his perfect nose. A powerful woman, Bert had said. Pure poison, Ligon had said. Greg had mentioned Samson.

Dora, no human woman, could be that powerful, Susan reflected, and then doubted her own conclusion. Dora *was* powerful. When her brown eyes grew hazy and dreamy Susan had an impulse to run for cover. So far she had controlled it.

Ligon slid the key into a pocket of his tweed jacket. Greg said, "I see you have the key to the gate."

"Why, yes. That is, just now. I'll put it back."

"Back where?"

Ligon frowned. "Back on the hook in the glass cupboard of the kitchen. There are several there, duplicates. Keys to the house door, too."

"How did you know that?"

"Milly told me. It seems she had been trying them on—never mind."

"On the liquor-cabinet lock," Greg said. "Well, anybody could have taken any key he wanted."

"Why, I suppose so, I—oh, I see. You're thinking of the man this young lady saw, or thinks she saw."

"I'm thinking of Rose's murderer. He must have had a key in order to lock that gate after him."

"Was it locked then when G.M. and Dora arrived Friday afternoon?"

"Yes," Greg said shortly.

Bert looked unhappy but spoke. "Seems odd they'd take such pains with guarding the front gate and then leave a batch of keys to this gate, even to the house door, where anybody could find them."

"He'd have to know where they were," Greg said slowly. "He'd have to take the time to search or somebody would have to tell him. Or Rose gave her key to him. Or he simply took it from her after the murder. It was not in her handbag, according to Lattrice. That seems likely, since the gate was locked."

"I expect you're right, but it doesn't prove anything," Ligon said. "Reporters gone?"

"All gone," Greg said. "So you needn't be afraid of the newspapers."

"I'm not afraid of publicity. My name is good."

"Nobody's name is that good," Greg said.

Ligon took it calmly. "All my business interests are open and above board. Anybody can tell you that."

"He's right, too," Bert said again unexpectedly. "Lattrice questioned us in Medbury Hills this morning early. They had the whole—what do you call it?—dossier—"

"Record." Ligon lifted an eyebrow.

"All right. Record. On him. On me, too," Bert said sadly.

Ligon glanced at him. "I certainly wouldn't have guessed that you are a former prizefighter."

"I wasn't for very long. In the lightweight class," he said, explaining to Greg and shoving his hands in his pockets. Lethal weapons, Susan thought again. But Rose had not been knocked out or strangled. Still, a hand had been used to grasp that gun (somehow, so Rose did not object, did not guess her danger—or more probably did not see it removed from the safe), aim it and shoot her.

"So the police dismissed you both with a clear slate?" Greg asked.

"I think so," Ligon replied.

"I don't think we're dismissed exactly," Bert said. "They said they would thank us to stay in Medbury Hills. They didn't say how long."

"Till they found out who killed Rose—and Snell, I should think," Ligon said. "I didn't want the money she left me. I don't need it and Rose knew it. What motive you would have, Mr. Prowde, I can't imagine. I wouldn't leave until after the services for Rose, however. I think G.M. would appreciate my presence. The services are set for Thursday—isn't that right, Mr. Cameron?"

Greg nodded. "In the city. Didn't G.M. or Dora tell you?"

"Milly, I believe. But Milly can be very inaccurate. Since the police have gone, I think I'll walk down to the gate. Sitting around in that house doesn't—I don't enjoy it," said Ligon.

"Who does?" Bert said bitterly. "I'll go with you."

"As you please." Ligon nodded politely at Susan and strode away, Bert keeping up with him. Bert's light and easy tread proclaimed his former profession.

"All right," Greg said. "I'm going to get G.M.'s big car. You can stay with my aunt if that makes you feel any better. Now, there's no use in being stubborn, Susan."

"But G.M.—"

"Forget about him for just an instant or two, can't you?" Greg said crossly and took her arm in a hard grip. "Now, go and get anything you want out of your room—No, no, better not! No need to let anybody here guess that you are leaving!"

"Greg, I told you—"

"Listen to another reason. Even if I had no thought for your possible danger—don't look like that, I mean it—there's another reason for your leaving. If anybody follows you, if anyone leaves here to find you, we'll know who that person is. By leaving, you can possibly exclude the whole Clanser outfit. Doesn't that make sense?"

It was an argument his aunt had made and had a certain validity. Excluding the Clansers as possible murderers would not only markedly relieve the Clansers, which Susan did not much care about, but it would relieve G.M., and she did care about that. Greg, however, gave her no chance to consider. He drew her around the house toward the garage and stopped. A police car stood in the driveway.

"All right," Greg said after a moment's pause. "We go without telling G.M. He'll not mind my taking the big car. I'll explain to him later. I'll not tell anyone though where you are going. Come on!"

She went with him. She thought vaguely that it was a good thing she had worn a warm brown suit. He had the keys for the big car. It had slid out of the garage, passed the police car and swept to the gate before she said, "But Greg, the dogs!" Greg glanced down at her with a smile which seemed rather unwilling. "All right. Col will see to them. He did before."

The gates were open, but Col came lounging out and peered at them. "Going someplace?"

"Another errand for G.M.," said Greg, lying.

"The police are here. That is, that Lattrice is here and I think a state detective. Seems they searched the woods near where Snell was found killed and finally found a—a rock." Col looked rather sick. "Seems it has gone to the police laboratory, but they're sure it's the rock that was used to bash in Snell's head. There were signs on it—"

"All right," Greg said hastily. "We get the idea. Col, will you see to the dogs and cat if we don't get back till late tonight?"

"Oh, sure," Col promised and Greg shot out the gates, leaving Col staring after them, the gluttonous Clanser curiosity on his face.

"I don't think this is the right thing to do," Susan said after the first few miles.

"I do," Greg said. Later he asked the address for her apartment. "You can pick up anything you need there. I'll phone Aunt Lalie."

It was almost dusk by the time they reached the glittering lights of New York. Her apartment was in a remodeled brownstone, a small apartment but one that Susan thought was charming in its way. It was a walk-up, two flights. She didn't have the key, but she had made a practice of hiding an extra key under the hall carpet. She dug it out, aware of Greg's amused chuckle. "Taking no chance of locking yourself out," he said and glanced around the living room with its few pieces of good furniture, its snowy curtains, its bookshelves. "The phone is in the bedroom," she told him.

He made for it quickly. "Hurry up, will you? I ought to get back soon enough so nobody is too curious about where I went. That is—of course they'll guess that I took you somewhere. But they needn't know too much."

He dialed as she began to fling a few things into a small suitcase. He put down the phone. "Come on. Aunt Lalie wants you. I'll take that suitcase. I didn't give you a chance to get your handbag. Have you got any money?"

She had picked up another handbag. She opened it, but it was dismally empty. "Here." Greg got into his pocket, took out his billfold and shoved some bills into her handbag. It gave Susan an odd and unusual feeling; her father had supplied her with what money she needed, but nobody else. The matter-of-fact way in which Greg put the bills in her handbag seemed to establish some link between them; she felt—why, she felt cared for! He locked the door and put the spare key into her handbag instead of its usual hiding place under the hall carpet.

"What are you going to tell them all—"

"To explain your absence? I'll say I took you into New York because G.M. had some chores in the office he wanted you to do. That's easy. G.M. will back me up."

"Then you'll tell him the truth?"

"Oh, yes. Susan, G.M. didn't kill Rose. He may have wanted to but he wouldn't have done it in that way even if he had—gone over the line and decided on murder, as I'm sure he didn't. Get that little idea out of your head."

"I don't need to get it out of my head. I'd never, never suspect G.M. of murder."

"He has certainly made himself a place in your regard, hasn't he?"

"Yes!"

He drove through the heavy evening traffic. He knew just where to find a parking place near his aunt's apartment, and his aunt was waiting for them, quickly opening the door when Greg rang. She put out both hands and drew Susan into the living room.

"I've got to hurry back," Greg said. "There's something though." He hesitated. "I don't know—Susan may want to go out or—oh, anything. I mean—"

His aunt was quick. "A wig," she said firmly. "Easy. Those dark wrap-around glasses. Nothing to it. She'll be free as the air."

Greg looked dubious. Susan felt another wave of complete disbelief: a wig, dark wrap-around glasses, so nobody would recognize her.

Greg nodded. "It might help."

"Does anybody at the Manders' place know my name?" Aunt Lalie asked.

He paused again, troubled. "Dora might. G.M.—no, I'm not so sure. Somebody in the office, although I doubt it. Oh, gosh!"

"What?" his aunt asked sharply.

"The doorman at my own apartment house. He knows it. If there's any inquiry—"

"I'll see to things. Go on now, Greg."

But Greg paused to take Susan's chin in his hand. "Now, stick to it. You're doing the right thing."

"I'm not a bit sure. You did rush me."

"Do you want to be killed?"

"What a silly question! I didn't like leaving the house—"

"Or leaving G.M.," Greg said and walked out. He came back to stick his head in the door Aunt Lalie was closing and say, "Thank you, Aunt Lalie."

"All right. Now Susan, I have a tiny guest room. You'll want to freshen up before dinner. You do look rather as though you'd been through a wind tunnel. I'm afraid Greg is impetuous sometimes. But sensible," she added firmly. "It's this way."

It was a tiny but charming room with an adjoining bath. By the time Susan emerged, Aunt Lalie had cocktails on a tray.

"I can't call you Aunt Lalie," Susan said unexpectedly after her first cocktail.

"My name is Mrs. Rogan." Aunt Lalie smiled and poured another cocktail for Susan and a second for herself. "But I expect Aunt Lalie would come more easily to you."

"Thank you," Susan said and meant it.

Dinner was served by a neat maid and it was good. They went to bed early; there were books in the guest room, but she was too tired even to read. She missed Belle and Beau and even Toby. She missed G.M. She missed—yes, she missed Greg.

In the morning Aunt Lalie sent her firmly to find a wig and glasses. "Makes more sense than it may seem to you," she said kindly but resolutely. "You can't stay cooped up in this apartment for heaven knows how long. I'll ring down for a taxi."

Susan was thankful for the money Greg had put in her handbag. She selected a blond wig and had it carefully fitted to her head; she found some enormous dark glasses. She returned to Aunt Lalie's apartment, feeling rather peculiar when she caught a glimpse of the blond curls and black glasses in the mirror of the taxicab. She got out, paid the driver and saw the running man.

Sixteen

At least she thought she saw him; she was so sure that her heart jumped up into her throat. It was only the barest glimpse of a man's figure, sliding out of the way into the foyer of the next-door apartment house. He did it quickly, yet in a way which instantly brought the running man almost before her eyes.

But it couldn't be, she told herself.

After she had almost fled into Aunt Lalie's apartment house, she decided that she could be right, for the doorman said politely that someone—he paused as if he had started to say "gentleman" and substituted a more suitable word—"a person was here a moment ago, inquiring about the young lady who is Mrs. Rogan's guest. He's just gone." He stared rather impolitely at her wig but seemed to put it down to feminine vagary.

She swallowed hard. "Did he leave a name?"

"No, Miss. He left rather hurriedly, just as your taxi came up." The doorman hesitated and clearly broke one of his rules of discretion. "I don't think he knows Mrs. Rogan."

"Did he say he'd be back."

"No, Miss."

The elevator came; she thanked the doorman and went into the elevator and didn't stop shaking even after she rang the bell of Aunt Lalie's apartment.

The maid came to open the door and stopped for a second or two, apparently stunned by the enormous blond wig and the dark glasses. She was too polite to mention either, and Susan jerked off the glasses. The maid recovered herself, although she said on a questioning note, "Miss Beach?"

"Yes. It's only a wig."

"Of course. There's a message for you. Mr. Greg phoned from the country. He wanted to know how you were. I told him you'd gone shopping, I thought. He said not to call him, he only wanted to remind you about the services for Mrs.

Manders. Ten o'clock tomorrow morning, he said. He said you'd know where."

"Y–yes. Thank you."

"Mrs. Rogan said if you got back before she did I was to tell you that she was going to get you a different dress."

"Different—"

"That's what she said."

A different dress; a wig and dark glasses. But it wasn't likely that the running man or anyone else would remember her brown suit. Aunt Lalie was thorough. Perhaps Susan still did not quite believe in her own danger.

She thanked the maid again and sat down to debate her course.

Should she telephone Greg and say she thought—only thought—that she may have seen the running man? She thought—only thought—that he must have discovered Greg's name and address, and thus by adroit questioning his aunt's address. No, she was utterly sure, down to her bones.

The "person" had inquired about her; he had questioned the doorman. She felt a paralyzing sense of near, immediate danger. She must escape, and she could not expose Aunt Lalie to that danger. A man who murdered twice is not likely to pause if he sees a need to protect himself. She wrote a quick note. "Dear Aunt Lalie, I have to leave. Don't open the door for anyone. I'll be safe. Thank you. Susan."

It was inadequate. She knew the maid was busy in the kitchen; she crammed her few small belongings into her suitcase again, straightened the blond wig and went down to the street. She was in luck, she thought dimly, for the doorman she had talked to that morning was probably having his lunch; the elevator man took his place and whistled up a taxi. She jumped into it.

She went to the park entrance of the Plaza and thought of her lunch there with Greg, only Sunday. It seemed weeks away, yet today was Wednesday and the services for Rose were to be on Thursday. She didn't know whether or not she was followed, but she ran up the Plaza steps, mingled with the lingering noonday crowds of people, went straight through to the opposite entrance—used little really, except for people attending parties in the great ballrooms—flashed across the street toward Fifth Avenue and into Bergdorf's.

Here she bought a wide, swooping hat which all but covered her face.

So now what was she to do? The suitcase, lightweight and

loaded with only a few articles, was a handicap, impeding her actions. However small and light it was, still it was baggage; she could check in at a hotel. Yes, she'd go to a hotel, get a room and simply stay there; room service would supply meals, although just then she felt she could never eat again. She went on through the Delman shoe section, turned left through the section devoted to men's apparel, passed some handsome shirts and dressing gowns, and went out the small Fifth Avenue door. The big Fifth Avenue door was thus behind her. She paused as if to look in the VanCleef and Arpel's windows, had one glimpse of a magnificent array of jewels and peered swiftly over her shoulder. Through the drifting groups of shoppers she saw a man, standing perfectly still, precisely at the corner of the sidewalk. He was in such a position that he could see both the Fifth Avenue and Fifty-eighth entrances to Bergdorf's. Just then he was not looking her way, but he would glance that way in a second. She could see only a figure of a man, still, intent as a hunter, his hat low over his face. The sense of near and immediate danger caught her again.

Nobody could hurt her there on the broad avenue with its shoppers, its policemen! But she went swiftly along the street; she crossed at Fifty-seventh Street merely because the light was green; she went along too rapidly, her suitcase bumping her knee. She felt that she encountered rather surprised stares from the people she met; she knew that she struck someone with the suitcase, hurriedly apologized and went on. Here was Mark Cross's and again the light was green; she sped across the street. She'd go to the St. Regis, take a room and—and a line of taxis stood at the curb.

Without thinking, with only the instinct of a hunted animal fleeing for its lair, she jumped into the first available taxi and gave the driver her home address.

It was fortunate that Greg had placed her spare key in her handbag.

If the running man *had* contrived to follow her to the St. Regis and *had* seen her take a taxi, surely he would assume that she was returning to Aunt Lalie's apartment. If it really was the running man!

She couldn't be sure of that! But she *was* sure.

Then she ought not return to her own apartment. If he had found Aunt Lalie's apartment, he could certainly find her apartment; her number and address were in the telephone book.

She peered back over her shoulder, but there was only the usual stream of traffic. The taxi couldn't go north on Fifth Avenue; it had circled around to Madison, crowded everywhere.

Her suitcase alone could easily have identified her to the man following her. He could have seen it and her and failed to be deceived by the floppy hat. He could easily have seen her leap into the taxi. But certainly he couldn't know where she was going.

The taxi went on and she went on with it and when she arrived at the converted brownstone where she lived, it seemed a haven of refuge. No taxi drove up behind them. She examined the street behind before she paid the taxi. The taxi driver gave her an odd look. "You all right, lady?" There was genuine kindness in his voice.

"Yes. At least—you didn't see a taxi following us, did you?"

Nothing disturbs the aplomb of the New York taxi driver; he has seen too much. He shook his head, glanced in the little mirror and shook his head again. "I wouldn't have noticed it unless he got too close or tried to pass me. But—no, there's not a taxi in sight now. But you're scared. You'd better hop inside the house while I stay here and keep an eye on you. This your home?"

She nodded. "A small apartment here."

"Plenty of locks and bolts to the doors?"

"Only one door. But, oh yes—everybody in New York locks and bolts."

"You got friends? Sure. Then you just hop across. I'll be sure you're safe inside. Then you go into your place, lock and bolt the door. Phone some friend you can trust to come and stay with you. Now, that makes sense, doesn't it? You can't go running around the city in a state of nerves, can you?"

"No. I—thank you. Indeed, I do thank you."

"It's all right, lady. Run on, now."

She still had some of the money Greg had given her. The taxi driver took the bill she gave him, thanked her when she said to keep the change and watched her, she was sure, as she ran across the sidewalk, the suitcase bumping her knee again. As she opened the big main door, she turned back and waved at him. He grinned, held up thumb and forefinger in a cheerful circle, and drove away.

She went up the stairs. She got out her key, unlocked the door to her apartment, locked it again as she went inside and thrust on the bolt which the man who sold it to her said was unbreakable.

She wasn't too sure that any bolt was unbreakable if anybody really wanted to get in. Didn't firemen take a special course in breaking into locked and bolted doors?

Why not the running man? The thing to do was to telephone Greg at once.

Dora or any Clanser might answer. G.M. might answer, and he would know what to do and see that it was done. G.M. would send a whole platoon of protectors if she talked to him.

She dropped her suitcase and handbag, yanked off her swooping hat and enormous wig, and went into the bedroom where the telephone stood on a bedside table. She snatched it up as if it were a life line and dialed—and dialed. She clicked down the telephone, waited a second and began to dial again. The line was dead and remained dead.

Only half believing, feeling as if she were in a dream, she got down on her knees; she followed the telephone wire to the baseboard, where it was rather raggedly but successfully cut. A small kitchen knife lay as if tossed down beside it.

So someone had already entered her apartment. Someone had already made sure that she wasn't there—and if she returned she could not telephone for help, for anything. There was something chilling about that sharp kitchen knife and the arrogant way it had been used and then simply tossed aside, as if the person who had used it had certain confidence in his own ability. She got to her feet, feeling rather as if she'd been sandbagged. There was no other sign of entry. She looked carefully, if unsteadily, all over the small apartment. There were no signs whatever of forceable entry.

But the bolt on the door which she believed was safe was on the inside of the door and could not—she hoped and believed—be manipulated from the hall outside. The lock could have been manipulated by someone who knew how. At least it had been.

Her own key could have opened it! She had left a handbag in the room she used at the secret house. Another key had been in that handbag. Anybody in the house could have given it to the running man.

First she must make a complete survey of the apartment, familiar as it was to her. She must make sure there was no other means of entry than the door from the hall. This was quick and simple. The tiny kitchen had only a ventilator; the bathroom had a window which looked out into the space between the brownstone and a huge apartment house. The two windows of her bedroom had the same outlook. The brownstone was built after the fashion of its time, which meant that there were, first, stairs up from a kind of half basement and a first floor; then stairs up to the second floor. So, figuring roughly, anybody would have to have a ladder of about thirty feet to reach her windows. They were locked simply because she had succumbed not only to the present New York phobia about crime but to keep out dust and smog, another New York phobia. A window would have to be broken in order to take off its solid lock. The sound of the breaking would give her time to escape by way of the hall and the massive front door and into the street. Wouldn't it?

How about the fire escape? That offered no means of entry; its door stood at the end of the hall. She peered from her bedroom windows and did not believe that anybody in the world could leap across at least ten feet of space from the fire escape to the nearest window. She wondered briefly about the efficiency of that particular fire escape; she had not given it a thought before then.

She began to feel reasonably safe. It might be a trap for a gibbering and terrified mouse, but all the same nobody could get in without her knowledge and without giving her a chance to run.

She took off her brown jacket and wondered vaguely what kind of dress Aunt Lalie had chosen for her; obviously it would be something that did not suggest Susan's brown suit, which she had been wearing when she saw the running man—and when he saw her. He could have had no more than a glimpse of her, standing staring in the kitchen window. It was all too clear, however, that that one glimpse had been enough.

It was like what she knew of Greg's aunt suddenly to think of a different dress and go straight out to buy one. It also put a stamp of validity—if she needed such a stamp—on her own danger.

She made herself some tea. She always kept a few things in the refrigerator-freezer and a few cans in a cupboard. In any event, she couldn't have starved until the next morning. Besides, Greg's aunt would read the note she had left and almost certainly phone Greg. Greg would guess where Susan had gone. Surely he would try to telephone her apartment and when there was not even a ringing, he too would realize that the line had been cut—and come to her.

G.M. would send a whole body of police if needed.

She smiled at that and began to recognize her extreme weariness; her muscles seemed to collapse almost of themselves. She drank another cup of tea.

Of course Greg might think she had hidden herself in some hotel; but she would have to count on his trying to phone her apartment. She wouldn't cross bridges until she came to them.

It was a long, listening and unnerving afternoon. It was dusk before she decided that the running man had to be Bert Prowde. He was slender but muscular; the point, however, was that he could move with the swift ease of his one-time profession.

It was not pleasant to think of his potentially lethal hands.

If Bert had said he had some pressing errand in New York, she doubted whether the police would keep him in Medbury Hills; perhaps they could and had. But whoever had gotten into the apartment, cut the telephone wire, inquired for her at Aunt Lalie's apartment, and followed her that day couldn't have been a Clanser. The police wouldn't have permitted a Clanser to leave—would they?

Whoever it was, it wasn't Milly, not enormous and unwieldy Milly who had the best motive of anyone for killing Rose.

Col and Wilfred would have had to come up with some very convincing excuse for leaving Medbury Hills.

Ligon? She supposed since the police had apparently cleared Ligon's slate for him, he could have made an excuse to come to the city, but the stealthily swift figure she had seen did not remind her of Ligon.

She liked Ligon the least of any of the Clansers; if she'd had to make a choice among them for a candidate for Rose's—and Snell's—murderer, she would have plumped for Ligon. It struck her that in spite of the fact that Ligon seemed prosperous and in no need of the money that would come to him from Rose's estate, still there were times when even the most astute businessman could suddenly need cash.

Yet the police had thoroughly investigated Ligon's affairs and had given him a clean slate as to money matters.

Money, she thought, must be at the root of a motive for Rose's and Snell's murder. And if in fact Snell had tried to blackmail anybody, it obviously had to be somebody who had money. Ligon?

Suddenly she remember something G.M. had said at some time; he had said it rather sadly while he was dictating a letter to her, an answer to one of the many begging letters which came to him. "Money is a danger," he had said wearily. "You think when you're earning it that it's a way to make yourself safe from—oh, anything. But a great deal of money is—well, call it danger money. It invites some really ugly things—blackmail, threats, even murder."

Danger money, she thought coldly.

She could hear the rasp of the key, the tiny movement and rustle outside. Her throat closed up. She couldn't have screamed even if there had been somebody to hear—somebody besides the person who was working at the lock and, as it clicked, pushing the door.

But there was somebody to hear! A woman's voice floated clearly from the hall. "Are you looking for Miss Beach?"

There was a kind of murmur, an assent probably, some reply. The pressure on the door ceased. The woman who spoke was Mrs. Liley, who lived above Susan; her voice was unmistakable, light and drawling. She and Susan weren't precisely friends, but they spoke and exchanged comments on the weather when they happened to meet. "I think Miss Beach is in the country," Mrs. Liley said now, clearly.

She knew Susan was in the country; she might have seen her leave, but it was likely that she had read the newspapers.

In any event the person—the man, Susan was sure—who had the key seemed to feel obliged to leave the door. He spoke to Mrs. Liley; the voices dwindled away down the hall and almost certainly down the stairs. She ran to the window of the living room that overlooked the street and pressed her face against the glass. The massive front door was never locked; locking it had proved too much of a nuisance to the tenants, who preferred locking and bolting their own doors. But Mrs. Liley merely crossed the sidewalk, foreshortened in Susan's view; she was going to a party; she wore a short silk dress and fur wrap and high-heeled slippers. She waited for a taxi, which was a good thing, for whoever had tried the lock on Susan's door couldn't simply stand there and wait without incurring a longer and keener observation from Mrs. Liley than he could have wanted. Susan couldn't see him leave however; he must have moved very close to the apartment house—and moved very swiftly.

The episode had happened too suddenly. Now that the chance was gone she didn't understand why she had not screamed out to Mrs. Liley, screamed for help, screamed. What could Mrs. Liley have done?

Perhaps she had saved Mrs. Liley's life by her failure to scream! It was now too late to do anything, but the experience jolted her out of her comparative calm. Fortunately the strong bolt had held. There was no doubt about that. The salesman had told her the truth.

There were two more attempts to get into her apartment.

She was cooking some eggs when her doorbell rang. She went very quietly to the door. A voice outside called, "Miss Beach—Miss Beach, flowers to deliver." There was a pause and Susan held her breath. The voice came again, "Flowers to deliver from Christatos, Miss Beach." She did not recognize the voice, only that she thought it was a man's voice. There were ways of disguising one's voice.

After a long time there was the faintest sound of movement in the hall and then silence. Did the person out in the hall really think that she could be so deceived as to open the door? Did he actually believe that she would not suspect anyone approaching the door with a patently false excuse? Bert was swift enough physically, she supposed; she didn't have much regard for the swiftness of his thinking.

She felt in every instinct that whoever had been in the hall was now gone, and after listening and listening she left the door, but when she got back to the kitchen her forehead was wet. The omelette was sunken and brown. She forced herself to scrape it out of the pan and make another. She was staking her life, she thought rather wildly, on the word of a salesman of locks and bolts.

The next attempt came about ten o'clock. This time the voice announced that there was a delivery of liquor. When she didn't respond, there was again the click of the lock being turned; there was again the stealthy but hard pressure against the bolt, and again the bolt lived up to its claims.

Again she couldn't identify the voice; it was a man's voice, she was sure—reasonably sure—and it sounded rather nasal, as if the speaker held something over his mouth or pinched his nose together.

Bert's beautiful nose? Bert's potentially lethal hands?

It was midnight when G.M. came.

He rang the door buzzer; he called through the door. "Susan! Are you there?"

She couldn't have mistaken his voice. She was curled up in a deep chair near the old-fashioned fireplace. She listened, thinking for a moment that she had dreamed G.M.'s voice. But then she knew it was true and that G.M. had come to find her. She struggled out of the chair; her legs were cramped and stiff but she ran to take off the very efficient bolt and fling open the door. She didn't fling herself into G.M.'s arms, but all at once she was there, with G.M. holding her strongly. "We were terrified! Susan!"

"Somebody came—"

"Who?"

"I don't know. I couldn't see. It was a man. I didn't know his voice. He was here before. He cut the telephone wire. G.M. . . ." She burrowed her head into his shoulder. He held her close; she was so thankful for the warmth and safety of his arms that she nearly cried.

He said, "Here, have you any sort of drink in your place? Brandy, whiskey?"

A Clauser would have had something, she thought wildly. She didn't. G.M. said, "Never mind. Now I'm going to take you back to Greg's aunt."

By this time she was feeling less cold with fright, less like a harried little animal, pretending its lair was safe from predatory animals. "How did you know where to find me?"

"Greg's aunt phoned him. She told him you had gone and left a note. So"—G.M. shrugged—"we both came. Greg is combing the hotels. The trouble is we weren't sure you had registered under your own name. And then all at once I knew you had come to your own apartment."

It was like G.M. He always had been able to outguess anyone else. She moved out of his arms; she straightened her dress and tried to smooth her hair.

He smiled. "It doesn't matter how you look. Now then—oh, no, I can't phone Greg's aunt. We arranged to call her if one of us found you." His face grew hard and his eyes very cold when he looked at the frayed telephone wire and the kitchen knife.

"You didn't touch that knife."

"No, I couldn't. That is, perhaps I had some notion of fingerprints."

"You were too scared to think of anything. We'll leave the knife where it is for later investigation. Not that any criminal doesn't know enough not to leave fingerprints."

"It was the running man. I'm sure of it."

His gaze shot back to her own. "How do you know?"

"Because I caught just a glimpse of him once near Aun Lalie's apartment house, and I believe he had inquired for m there. And again at the Fifth Avenue corner of Bergdorf's After that I don't know, but I do know somebody tried to ge into my apartment. He had a key. My key."

"How did he get that? Oh, I see. You had left it in the country house. Yes, I see. Anybody in the country house could have taken it. Was this man Bert Prowde?"

"I don't know. I had only a glance at him—hat over his eyes and something about the way he moved. But I know it was the running man."

"Susan," G.M. said abruptly, "this is not the time, this is not the place. It isn't right—so soon after Rose's death. But I've got to tell you. I never knew about love before." He put out his hands.

Seventeen

'here was no mistaking the look in his eyes, the appeal of his ands reaching toward her.

She couldn't believe it. Yet she had always believed G.M.

But he was right; it wasn't the time, it wasn't the place. His ands slowly dropped. "I see. Is it because I'm too old for ou?"

She found her voice. "Oh no! Not you!"

"I didn't know, when I first saw you—I never thought, I ever realized how much you mean to me, until today, after ou had gone. And it was so—I was beside myself. I made .attrice let me come and look for you. Can't you undertand?" He paused and then said, "Of course it is too soon af- ɜr Rose's death. Good God, her funeral is tomorrow. But :ose had not been my wife in fact for years. I can't rememer really when our marriage just—just stopped. It's in the 'orst of taste to talk to you like this at this time. But I had) say it."

She felt as if she must be dreaming. G.M., the great man, nd little Susan Beach. The Cinderella feeling returned to her s it had when he had confided in her.

He waited. Then he said bluntly, "Is it Dora?"

She shook her head.

"Because all that is in the past." He watched her again for long moment. "All right. I'll not hurry you. Now I'll take ou to Greg's aunt. Get your coat." Her jacket lay on a hair. He picked it up, put it around her, saw her handbag nd the wig and said, "For heavens' sake, what is that? A 'ig?"

"I got it. Greg's aunt thought it a good idea. And dark lasses, too."

He considered it. "Well, it might have been a good idea. It epends on whether or not the running man actually got a lear view of you in the kitchen window. I think he must ave. You'll not need it now." He took up her small suitcase.

"I've got a car waiting and a chauffeur, a good hefty fello
You needn't be afraid."

She couldn't have been afraid of anything with G.M.'s ar guiding her, G.M. at her side. He saw that the door w firmly locked; he took her handbag and put the key in much as Greg had done.

They went down the stairs through the now silent, no safe house. A long car was standing at the curb; its un formed driver sprang out. It was obviously rented. They sp through quiet streets with only the lights from apartme houses and cars and the red and green traffic lights.

G.M. spoke once during the ride uptown. "The man yo saw just could be Bert Prowde. I don't remember seeing hi at the country house today. But I don't think it was one the Clansers. It seems to me that they were all there, in an about all day. Here we are."

He told the driver to wait; he wanted to be taken back Medbury Hills. He took Susan to Aunt Lalie's apartment a ter he had told the night doorman to announce them. Au Lalie was standing in the open doorway. "You poor chil Come in—Greg is on the phone right now. I'll tell him."

G.M. didn't wait for Aunt Lalie to tell Greg that he ha found Susan; he took the telephone himself. "She's all righ She was in her apartment after all . . . No, no, I tell you she all right. She's here. Where are you? . . . I'll pick you up the and we can get back to the country. I think we'd better g now. Lattrice ought to know of this at once . . . I tell yo she's all right, but"—he turned to Susan—"He wants to spea to you."

She went across the room; her legs were wavery; G.M. pu out his hand toward her, which she took gratefully. "Greg—"

"Susan we've turned out the town—"

"I'm all right. G.M. found me. I'm all right."

Greg didn't say anything. She cried, "It's really all righ Greg. I heard G.M. say that he'd pick you up and—"

"I want to see you for myself."

"Will you believe your aunt?"

"I believe you, but—all right. Tell G.M. I'll be waiting."

He didn't say good night. He simply hung up. Susa waited a moment and G.M. took the receiver out of he hand. "You ought to get to bed now. You'll be safe here."

"I'll see to that," Aunt Lalie with a glint in her eyes whic made Susan think of a certain occasional glint in Greg's eyes.

G.M. put a hand on Susan's shoulder. "Now, take it easy

:'s all over. I'll see to it that nothing like that happens again. Good night. Good night, Mrs. Rogan."

It was like him, too, to remember Aunt Lalie's name. She aw him to the door, closed it, put a very sturdy-looking bolt cross and said, "Now then, into bed with you. Would you ke a hot drink, a toddy, milk, anything?"

Susan let out her breath in a long sigh. "Bed," she said as ' she couldn't say another word.

Aunt Lalie helped her out of her suit and into the night-own from her suitcase. She took a hanger out of the closet nd showed Susan a dress, coral wool, handsomely made with short jacket. "I told them ten was the right size. Is it?"

"Oh, yes. I never thought of a different dress."

"Neither did I until you'd gone for the wig."

"I must pay you for it. I've been using Greg's money. My andbag with some cash and my checkbook are in the coun-ry—"

Aunt Lalie was too well bred to quibble. "Of course you hall pay me. Now then, I'll leave the light on. If you get neasy or—oh, dream or anything just call me. I'm in the ext room."

Again she left a sense of comfort and ease and a faint race of some light, flowerlike scent.

Too much, Susan thought; too much had happened. Too oon, G.M. had said. G.M. with his power, his kind wis-lom—yes, she felt like Cinderella. She went to sleep as if he'd been drugged.

Aunt Lalie woke her. "I'm sorry. You looked so desper-tely tired. But Greg tells me that the services for Mrs. Manders are at ten. I think you'd better be there. It's now ine-thirty, and here is your breakfast."

The pleasant-faced maid came in on the word; there was ot the smallest flicker of curiosity in her kind face. She put tray over Susan's knees.

Aunt Lalie accompanied her. "If you don't mind," Aunt Lalie said in the taxi. "Greg said to go in a side entrance. Re-porters." They did not quite escape the alert reporters and photographers who also knew of the quiet side door. There vas the rapid click of cameras.

Inside, G.M. and Dora, all the Clansers and Bert Prowde, ooking even more miserable than Susan had yet seen him, tood in a cluster. *Could* Bert Prowde have been the running nan? *Could* he have cold-bloodly killed Rose and Snell? *Could* he have tracked down Susan the night before and tried stupid excuses to get into her apartment—after he had a ready visited it and cut the telephone wire with that smal sharp kitchen knife? She couldn't accept it, not when she sa Bert. Greg came to meet them and took Susan's arm. The were a number of other men, none of whom Susan knew bu who, she surmised, were business associates of G.M.'s.

The small, solemn chapel smelled sickeningly of lilies. Th service was mercifully brief. Susan, Greg and Aunt Lalie sa in the third row of tiny seats. Ligon, no longer in his tweed but in a dark business suit, sat just ahead of them with Dor Bert Prowde and some other men, also clothed in discre dark suits. She couldn't see G.M. from where she sat, bu Milly's bulk with Rose's fur wrap around her shoulde loomed up in the front row, surely next to him.

She was thankful when they could leave the smell of lilie and the solemn tones of an unseen organ. Greg helped he and Aunt Lalie into a waiting car; they sped back to Aun Lalie's apartment.

"Now then," Greg said, "get some of your sherry, Aun Lalie. I want to hear everything that happened yesterday And last night."

"So do I," Aunt Lalie said frankly and brought out a hand some decanter and glasses.

Telling it was like telling of a nightmare; it was almost a unreal as a nightmare. When she finished, Greg said thought fully, "Bert Prowde wasn't in the house yesterday—at least don't know if he was. I believe all the Clansers were there. don't think one of them *could* have got to town."

"A hired killer?" Aunt Lalie said.

"If that's it, the police have their hands full."

"Perhaps not." Aunt Lalie poured herself another glass o sherry. "Have the police examined G.M.'s helicopter very very carefully?"

"Why, yes, I suppose so."

"Hmm." His aunt drank, thought and said, "Get you things together, Susan. You'll have to be starting back to th country house. That is, if you really want to go back there."

"Oh, yes, she wants to go back there," Greg said; there wa an edge to his voice. "She thinks it would be disloyal to G.M if she left the place now. Or rather left him."

Aunt Lalie's eyes sharpened again. "In a way it would b disloyal. However, that's Susan's decision to make."

But of course I'm going back, Susan thought, thrusting he few belongings into the little suitcase. G.M. wants me.

For an instant visions of a future with him seemed to fly through the air. His hostess, presiding at dinner with the greats of the world. Travel, always in deluxe fashion. Luxuries such as she had never dreamed of. G.M. and his kindness, his reliability, his wisdom.

She couldn't quite picture him as a husband. In fact her flying imagination came to a jolting stop at the bedroom door. Yet she was no dolt. How could she fail to know that she had felt only warmth and tenderness when he held her in his arms the previous night? There hadn't been the slightest quiver of physical revulsion, so why boggle at marriage? Oh, shut up, she told herself angrily. Shut up and pack.

The smooth-running car swept them along through the city, along the parkway, back to Medbury Hills and the secret house. Greg said almost nothing.

Col had certainly attended the funeral, but he appeared instantly at the gate with the news that G.M. had arrived some time ago. He didn't go so far as to ask where Greg and Susan had been, and why they were so much later in returning than G.M., but the Clanser curiosity glittered in his little eyes.

The car swept on along the driveway and at the door to the secret house, G.M. himself stood waiting for them. The dogs were with him and leaped upon Susan as she emerged from the car. Even Toby came strolling from some shrubbery and eyed her with an intent blue gaze which did seem to express a certain friendliness. But G.M.'s greeting was like a warm and sustaining authority, welcoming her. Greg reached for her suitcase, but G.M. took it at once.

"So you got here," G.M. said. "I'm glad."

Greg said good morning rather stiffly and then asked if he could continue to use the car. "I want to go to Medbury Hills."

G.M.'s eyes flashed an inquiry; he didn't ask it but merely nodded and took Susan's hand. Greg turned back into the car, and it glided away again.

The dogs romped around Susan and G.M. Toby came after them in a more stately but nevertheless interested way. G.M. said, "I've been waiting. I thought you'd never get here. Oh, it's all right, Susan. I'm not going to bother you. I only want you to know how very glad I am to see you. To tell you the truth, I was rather afraid you'd decide not to return here."

"No, I couldn't do that."

"I'll take your suitcase to your room."

She went with him into the hall, leaving the vestibule door

open so dogs and cat could have the freedom of the house. She couldn't help looking behind her as she went up the stairs; she had a glimpse of the living room in all its beautiful luxury.

G.M. led the way to the room she was using and put down her suitcase. "You really are all right?"

"Oh, yes. The house seems so quiet."

"Not a Clanser on the place as yet except Col. The rest of them went out to the cemetery on Long Island. I got snarled up with reporters and by the time I had coped with them as well as I could, I decided to come straight back here. I'm not sure I coped very well. Susan, I don't believe it was Bert Prowde yesterday. Your running man. I talked to Lattrice by phone late last night. He can't be perfectly sure that Bert was in Medbury Hills all day yesterday, but he thinks he was. I'm inclined to believe that Lattrice's thoughts are likely to be accurate. Let's go downstairs."

The house was so wonderfully silent; she could scarcely believe that a drinking, quarreling Clanser would not show up. G.M. was in an expansive mood. He showed her the paintings over the fireplaces and talked knowledgeably and with affection of painting. He showed her the chairs in the dining room and then suddenly chuckled, ruffled up her hair and said, "I'm behaving very badly. It's like taking you to the top of the mountain and showing you the pleasures of the world which I can give you. All the same, I can give you so much. Everything you want. No more hole-in-the-corner apartment for you. We'll have the Fifth Avenue apartment completely renovated—changed, everything. Or better—I'll sell that apartment and buy another, anything you want."

"But—but, G.M.—"

"I promised not to hurry you or harry you. I'll keep my promise."

Nevertheless she could not help seeing herself as mistress of this beautiful hidden house, mistress of a handsome luxury apartment. Her imagination took its flying course through the fantastic luxuries that marriage with G.M. would give her—her, little Susan Beach.

His piercing eyes saw too much. He shook his head. "We'll take time, all the time you want. Why did Greg want to go into Medbury Hills?"

"I don't know. I didn't know he was going."

"There must be a reason, and if I know Greg, a good one. Have you had lunch?"

She shook her head. He was pleased. "I thought perhaps you wouldn't have had. I stopped on Madison and bought a quiche Lorraine and some salad stuff and fruit. All we have to do is heat the quiche Lorraine. Sherry?"

He had also set out a decanter and two glasses. He gave her sherry, smiling down at her boyishly. "I felt that you'd like a change from whiskey."

She sat back, sipped the sherry and thought, None of this is real. This beautiful room, G.M. looking so young, so pleased, the dogs settling down near her and looking pleased, too. Even Toby sat nearby, his eyes almost closed so there were only contented blue slits showing. A beautiful room. A handsome man, kind, brilliant—and yes, in love with her.

And very, very rich; he would give her anything and she'd be a great fool not to take it.

He did have an uncanny gift for reading thoughts, for he said quietly, "Don't take me because I have so much money. Take me because you like me. I ought to warn you, though, I'm not always a very satisfactory husband. I do like business, I do like my various interests. Sometimes I'd have to leave you alone. Or—" He turned his sherry glass in his fine hands and continued casually, "Or ask Greg to see to you. Take you to dinner, something like that."

She finished her sherry; she put down the glass sharply. She said sharply, "No. No, that would not be a good idea."

It struck her, but in a distant way, that he had spoken perhaps too casually in suggesting Greg as an escort; it struck her too that she had replied too quickly and too vehemently. It was only a fleeting notion, however; she said, "I'm starving. Shall I heat the quiche Lorraine?"

"I will." He shot to his feet with the alacrity of a boy again. It seemed wrong, so shortly after Rose's death; it was not right for him to behave as if he'd been released from a dreary kind of burden. Yet that was a fact and there was no dodging its truth.

In the kitchen he was still what seemed his natural self, as if his younger years had been restored to him. He was the G.M. she had known, in a way; she knew he could assume his mask of dignity and command at any instant. But they heated and cut the quiche Lorraine; they mixed the salad; they chatted of the food, of anything but murder. They sat at the long table in the dining room. G.M. knew where the silver was; he knew where there were crystal goblets. He had also got out wine that sparkled like the autumn day. She felt her cheeks begin to grow warm. G.M. said, “Now you look like yourself. Color in your face,” and held up his glass. “I promised not to hurry you. But may this be only the first of years of enjoying being together.”

As if on a reminding cue the Clansers returned with a burst into the vestibule.

Toby gave them the first warning of their arrival, for he had been stealthily ensconced under the table, on the alert for any inadvertently dropped crumb. He shot out, a streak of beige and black, and disappeared as the vestibule door clanged, voices and footsteps came in and Milly appeared in the dining-room door.

Her bulging eyes took in the little meal, the glasses, the wine. She cried, “The very day poor Rose was buried! I don't care what you are, G.M., or anything about your money or—but this is disgraceful.”

G.M. rose courteously. “I'm afraid we've eaten all the lunch. But there must be more food.”

Dora was suddenly beside Milly; her eyes were dreamy as she, too, took in the glasses, the atmosphere of friendliness which did indeed exist. She said nothing. And Greg came in.

Another swift glance swept across the table, the plates, the glasses, G.M. and Susan. Greg said, “I'm hungry. I hope something is left.”

Dora said icily, “We stopped for food along the way. Col had come on ahead of us. But Milly thought we ought to go to the cemetery. I'm sorry you were too—too occupied, G.M., to accompany us.”

He took that, too, courteously and with his reassumed dignity. “I was held up. Greg, did you see Lattrice in Medbury Hills?”

Greg nodded. “Yes. I'm going to get something to eat.” He disappeared into the kitchen.

G.M. said, “Dora, I have some chores that have to be done. Will you help me, please?” He went out, dignified, kind and utterly unapproachable.

Dora's eyes were dreamy as she looked at Susan, and Susan on a sudden impulse looked back at Dora with defiance. Dora could no longer frighten her. Dora could no longer give her directions.

Dora must have read that; her mind was swift, too. She whirled around and followed G.M. downstairs to the room with the bridge tables and private wires.

Susan went up to her room.

No one came, no one followed her, nothing happened until Belle came scratching at the door and bounced in when Susan opened it. Beau followed at a more dignified pace. Toby followed Beau. All three sat down then and looked at Susan, who realized all at once that she was not only a purveyor of food, she was a purveyor of water. She filled the bowl again and all three lapped, their stylish noses peaceably together. She put on the coral pink dress, which was becoming and lifted her spirits. She looked in the handbag she had left in the house; her key was not there. She had known it couldn't be there, but her spirits went down. So a Clanser had taken it and some way given it to the running man.

Late in the afternoon from her window she saw Greg and Ligon strolling through the gate, which this time Greg unlocked. They had both changed from their decorous clothing of the morning. Greg was in his usual slacks and sweater; Ligon had resumed his tweeds. They were not talking, merely strolling; Greg did not look up at her window.

Greg was quick on the uptake, too, as quick as Dora. She was sure that he had guessed much of what G.M. had said to her. He had also guessed, wrongly, that she had already promised to become G.M.'s wife.

This proved to be reasonable. Greg himself an hour or so later came to her door, knocked, said, "It's Greg. It's all right to open the door," and when she opened it he said quietly, "I must congratulate you. Or rather G.M."

Eighteen

"But—but, Greg—"

"I guessed right, didn't I? G.M. is so changed and so are you. You'd be very silly not to take him. You'll never get such a good chance again. Lattrice is here."

"You don't understand—"

"Oh, I understand. Lattrice wants to ask you about the man you saw yesterday." He turned abruptly and went down the hall and away; she had no chance to call him back and say—all right, say what? she asked herself. Tell him yes, G.M. had asked her to marry him. Tell him that she intended to say yes.

Apparently Dora passed him in the hall. She heard Dora's voice. "Talking to Susan, Greg? You'll have to talk very fast."

Greg muttered something Susan couldn't hear. Dora flashed into sight and came to her. She also flashed into the room; she settled herself with composure in the lounge chair and looked stunningly beautiful and also angry. Her eyes were like creamy brown fudge but with no suggestion of a sugary flavor. She attacked at once. "You've been doing your best to get G.M. into your clutches! G.M. is not for you. Why, you little fool, don't you know that Ligon divorced me! I didn't divorce Ligon. He divorced me because of G.M. Didn't you know that?"

Susan got her breath. "This has nothing to do with me."

"Oh, doesn't it! Don't you know G.M. well enough to know that he'd never forget an obligation? Haven't you seen the way he has let the whole Clanser family fasten upon him simply because Rose gave him his start to a fortune? He would never have even mentioned a divorce to Rose."

"Did you want him to?"

"You feel very secure, don't you! Let me tell you something you ought to have sense enough to know. G.M. cannot get along without me!"

"Nobody is indispensable."

"I am indispensable. He needs me. No matter where he goes or what he does he needs me. I know more of his business than anybody. He'd never want anyone else to know the things I know."

Susan thought and decided swiftly. "That sounds very much like blackmail."

Dora rose; she lifted her lovely head. "Let it sound like anything you like. I mean what I say."

"Suppose I tell G.M. what you've just said."

Dora laughed. "Do you think he'd believe you? He's known me too long. He knows he can trust every word I say and everything I do for him. He'll never trust anyone else like that."

She went gracefully away, her hips moving in a kind of swagger. In all probability she was right. Certainly Dora knew the ways through the vast labyrinth of G.M.'s business affairs. But as to blackmail—no! Susan could by no stretch of the imagination think for an instant that G.M. would indulge in any sort of double-dealing or chicanery, certainly not outright dishonesty of which Dora knew. Yet she knew in her heart that there must be a streak of ruthlessness in G.M.'s make-up.

One thing Dora had made extremely clear; she might try to threaten G.M. by saying she would marry Bert Prowde; she might say that merely to frighten G.M. into marrying her himself. But whatever she did, marry Bert or not, she had not the slightest intention of leaving G.M.

With a start, Susan remembered that Lattrice was waiting to question her and went downstairs; Lattrice and G.M. were in the library; Ligon was with them, and he was angry. "I tell you there's a thief in the house. And if you want to know who, I'll tell you. It's this young Prowde."

G.M. motioned Susan to a chair near him. Lattrice spoke to her pleasantly.

G.M. looked rather puzzled. "But, Ligon, do you mean that you had brought a suitcase—clothes—here? You've been staying at the inn."

"I'm still staying there. There's a vacant room upstairs here but Dora won't let me use it. I don't see why—well, yes I do. I understand that Rose was found shot in that room. But most houses have rooms where somebody has died—"

"Not in that way," G.M. said.

"No, no! I only thought—"

"Where were your clothes when, as you say, they were stolen?"

"I'm telling you. I had put on a dark business suit for the funeral. I couldn't have attended dressed like this—sports coat, slacks—"

"So what did you do?" G.M.'s patience was wearing a little thin.

Ligon said defensively, "Naturally I wore a dark suit. But I knew I'd be coming back here after the services, so when I came here this morning to join all of you in order to go to the city, I brought my coat and slacks—what I'm wearing now. As soon as we got here I changed. I put on more comfortable and suitable clothes. I hung up the business suit I had worn into the city in the closet of that little room with the safe. And now it's gone. Gone completely. Bert Prowde took it."

G.M. sighed. "But I can't see why Prowde would steal your clothing."

"He'd steal anything!" Ligon didn't shout but gave that effect. "I tell you he's no good. Why, he's an ex-union official—"

"Nothing wrong with that," Lattrice said. His dark eyes sparkled.

Ligon sputtered. "I said *ex*, didn't I? He was fired after he nearly killed somebody. I know that Prowde is also an ex-prizefighter. It's against our law for him to use his hands in assault."

"Yes, we know," Lattrice said, so quietly that he seemed to take the wind out of Ligon's sails. "You were there when he told us that."

Ligon dropped into a chair. "Bert Prowde stole that good suit! Made to order. An expensive suit!"

"Did you see him take it?" G.M. asked.

"No. No, I didn't see him take it. But there's something else. That safe in the room upstairs! It wasn't locked, so I looked in it. It's empty. Not a thing in it!"

The safe and the ring bought for Dora! Susan sprang up. "It can't be!"

"All right, Susan," G.M. said quickly. "I'll see to it. Now then, Ligon, I'll pay for another suit—made to order." He didn't mimic Ligon's indignant voice, but his words stung Ligon.

"I can pay for my own clothes, thank you!" Ligon cried. "But I wish you'd get rid of Bert Prowde."

"He's to marry Dora," G.M. said.

Ligon turned slightly purple. "How can you stand by and see Dora marry him! He's no good! And Dora—I couldn't get along with her myself, you know that. We weren't—weren't compatible," Ligon said with dignity. "But you'll do well to marry her yourself. She's been faithful to you and your interests ever since she started to work for you."

"Yes," G.M. said. "That is true."

"Why, she wouldn't ask for time off even to get our divorce! I did it myself. I could take the time to go—"

"Where?" Lattrice asked.

"Reno. All square and aboveboard. I was sorry about it but, as I say, we were simply not compatible. I respect her, just the same. I have her interests at heart. Marry her, G.M. Don't let her marry that—that . . ." Ligon spluttered to a stop, wiped his forehead with a spotless handkerchief and finished rather lamely, "That sissy."

G.M.'s smile twinkled in his eyes. "You just now suggested that he is a dangerous felon."

"I'm not afraid of him," Ligon blustered. "But Dora—after all, she was my wife. I have some regard for her future."

"I'm sure of it," G.M. said politely. "Now, Ligon, Sergeant Lattrice wishes to talk to me." He didn't say, he wants to question Susan.

Ligon drew himself together, made a polite kind of bow in everybody's direction and left.

Susan said, "But, G.M., the ring!"

"Forget it. Now then, Sergeant—"

But knowing the cost of the ring, Susan's prudent nature couldn't brush off its loss. "I did close the safe. I turned the dials."

G.M. nodded. "It's all right. But Ligon's suit—I really don't know what to make of that. Seems—well, Lattrice?"

It was a long interview. At the end of it she could not see that she had advanced in any way the task of identifying the running man. She had only told Lattrice that she was sure she had seen him and that he must have followed her.

It was by then full dark; G.M. had turned on lights in the library when Wilfred and Milly came clanking in with the tray of bottles and glasses and the ice bucket. Lattrice thanked Susan and G.M. and left.

He looked no wiser, but then it was hard to tell what Lattrice felt.

Again, as if drawn by the same magnet the whole tribe of

Clansers—or what was left of them—assembled, followed by Ligon.

They took up their usual occupation and were indeed fairly well launched upon it when Greg came in. He didn't so much as look at Susan. The dogs came in with him and settled down with their usual air of pleased participation. Only Bert Prowde was not there and Wilfred explained it. "That young Prowde said he was very tired, and he got Col to take my car and take him to the inn."

Col was pouring a drink in the practiced Clanser manner. "I don't see why you want to marry him, Dora. He'll never make anything of himself. No guts."

"He was a prizefighter," Dora said softly.

Col nearly dropped the bottle he held. "You've got to be kidding!"

Dora shrugged daintily. "You don't have to believe it. Look out, you're pouring whiskey on the rug."

Col righted the bottle, much more upset at spilling whiskey than at any possible spot on the rug. "Really, Dora, you act as if this whole place belonged to you!"

"Not at all," Dora said sweetly. "I only have had the care of it."

Milly said, "Don't quarrel! I'm so tired. It was a beautiful funeral, wasn't it? Who sent that whole sheaf of orchids, I wonder. One of your friends, G.M.?"

"I have no idea," G.M. said firmly. "I don't wish to talk of Rose's funeral, Milly."

She gave him for once a startled, almost frightened look. It was clear that G.M. had rarely used that particular steely voice in her hearing. She was flustered, she fumbled with her glass, dribbled on her vast bosom and said, "Oh, certainly not." But then she rallied a little. "Now as for poor Snell and the family lot—"

"Stop it," G.M. said.

Milly stopped. Dora said softly, "Shall I turn on the television news?"

"No," G.M. said, steel in his voice again.

Ligon had been quietly drinking but also apparently brooding in the big chair he seemed to have taken a personal lease on. "But I'd like to know who stole my clothes."

"Stole your clothes!" Milly shrieked it. Col and Wilfred stared. Dora's lovely eyes clouded over hazily.

"But how—how funny!" Milly began to laugh, wouldn't

stop. Col hit her a resounding whack over the shoulders. She choked but kept on laughing.

Ligon scowled. "I can't see anything funny about there being a thief in the house."

Susan couldn't either. She didn't care about Ligon's suit, but she was concerned about the beautiful and costly ring she herself had put in the safe.

Dora took decisive charge. "Stop that, Milly. Go and get dinner. You've all had enough to drink. Greg, please take the bottles away and lock up the cupboard."

But again Milly was too swift; she clutched at a bottle and held it defiantly to her purple-clad bosom. "Oh, I'll cook dinner. There'd be nothing to eat in this fine house if I didn't see to it. But"—laughter caught her again in a vast giggle—"but I don't think it would be any treat to see stuffed-shirt Ligon without his clothes. I can't help it if I think it's funny."

There's going to be another murder this minute, Susan thought, alarmed at Ligon's red face.

Greg said, "All right, Milly, if you want to get yourself bumped off just keep on acting like that. It's all right." He nodded peaceably at Ligon. "She's only drunk again."

"Only halfway. She cooks better when she's like that anyway," Col said peaceably, too. "I'll help you, Milly."

"You'll not get this!" She clutched at the bottle. Greg coolly removed the tray and went out with it.

Another Clanser quarrel; another Clanser drinking bout. Susan wondered how G.M. had stood it, year after year; the answer was, of course, that he hadn't; he had quietly removed himself to a hotel apartment.

Dora snapped, "If you're going back to the inn, Ligon, you may as well go now and have your dinner there. A better dinner than Milly will give us."

"You might offer to help her." Ligon rose, however, with offended dignity. "I'll walk down to the gate with you, Wilfred. You can phone for a taxi for me there." He marched out with Wilfred. Dora forgot her own sedate dignity and laughed, looking so utterly lovely when she laughed that Susan did not understand how any man on earth could fail to fall a victim to Dora's beauty and the charm which, for Susan's observation, was rarely turned on.

She remembered, though, Dora's threats that approached blackmail. Dora broke off her musical laughter and turned to G.M. "Have the police really gone through all Ligon's business affairs? It's perfectly possible for anybody in business, no matter how successful, to get into a tight spot now and then."

Did she mean G.M.? Susan thought. Was this a covert reminder to G.M. that there had been times in the past when G.M. needed cash, even a relatively small sum, so much that he might have gone beyond the law to get it?

If it was such a reminder, G.M.'s face gave no evidence of it; he said quietly that he'd like Dora to help him at the telephone downstairs. "There's a wildcat strike threatening at the Manders' Jig and Dye Works. The manager phoned me this morning. I think we'd better smooth things out. You're very good at that, Dora."

Dora smiled. "That's how I met Bert," she said smugly. "Remember? There's nothing like personal diplomacy and, if I do say so, know-how. I can give that. Can't I, G.M.?" She didn't wait for his grave nod but went on. "That first Jig and Dye strike, I had to cope with myself. You were in California, G.M. That's how I met the union representative, Bert." She smiled into G.M.'s eyes. "I expect we can settle this thing before the strike really catches on and spreads."

The Manders' Jig and Dye Works, Susan knew, was the first company which G.M. had bought outright. The title had a jovial suggestion of a macabre dance, but from what correspondence Susan herself had typed, she had learned that G.M. had bought the company at a time when a coming surge of need for machine parts was just on the horizon. G.M. was already in the market to supply that need, and the small company had grown. From there, of course, he had gone on and on until he became a power. But it was a quiet, behind-the-scenes power, nothing that he himself gave evidence of or, she thought, in fact wanted once he had it. Danger money, he had said.

G.M. followed Dora out through the living room and down to the basement room with its telephone lines. Susan sank back in her chair, feeling again, as she so often did with the Clansers, as if she'd been through a rather frenzied hurricane.

If she married G.M., there would be no more Clansers in this beautiful house. They were now, with Rose's death, all paid off. They had no more hold on G.M.

Being G.M. he would in all likelihood try to see to them; he would never get over his feeling of obligation to Rose and thus to her family. But he wouldn't feel required to keep them underfoot. This beautiful house, she thought again, relaxing in the comparative peace of the library. It was a long time before she became aware of canine and feline eyes fixed upon her. She sat up and looked. The two dogs and the cat again sat in a patient but demanding little group before her. Food, of course, this time.

"All right," she told them.

They followed her, the dogs prancing, the cat sedate and dignified but also determined. In the kitchen Milly was broiling some chops while Col peeled potatoes. Neither paid any attention to her.

The dogs wolfed their food; the cat gulped it with voracity. When they finished and Toby sat down to wash his face, she picked him up—to his annoyance—called the dogs and moved them out to the vestibule. She ought to take them out.

She was no longer afraid of the Clansers; all the same she didn't want to go out alone.

She sat down on the bench in the vestibule; Toby, released, gave her an indignant blue glance and resumed his vigorous washing. Both dogs, however, stood at the door expectantly. At last she rose and started out, but then Greg called to her from the stairs in the hall. "Wait, Susan, I'll go with you."

He came through the hall and into the vestibule. "It's cooler. You'll need a coat or a sweater." He knew thoroughly all the ways of the house; a small coat closet opened off the hall, under the stairs; she had never noticed it before. He pulled out a man's coat and threw it around her shoulders. "I'm sure G.M. won't mind your wearing his coat."

He opened the vestibule door and the dogs dashed out. Toby followed. "I wonder when Col let them out last," Greg said. "They really are very good little things. They never got any exercise to speak of before."

She pulled the coat closer over her shoulders; its soft cashmere folds seemed to shield her as if G.M. himself were there. She said abruptly, "Greg, the ring we bought for Dora. It's gone."

Greg walked on. It was later than she had thought and very dark, for it was a cloudy night. They left the streak of light from the vestibule door behind them. The dogs and cat had vanished into the shadows.

Finally Greg said, "Does G.M. know?"

"Oh, yes. He seemed to make nothing of it."

Again they walked on for a space before Greg spoke and voiced Susan's own thought. "It's his money. If he doesn't care what happened to it, it's nothing to me. It may be something to you, of course."

Susan ignored that. She went on, "Ligon says a thief is in the house. He accused Bert Prowde. He said a suit of clothes belonging to him was taken and he had put it on a hanger in the closet of the room where Rose the room with the safe. He said the safe was open and he looked in it and it was empty."

"Rather nosy of him. Still, if you are a Clanser and see a safe standing open or even half closed, I suppose it would be impossible to resist an impulse to look inside it."

Susan mutely agreed. The Clansers were nothing if not inquisitive. They walked on again. Finally Greg repeated, "It's G.M.'s money. His loss. He can afford it. There may be some reason why he doesn't take the loss of the ring very seriously. A wife can't be made to testify against her husband."

"A wife!" She stopped to stare up at his face which, however, the darkness veiled. She could only guess at a kind of anger in it. "What do you mean by that? Dora?"

"Possibly," Greg said.

"But he said he wouldn't marry her. And besides—you don't understand—"

He caught her arm and turned her to face him. "You mean that you *are* going to marry him, don't you?"

"Is that any business of yours?"

"Why, yes, I think it is. Oh, to be fair to G.M., he makes his own conventions, sometimes his own laws. If he felt it was not too soon after Rose's death to talk of marriage, then that's the way he felt. And of course it's true that Rose hadn't been his wife for a very long time. It's only fair to G.M. to admit that. Are you sure you love him enough to marry him?"

"Greg, how did you know? How did you guess? You said you wanted to offer congratulations."

"How could I help guessing! I've got eyes in my head. Besides, I know G.M. He's got something that women like. Magnetism, whatever. I've got to be fair again. It's not only his power and his money."

She said presently, feebly, "Nothing is settled yet."

He laughed. "You are trying to evade. Don't."

"I'm not!" She flashed angrily but knew that she was doing her best to evade his questions and her own vacillation. If she had any sense she'd jump at the chance G.M. gave her.

Greg said it. "He'd give you everything any woman can

want in the way of luxury. Jewels, furs, gorgeous homes anywhere. He's got the money for it."

"He told me I mustn't think of that. He said he might not be a good husband. He said there were times when he was so engrossed in business that he might not pay much attention to—to me."

"And naturally you said you wouldn't mind."

"I don't know—I really *don't* know what I said. He—it was all—"

"All so unexpected!" Greg said, jeering, and then all at once exploded. "Good God! He really is the most devilish, cunning old rattlesnake that ever lived!"

"Who's talking of rattlesnakes?" G.M. said behind them and as they whirled back he loomed up in the darkness, tall, slim and laughing gently. "We have no rattlesnakes in this part of the world, Greg. At least we have only the human kind, which we know how to deal with." He put his arm possessively around Susan's shoulders and pulled his coat a little closer about her. "You have my coat. Good. It's much cooler tonight. We'll walk on a little. Greg, I believe dinner is waiting."

"Oh, I'll just stroll with you, if you don't mind," Greg said with cool politeness.

But G.M. only laughed. "Can't stand Milly? Or Col?"

"I can't stand any of them, if you want to know," Greg said with a ring of sincerity in his voice.

"Neither can I," G.M. said good-naturedly, holding Susan's arm. "But then I'll not have to much longer. As soon as the police get busy—"

"They've been very busy," Greg said.

It seemed to Susan oddly that there was some significance in Greg's words or in his voice which G.M. heard and understood but she did not. They walked on, the three of them quietly, with only the *pad-pad* of their steps on the driveway breaking the silence. Then G.M. said, "Do you think the police will soon have results?"

"I think it possible," Greg said.

G.M.'s grip on Susan's arm tightened; he turned her around. "Let's get back to the house."

Nineteen

Milly had disappeared. Dora was sitting in one of the stately wing chairs in the living room, looking like a very beautiful, very self-possessed queen of all she surveyed.

Wilfred had apparently gone, too.

"There's still some food," Dora said pleasantly. "You'd better eat, G.M. And you, Greg. I can't say it's very much of a dinner. Really, G.M., your notion against steady domestic help out here is too absurd."

G.M. shrugged and took the coat from Susan. Dora eyed it and Susan and for just a second her brown eyes turned hazy again.

Greg said, "I'm hungry," and went to the dining room.

Susan, G.M. and Dora followed. Dora served G.M. from dishes which had apparently been kept hot.

Greg commented on it. "You're getting very domestic, Dora. You actually put things in that handsome warming oven in the kitchen."

"Of course," Dora replied with surprising amiability. "G.M., I think I've got the strike fixed."

"Good," G.M. said. "I only wanted to stop it before it spread. Let's have some wine. I can stand some of Milly's cooking, but not too much."

Greg got out a bottle of wine. G.M. opened it, poured some in one of the glasses Dora had brought from the kitchen, tasted, nodded and filled the other glasses. It was a little like their lunch, Susan thought, yet it wasn't at all the same. She and G.M. had been alone; it had been a happy lunch. Perhaps, she thought soberly, G.M. had both coaxed and cajoled her but he had done it so adroitly, so kindly that she had felt only warmed and protected.

Surprisingly Wilfred's hound-dog nose for liquor did not extend as far as the gate. Susan half expected him to appear, tongue hanging out, in the doorway as G.M. lifted his glass. Milly, not so surprisingly, did not appear; she was almost certainly swigging away at the bottle she had contrived to snatch before dinner.

The wine was reviving. It even induced a kind of friendliness between Dora and Susan, for without speaking of it they automatically cleared off the dining-room table and straightened the kitchen. Greg and G.M. had disappeared when Susan and Dora emerged from the kitchen. Dora looked at her white hands. "One thing I promised myself long ago never to do, and that is wash dishes."

Her white hands were obviously bare of a lovely star sapphire.

"Good for you," Susan said rather hazily. The wine had gone to her head a little; she decided she was becoming a candidate for the Clanser tribe and went rather unsteadily up the stairs.

Dora followed her, sliding her ringless white hand along the red velvet on the banister. At the top of the stairs she said dreamily, looking at nothing, "Now you see the kind of thing I can do for G.M. I settled that strike. I know all the ropes and all the strings to pull. G.M. needs me."

Susan nodded. This was clearly the truth. It was also very likely that if any bodies were buried in G.M.'s fantastically successful career, Dora knew where.

Then the thought of Rose's death and Snell's made the merely familiar phrase take on an ugly and literal meaning which in fact in this instance it did not have. She said good night abruptly and bolted her bedroom door. The house seemed remarkably quiet. Probably G.M. and Greg were down in the basement room, busy with those private wires.

She hesitated about turning off the bedside lamp, gave in to a cowardly impulse and left the light shining, then drifted into sleep, lulled by the cool night air and half dreaming of the magic world which opened before her because G.M. wanted her to marry him.

The next day could have been any day in the city office. G.M. and Dora worked in the room downstairs, G.M. dictating, Dora typing. Greg spent most of the time with them, although he made one trip, Susan supposed to Medbury Hills, with a bundle of letters in his hand. Milly drifted around; Col apparently remained at the gate. Wilfred did not turn up at all. Neither did Bert Prowde or Ligon.

Neither did the police, or at least if any police or if Lattrice himself came, Susan did not know it. She helped Milly cook lunch and told her the truth: she knew nothing of the key to the liquor cabinet or to a wine cellar downstairs. Milly sulked.

Over lunch, however, Greg began to talk of keys again. How many keys were there to the back gate?

Dora said she couldn't remember how many keys. It didn't seem important. Either Col and Wilfred was at the gate at all times. Nobody could have got into the house without their knowledge.

"But somebody did," Greg said shortly.

Dora was offended. "Really, Greg, this was not an oversight! Of course Col and Wilfred have keys, they had to have keys in order to get into the house and clean it. You know all this. Rose had a key. I have a key. G.M. has a key."

"Too damn many keys," Greg said.

The obvious fact was that anyone who had ever entered the house presumably had had access to the duplicate keys.

G.M. and Dora returned to work, G.M. with a kind of apology to Susan. "I've let work stack up. I've got to get some of these things done. You'll be all right this afternoon?"

Susan nodded and he went back downstairs with Dora. This was like G.M.; even at such a time he could and did concentrate on business affairs. Presently the tap of Dora's typewriter started up again.

It was a long, strangely peaceful afternoon. Susan spent most of it in the library, although once she walked the dogs around the house as she had done before.

It was a beautiful, slightly hazy fall day. The dogs romped and played but returned to the house with her. Presently the evening ritual began; it was not quite the same, for there was only Milly to make real inroads on the supply of whiskey.

Nothing happened. There was almost no conversation at dinner. After dinner, however, G.M. suggested that he and Susan take the dogs out. "I want some fresh air," he said.

She was aware of Dora's fixed look as G.M. draped his coat around her again and they went out. G.M. held the door open for the dogs and the cat.

But in the shadow of the pines G.M. gave her the star sapphire. He did it directly and simply, taking her hand, fumbling in his pocket, taking out the ring and putting it on her finger. "There," he said. "That settles it."

"But it was gone! Somebody took it."

"I did."

"I thought Dora—"

He chuckled. "Don't you like it?"

"It's beautiful. But you said Dora—"

"I'll make it up to Dora. Buy her another one."

Greg came walking briskly along behind them. "Oh, it's you," he said far too casually. "I thought I'd get a little walk before going to bed."

"Good," G.M. said, but not very heartily.

They walked as far as the gate where Wilfred hailed them briefly, probably to show G.M. that he was on the job and the gates were locked. They called the dogs and went back into the house, the dogs romping ahead. No one noticed that the cat did not follow them.

But Greg at once saw the ring on Susan's finger. He said nothing; he only turned away but with such a complete finality that he might have been saying goodbye forever.

Dora saw the ring too. She came from the living room, her eyes dancing. "I phoned Bert. He had just licked Ligon. Ligon accused him of stealing a suit of Ligon's clothes. Bert forgot himself and pasted Ligon one in the eye. Then he realized what he had done and so did Ligon. Ligon threatened him with arrest. They finally settled it—guess how? By playing gin rummy all day. That's where they've been. Ligon always fancied himself good at cards, though he was cautious. But Bert has had more experience. Actually I expect Bert is a born gambler. Anyway, he took Ligon for—" Her dancing eyes had got around to Susan and she, too, saw the ring.

She stopped dead still; her face turned to stone. G.M. said pleasantly, "We've all had some tiring days. Good night, Susan." He underlined her wearing of his ring, purposefully, Susan felt. He took her in his arms, kissed her, as Dora watched, and went upstairs. Dora did not move. Greg had disappeared. Susan dropped G.M.'s coat over a chair and went upstairs, too. Dora was as still as a statue, watching her.

Susan turned on the lights in her room and again bolted the door. Then she sat for a long time looking at the ring. It was a beautiful bond. She began to feel as if she were tied, sealed and all but delivered—to what? To a sensible course. Sensible, certainly.

Finally she roused herself and went to bed. It seemed to take hours before she could sleep, yet she must have drifted off at last into an inexplicably troubled slumber when a raucous, angry but frightened scream awakened her sharply. She jerked upright in bed and the scream came again. It had a curiously inhuman tone but it was desperate.

The cat! He was directly below her window. He had to be

there. The scream was choked off but began again. He must have been caught in some trap set out for a marauding animal. She sprang out of bed, seized her dressing gown and took off the bolt of her door. As she started down the stairs a self-protective instinct stopped her; she wouldn't go out in the middle of the night alone. She forgot that Greg had looked as if he never wanted to see her again. She knew which room Greg was using and she fumbled her way to it, opened the door and whispered. He came, turning on a light, his hair tousled, in pajamas. "What is it?"

"The cat. He's outside. Oh, Greg, he's caught in some trap or something. He's in pain."

He snatched up an overcoat which lay over a chair. "All right. I'll see to him."

"I'm coming too."

He didn't hear or at least did not reply but ran down the stairs ahead of her. She followed. Greg ran through the hall and then turned on a vestibule light. Here the dogs were sleeping; Belle sprang up and wagged her tail, delighted at this arrival of friends; Beau, however, stood at the door, sniffing and growling softly. Greg thrust open the door and started down the drive but Susan caught him. "No. He was right under my window. At least that's what it sounded like. This way."

She ran around the end of the house. The lamp from her window above cast a patch of light on the grass. She didn't see the cat. She called him, "Toby! Toby!" and turned to speak to Greg. Greg was not there.

There was nothing but blackness except for the patch of light from her bedroom window on the lawn below it, and nothing moved within that. She ran back around the end of the house and reached the driveway; suddenly her bare feet felt cool concrete. Here there was a diffused light from the vestibule. She ran toward it, stumbled on something, went down to her knees and knew that Greg was lying there. "Greg!" She groped for him in the blackness; she must do something, tell someone, call for help. She started to her feet; suddenly she heard a crash like thunder, saw a wild outburst of stars shooting everywhere, and felt herself crumpling into a heap; then the stars, the thunder, everything vanished—even her breath was cut off by strong hands.

Someone began to shake her. A woman was calling for help, calling Wilfred. Her voice shrieked out into the black void around Susan. "Wilfred! Help! Wilfred!"

It was Dora. It was Dora's hand reaching for her pulse, Dora's hands pulling at her, Dora's voice calling, "Don't move! Wilfred is coming. I can hear him."

Susan could hear footsteps pounding along the driveway. That would be Wilfred. She tried to speak and heard her own voice whisper, "Greg—"

"I think he's all right. Knocked out, but all right. Just lie still. Wilfred will get help."

Greg muttered, sat up and put his hands to his head. "Gosh," he said.

A wave of something vital flooded Susan. He was alive.

He said, "What hit me? Is that you, Dora? Where's Susan? Where—"

"Here I am, Greg." Susan's voice came out in a whisper; her throat was agonizingly painful.

"Somebody—" Greg said and got to his feet. Wilfred thudded up to them. Greg said, "Get back to the gate, Wilfred! Have your gun ready and use it! But let in the police. I'll call them now. Come on, Dora. We'll get Susan into the house."

It was mainly Dora who helped Susan to her feet and walked her into the vestibule. Toby shot in after them. He was an enraged, angry Toby, and he had been a fighting Toby. His eyes blazed red; his black tail lashed furiously. Susan had a flashing notion that his claws might be red, too. She tried to explain that she had heard him crying, screaming for help. Dora said, "Don't talk. Come on into the living room. Your throat—I'll get some ice and towels."

She maneuvered Susan to a chair, then ran toward the kitchen. She came back with a huge bowl of ice cubes and towels. Susan could hear Greg's voice from the telephone in the library. "Lattrice? We've got him, I think. He's got to be here. He tried to kill her just now . . . Oh, you did get all that evidence? Good then . . . Yes, right away."

Dora touched Susan's chin gently, tipped her head a little backward and began to apply cold towels gently to Susan's throat.

"You saved my life," Susan whispered.

"Yes, I suppose I did," Dora said matter-of-factly. "Did you get the police, Greg?"

He came running from the library. "They're coming. They've got evidence. You're not going to like it, Dora."

Dora gave him a long, still look. Yet Susan felt that her

swift intelligence was racing. Finally she said, "So it's that way. But I can't see why."

Greg didn't reply; he sat down beside Susan and she looked at him to convince herself that he was there, alive. Not undamaged, however, for he took one of the icy wet towels and pressed it against the back of his head. "I'll have a lump like a baseball." He patted his head and winced.

Milly shouted from the stairs, "What's going on down there?"

Nobody answered. Susan had to put her hand over Greg's just to be sure he was there. Greg's hand turned and caught her own.

Dora noted it and did not so much as smile but dipped a towel again into the bowl of melting ice cubes. It was a curiously domestic setting for a nightmare.

Susan whispered, "The cat screamed. The cat was hurt. I thought he'd been caught in some trap."

"It was a trap for you," Greg said.

Milly appeared in the doorway and then just stood there, her eyes popping. Toby gave a yowl from somewhere; Susan discovered him under a chair, his fur still on end, his tail enormous, his eyes red and glaring. As she looked he yowled again and then hissed venomously. Milly heard it, saw him and moved back. "That terrible cat! He looks as if he's going to attack me."

"Not you," Greg said shortly.

"But what's happened? What are you doing here? What's the matter with Susan's throat?"

"Oh, be quiet, Milly," Dora said, then relented and explained. "Susan heard the cat. He was being hurt and yelling. She woke Greg, I suppose. At least I saw them coming out of Greg's room and down the stairs. I waited a moment. Then I put on something and came down too. Greg was hurt. Susan was hurt. So sit down, Milly, and be quiet."

"Do you mean the—the murderer—"

"Be quiet," Dora said again with such savage determination that Milly put a fat hand over her mouth and sank in a heap in a chair. Toby took this as an insult and spit again in her direction.

"What on earth?" G.M. said from the stairs in the hall and came into the room. His hair was neat; he wore a scarf with his handsomely tailored beige dressing gown. "What's been going on?"

Greg said, "You'll hear in a minute, G.M. The police are coming."

"I think you'd better explain now," G.M. said in his cool voice of command.

Whoever had attacked the cat must have scratches on his hands, Susan thought vaguely; Toby was obviously a fighting cat.

Without intending it really she looked at Milly's fat hands, at Dora's pretty hands ministering to her, at G.M., whose hands were thrust nonchalantly in the pockets of his dressing gown. There was nothing nonchalant about his face. "Tell me, Greg."

Milly cried, "Somebody tried to kill her. That's what Dora meant. And somebody tried to kill Greg!"

Greg stopped her with a faint echo of his natural humor in his voice. "I have a hard skull. Luckily. But I don't think murder was meant for me. Definitely yes, for Susan."

"Go on," G.M. said in a hard, demanding voice which could be suave and persuasive. Greg said, as cold and firm as G.M., "Lattrice will explain. He's on his way."

"He's here," Dora said, sitting back on her heels beside the bowl of ice cubes.

He was there. He must have been expecting something to happen, Susan thought dimly. He couldn't have come so soon otherwise.

But then why hadn't he stopped it? Lack of proof? If it hadn't been for Dora, she herself, Susan Beach, would have supplied far too convincing proof.

Someone opened thc vestibule door. Lattrice must have brought the Medbury Hills police or state troopers or both, for she heard him giving quick orders. They were to search the whole place. They were to guard the gates; they were to use every force. That meant guns, Susan thought.

Why then, if he had expected a murderous attack upon her, had he waited so long?

Lattrice explained that at once. He came in, looked at Greg and said, "You were right. We have at last got all the evidence we need—or most of it. We had to pull some wires, overcome some resistance, wait for the report of the helicopter and have that and other things gone over with a vacuum. We were ready to work all night when you phoned. But we did find just what you thought we'd find. And I believe we have identified the running man. It took a little time." He turned to G.M. "His name is John Nelson; at least he has been going under that name since he was detected in embezzlement. He'd have been easy to hire; the threat of disclosure to the police would have been enough to put him in prison. He had to do what he was told. He can manage a helicopter. After he was fired, he took lessons in running a helicopter; he's been making his living by taking tourists for rides."

G.M. said, "I think you'd better explain."

"Why certainly," Lattrice said politely. "But your young man here, Greg, gave me the information we needed."

Greg said soberly, "Not me. My Aunt Lalie. And the cat."

Twenty

G.M.'s eyes were beginning to snap. Milly was leaning forward, gasping. Wilfred came in, gave one scared look around and said to nobody in particular that he hoped it would be all right with the police if he had to shoot.

Lattrice gave him a short nod, but it was so decisive a nod that Wilfred backed out again hurriedly. Lattrice came to Susan, tipped her head back gently as Dora had done, scrutinized her throat and said, "You're a lucky girl."

Suddenly Greg's face blazed into anger. "You should have been here! You should have had a guard here!"

"Yes," Lattrice said. "I should have known, but I didn't. As a matter of fact it took considerable pressure yesterday and today to get the records we had to have. But we got them. That is, all but one which I'm beginning to believe does not exist. If it does not exist there is a possible motive for your wife's murder, Mr. Manders."

"Get on with it," snapped G.M.

But Lattrice turned to Dora. "Why were you divorced from your husband?"

"Because we didn't get along. My husband got the divorce. He could take the time from his business. I was working for Mr. Manders and couldn't take the time."

"Do you have a record of your divorce?"

Dora's brown eyes became very still yet her lightning swift intelligence raced again. "I never thought of that. So that was it."

Lattrice nodded. "A possible motive, certainly. He did want you to marry Mr. Manders, didn't he?"

Greg said suddenly, "I ought to have guessed! I ought to have known when Susan told me that he had said if Dora didn't marry G.M., he'd have her back on his hands again. Dora, there really was no divorce."

"Wait," Dora said. "Wait—no, I have no record of it. I believed him. I do know that he wanted me to marry G.M."

"And make myself liable for bigamy, is that it, Lattrice?" G.M. said.

"I'm rather afraid so, Mr. Manders."

"But what could he want? Not money." G.M. looked at Dora.

Dora said flatly, "He is very ambitious."

G.M. said slowly, "Could he have thought such a threat would have induced me to see that he advanced his ambitions?"

Dora nodded slowly. "He would have thought that. He mentioned running for Congress. And you do have the power to give him power."

Unexpectedly G.M. went to Dora, who was still kneeling beside the bowl of ice; he put a hand on her head. "You couldn't have known."

His fine hand bore no scratches; Susan felt a wave of shame for her fleeting suspicion.

Dora took a long breath. "I supposed he had got the divorce. I never questioned it. I was so thankful to be rid of him. Oh, he was successful in his way. Devious. Why, he must have looked ahead all this time since he told me we were divorced, hoping—"

Milly gave a gulp. "Waiting till G.M. might marry you! That's Ligon for you. But how did he get Rose to come here?"

Lattrice said quietly, "A number of possible ways. The most likely is that Ligon told her that Col and Wilfred were in some sort of trouble out here."

Milly thought it over and nodded vigorously. "Yes. Rose would have come to help anybody in her family. But she must have told him that I would be here."

"Oh, yes," Lattrice said. "That is likely, too. He had to run it fine. He thought the helicopter would get here much sooner than the car. It's possible he seized upon a chance to make you, Miss Clanser, the scapegoat."

"Me!" Milly squealed.

"He is a cruel man," Dora said slowly. "It would be like him to discover an embezzler—"

"He was a teller in a bank your husband owns," Lattrice said.

"All right, a teller. It was like Ligon to let him off but hold it over his head in case of need. So the teller was the running man, is that it? He brought Ligon here?"

"We think so," Lattrice said gravely. "We think that Ligon went to your apartment, Mr. Manders. He sat in a chair near the door where, later, Miss Beach sat, and his suit was covered with cat hairs. No one but somebody Mrs. Manders knew well could have induced her to come here. Once here and in the room with the safe in which there was a gun—and he had certainly plenty of opportunities to know that—he shot her. I think it would be easy enough to get her upstairs and into that room. All he had to do was possess himself of the gun and call her. Of course we can't be sure of these details until we get the murderer and induce a confession—if that can be done."

"It can't be done. Not with Ligon," Dora said, her face like stone again.

"The running man guessed that Ligon had shot Mrs. Manders. Ligon ran back to the helicopter; the teller—John Nelson—followed him," G.M. said. "Snell probably thought of a little backmail that would keep him in clover for the rest of his life. I suppose Ligon made some sort of arrangement to meet him in the road."

Lattrice nodded. "We think so. Ligon could have come and gone as he pleased in Medbury Hills. Snell knew only what Ligon had told him. Ligon must have given some excuse for using the helicopter and had probably given Snell money. Snell obligingly got drunk, as Ligon might have guessed he would. When we get hold of John Nelson, as we will, we'll have more evidence."

Greg said, "Ligon was in and out of the gates at least once, perhaps several times, certainly tonight. All he had to do was put a bottle of booze where Wilfred could see it. Ligon could have informed himself very easily of the electrical switch which operates the gates. He also knew where the duplicate keys to the gate were kept. He could have helped himself to a key and come through the woods. Then later the young teller, the embezzler, the running man, was sent to track down Susan in New York. He did it. Ligon took Susan's key and made Nelson meet him in Medbury Hills. Nelson was still terrified of what Ligon held over him. He couldn't prove that Ligon had shot Rose. But Snell knew too much. We always thought that. He knew that Ligon had paid him for the use of the helicopter. He knew that Ligon must have had something to do with Rose's murder."

Lattrice said quietly, "We found cat hairs on Ligon Clanser's dark suit. Greg engaged Ligon in a talk and a stroll outside yesterday while I took the suit. Cat hairs had been on it at the funeral service that morning. Greg's aunt saw them. Greg knew that there were cat hairs in a chair near the door of your apartment, Mr. Manders. It was thick with cat hairs. So we pulled every wire we could to make a hurried but much more extensive exploration of Ligon's affairs than we had up to then. Indeed, previously we had all but dismissed him as a suspect. Everything we first uncovered merely showed him to be a respected businessman."

"He wanted more than that," Dora said. "Power—and G.M. could give it to him. G.M. could get him—oh, almost anything. An election perhaps. Later he would have aimed high. He thought he'd have you, G.M., as he had this poor young teller."

Milly's mouth had been hanging open; it closed and then snapped open again. "But why would he try to kill Susan? Why would he set this dreadful young man, this embezzler, after Susan? Why—"

G.M. answered her. "Because in fact there were two running men. Ligon must have been just far enough ahead of Nelson so Susan didn't see him. But he couldn't be sure of that. No, he believed Susan had seen him. And also the police would never give up. Sooner or later, searching through all Ligon's affairs, they would uncover, as they did, the fact of Nelson's embezzlement and that Ligon managed to cover it up. When they found Nelson, Ligon knew that Nelson would accuse him. Only time and circumstance, I suppose, have saved John Nelson so far. But just now Susan was his greatest danger."

Dora said quietly, "After Rose, I suppose he could kill again. As he did."

There was a silence in the room. A man outside shouted and someone replied.

G.M. looked gravely at Susan, still clinging to Greg's hand. Suddenly she remembered something he had said at their lunch, so like a picnic lunch, and yet G.M. was never quite unguarded, quite unobservant. He had said (too casually, too observantly?) that he might be away from home, but if so, Greg could take her out, take her to dinner. She remembered her own too quick, too revealing a rejection of that. G.M. had noted it. G.M. would note it, as he now noted the way she clung to Greg.

An odd expression flickered over his face. It was not decision or indecision. She sought for a word and found it; the look was only philosophical, the look of a man who knows how to take either victory or defeat. However sincere G.M.'s words about marriage to her had been, and she thought that at the time they were spoken he had been sincere, according to his lights, certainly he was not a man to cherish a hopeless love. Not G.M.

Dora said, "Oh, yes, Ligon told me I must marry G.M. I'll tell the truth. I've always wanted to marry G.M. But he doesn't want to marry me," Dora said flatly, "so I'll forget it."

Susan clung harder to Greg's hand. "Dora saved my life. She frightened him. He ran away—"

Lattrice's neat head jerked up. Everyone gave a kind of jerk as if the same string controlled them, for there were sudden, shockingly loud gunshots from outside. Lattrice sprang for the door and ran out.

Milly said in the silence, which was almost as shocking as the roar of the gunshots, "I hope they got him. Much easier for all of us."

G.M. gave an almost imperceptible sigh. But he was again himself, sure and decisive, and content with his life and everything it had given him. He said, "Danger money. Yes. It's always like that. Money gives a certain power, but it invites danger and—never mind all that. I can only claim a talent for observation. Sometimes it's a helpful talent, sometimes it is unwelcome. However, I know when to take what life gives and be thankful for it." It was rather enigmatic, yet Susan was sure that she understood him. It was as though he had given her freedom from bonds which had enmeshed her almost without her knowledge of them.

A look of kind but firm resolution came into his face; it was a look Susan recognized; he had made up his mind about something.

He came to her, reached out and took her hand from Greg's. Gently he removed the ring. He even smiled. "You didn't really want it that way, did you? I guessed." He went to Dora. "Here's the ring I bought for you, Dora. Please take it. We'll forget all about Bert Prowde. He's not important to me. But you are."

"Do you mean—as your wife?"

G.M. put the ring on Dora's hand.

Susan suddenly gave a hoarse little laugh. "Why, G.M.! I think I'm being jilted."

G.M. laughed too, lightly. "Not really. I can only see more than sometimes people think I can see." He glanced at Greg and then at Susan. "But I'll dance at your wedding, my dear."

About the Author

MIGNON G. EBERHART'S name has become a guarantee of excellence in the mystery and suspense field. Her work has been translated into sixteen languages, and has been serialized in many magazines and adapted for radio, television and motion pictures.

For many years Mrs. Eberhart traveled extensively abroad and in the United States. Now she lives in Westport, Connecticut.

In April, 1971, the Mystery Writers of America gave Mrs. Eberhart their Grand Master Award in recognition of her sustained excellence as a suspense writer.